take three girls

take three girls

CATH CROWLEY • SIMMONE HOWELL • FIONA WOOD

STERLING TEEN
New York

An Imprint of Sterling Publishing Co., Inc.

ISBN 978-1-4549-3827-9

Distributed in Canada by Sterling Publishing Co., Inc.
c/o Canadian Manda Group, 664 Annette Street
Toronto, Ontario M6S 2C8, Canada
Distributed in the United Kingdom by GMC Distribution Services
Castle Place, 166 High Street, Lewes, East Sussex BN7 1XU, England

For information about custom editions, special sales, and premium and corporate purchases, please contact Sterling Special Sales at 800-805-5489 or specialsales@sterlingpublishing.com.

Manufactured in the United States of America

Lot #:
2 4 6 8 10 9 7 5 3 1
03/21

sterlingpublishing.com

Cover and interior design by Julie Robine

All images from Getty Images:
Cover: Bettmann: running girls; E+: Azndc (snake); DNY59 (cellist); Floortje (strawberry); Hudiemm (keys); Lambada (statue); Liliboas (roses); Mihailomilovanovic (cellphone); MStudioImages (girl); PetrePlesea (mixed bouquet);Stockcam (paper); Hulton Archive: George Marks (girls whispering); iStock: Cyclonphoto (moon); Denira777 (tangerines); Hawk111 (flowers); Ksenia_Pelevina (peonies); Lifelong (pink peony); MeggiSt (stars)Nosyrevy (fish); Santje09 (mixed bouquet); Starets (cactus); Turnervisual (mixed bouquet); Photodisc: boy; Vetta: CSA Images (pie, donuts)

p. v: Azndc (snake);Lambada (statue); Liliboas (roses); Mihailomilovanovic (cellphone); MStudioImages (girl); Vetta: CSA Images (donuts); MeggiSt (stars); Denira777 (tangerines); Lifelong (pink peony); Photodisc: boy; Lambada (statue); Hulton Archive: George Marks (girls whispering)

p. 2: DigitalVision Vectors: Powerofforever (university)

PSST

CHEAP DATES WITH ANA: TOP 10 HOT GIRLS WITH EATING DISORDERS

Have we missed anyone? . . .

1. Bec Houghton
2. Sav Mueller
3. Jessie Ong
4. Calypso Steadman
5. Helen Pringle
6. Antonia Tucci
7. Meg Riley
8. Issy Spillane
9. Georgia Lucas
10. Maddie Vincent

hungryjackoff: srsly only chicks could be this stupid
Feminightmare: Hey, guess what, you idiot—eating disorders are not gender-specific. Publishing this list is creepy, slanderous, dangerous
hungryjackoff: don't get yr panties in a not
Feminightmare: Let's see what state your panties are in when you dickheads get busted for publishing shit like this
b@rnieboy: fat sluts are hotter any day. skinny chix got no titz
sufferingsuffragette: Dear PSST, nobody cares about your tragic lists except other losers like you. PrivateSchoolSecretsTrackr is run by PatheticSadSexlessTools
Feminightmare: Anyone who needs help with eating disorders, call the Eating Disorders Helpline at (800) 931-2237 for confidential support and information. Real people know this is a serious condition and not a joke; we're there for you.

St. Hilda's

2 Illowra Crescent Hawthorn Victoria 3122 Australia

Dear Sophomore Parents,

I am delighted to advise you that your daughter will participate in the St. Hilda's Wellness Program during the third quarter.

Dr. Peter Malik will be giving the classes. Peter is known to many of you as our 12th grade psychology teacher. He is also the author of the forthcoming book, *Growing Up in the Digital Age: A Guide for Teenagers*.

The Wellness Program covers topics such as identity, self-image, personal growth, respect for self and others, productive communication, working as a community, bullying, friendship, and making good choices.

We urge you to continue these important conversations at home. To facilitate this, the course plan—including topics, dates, and desired outcomes—is attached to this email.

We all see, with grave concern, the extent to which a seemingly nonstop stream of age-inappropriate material assails this generation in the digital era. Hardly a week goes by without another report in the mainstream media about the prevalence of online bullying and its frequently tragic consequences.

It is one of our most profound responsibilities to equip our girls with the resilience and personal integrity to cope with whatever comes their way in these challenging times.

Please advise 10th grade guidance counselor Heather Yelland if any of the topics are likely to prompt the need for extra support or counseling for your daughter.

The Wellness Program is a co-curricular activity and, as such, does not take any allocated time from core curriculum subjects.

Further communications will follow regarding our two key social activities this term: the Winter Fair and the Sophomore Formal.

Yours sincerely,

Maura Gaffney

Principal

WEEK 1

IDENTITY

Wellness

Monday, July 11
Dr. Peter Malik

Week 1: Identity

Who am I?

Provocation

I celebrate myself, and sing myself,
And what I assume you shall assume,
For every atom belonging to me as good belongs to you.
—Walt Whitman, "Song of Myself"

Points for Discussion/Reflection

Each of us is an individual as well as a member of various groups—family, community, school, friendship. Our identity is developed through a combination of our personality, our beliefs and values, our cultural background, our opportunities and privilege, our experiences and actions, our defining moments.

- Are you happy with your identity?
- Do others see you as you see yourself?
- To what extent do you reveal yourself to your peers?
- Are you happy with the way others see you?
- How might your value system inform your judgment of others?

Task 1

Write your first wellness journal entry. Respond to one of the questions, to the provocation, or to any aspect of our class discussion. You may choose to keep journal entries private. Alternatively, I am available if you'd like to share or discuss your thoughts on any of our topics.

Task 2

Next week we will be revisiting an elementary school favorite: show-and-tell. Bring to class an item that tells your classmates something about you.

Clem

Monday, July 11

Monday morning, 6:30. Gray clouds bulge in the sky. Jinx says she doesn't feel the cold, but I can't stop shivering. We're walking to the new pool and, with each step on the frosty grass, I want to put myself in reverse. It's been six weeks since I've been to training. I only made it out of bed today because we're getting our new uniforms—part 1 of our reward for killing it at Nationals. We're also getting a trip to Canberra. Each member of the St. Hilda's Marlins relay team won in our individual categories. Unprecedented, apparently.

Jinx bounces ahead of me like she's on springs. "Lainie says we're getting bomber jackets."

I make a noise, enough so she thinks I'm contributing.

She stops suddenly to stretch. "Did you see the itinerary for Canberra?"

"Uh, I haven't looked at it yet."

Jinx goes back to bouncing. "You're gonna love the pool.

Remember how crappy the old one was? All the Band-Aids and hair ties floating around? This one's so clean. I *feel* faster."

Jinx doesn't have to worry about speed. Last time we raced, she beat me—clocking just over a minute for the 100-meter freestyle. She's so tall—the bitches at school call her Slenderman, but Jinx doesn't care. She can eat whatever. Nothing sticks. Next to her I feel like somebody's squat aunty.

The new aquatic center looms before us, all glass and concrete. We pause on the step.

Jinx puts her hands on my shoulders. "Go hard, Clem—Maggie's eyeing your slot."

I snort. "Maggie Cho! I could've beaten her with my cast still on."

I flutter my hand and feel a twinge, but it's just phantom pain, nerves. I broke my wrist back in May. For a while after the accident, I still turned up for training, but it was frustrating having to sit there while everyone else was thrashing up and back, so I decided I was on hiatus. And then something—someone—came along and stole my attention.

Jinx heaves the glass door open. I smell chlorine and competition. Steam rises from the surface of the water. When Coach Beazley sees me, she starts to clap, and the Marlins join in, slow at first, but by the time I reach them they've gone feral, clapping like I'm the second coming. Jinx bows because she's the one who brought me.

Beaz is all business. "How's the wrist, Banks?"

"Perfect," I say.

Jinx is right, the water looks crystalline. I should want to dive right in, but it's the last thing I feel like doing. I turn my attention to the new uniforms, join the frenzy of ripping into the plastic bags. The new suit is as green and shiny as a Christmas beetle. Our surnames are printed on the back of our satin bomber jackets. The relay team—me, Jinx, Lainie, and Roo—floor it to the locker rooms while the other Marlins look on in envy.

Some sixth sense tells me to use a stall. I have a warning feeling, a buzz in my brain that gets louder when I close the door. I take off my tracksuit, take a breath, and step into the new suit. I pull it up. It's tight. It's very, very tight. That breath I took—I'd better keep it in, like, forever, because, once it goes, all the stitching will, too. I take the suit off and I grab handfuls of fat from my stomach. I didn't realize it was this bad. It's like I've gone up a whole size. All the sleeping in and second helpings and no training to work it off.

I can hear the others admiring each other, and I imagine they look like sleek machines. I wait until their footsteps fade. Then I put my tracksuit back on and shove the new bathing suit in my bag. I try to walk casually past the pool, but Beaz strides after me.

"Everything okay?"

"Ah, there's an emergency." I can feel my face burn with the lie. "My sister, Iris. She's sick."

I shuffle faster until I'm practically running.

"Clem!" Her voice drowns in the sounds of swimmers.

She'll want to see me later. I'll get the call when I'm in English or history. Some junior will come in with a note and I'd better have a good reason. I guess I've got from now until then to think of one. I imagine telling her that I can't swim because my suit doesn't fit. She'll want to do the whole diet interrogation. In the fall Lainie lost 18 pounds—she did it by chewing her food and spitting it out into a napkin. I don't know if I have that kind of willpower.

Instead of going back to my dorm, I head for the old pool. I think I'll be alone there, but as I walk up I can hear music: someone is playing a cello. I linger by the deep end and see Kate—Iris's roommate—sitting on a chair at the bottom of the empty pool, bowing away. There's a laptop on the ground beside her. She bends down, presses a button, and beats sound. Kate has her back to me, but she's so intent on what she's doing that she wouldn't notice if there were a hundred people watching. Her live melody weaves through the recorded sounds. Something in the combination makes me feel . . . I don't know, like the world is about to end, like everything sweet must be remembered. I lean against a tree and let the melancholy wash over me. I'm thinking that nothing changes until everything does.

On our first day at St. Hilda's, when Iris and I were introducing ourselves to the other boarders, I said that my natural state was half-fish. Iris mumbled about her idol, Ada Lovelace. Someone said, "If you're twins how come you don't look anything like each other?" This is true. Iris is tall; I'm short. Iris is pale; I'm ruddy. Iris is flat as a tack; I'm all hills and valleys.

When our parents packed up and moved to Singapore for work, they decided it would be too disruptive to our schooling for us to go with them. They chose St. Hilda's because it's academic *and* sporty. Iris is the smart one; I'm the athletic one. Mum always says we can be anything we want, but that's what we are. Iris was expecting me to room with her, and she still hasn't forgiven me for choosing not to.

I'm thinking about this stuff, but, also, I'm thinking about Stu. He's the *someone*—the reason I broke my wrist—sort of.

How it happened:

I was running on the track by the river, and I literally crashed into him. I fell, landed, howled in pain. Jinx said she'd never seen my face so white. A few days later, I was slouching around my dorm when Old Joy, our housemistress, stuck her head in and told me I had a visitor. It was him! He was gorgeous. And he'd brought me a bunch of flowers. We sat in the lounge—the only place boys are allowed—and he was being very funny and cute even with constant interruptions and surveillance. He told me his name was Stuart Laird McAlistair, and he wanted to buy me a coffee. He wrote his phone number on my cast and drew a rambling rose.

"Never call before 11 a.m.," he said. "I need my beauty sleep."

No, I thought. *You really don't.*

I'd never seen a guy so beautiful.

Our first date was on a Friday after school. We had hot fries at the cafeteria. Stu did most of the talking. He told me he was 19, and a musician. He'd been studying community work, but had dropped out. When I told him I was 16, he scrunched his brow, faking deep. "That's a dangerous age." He teased me about my school uniform and, as he kissed me goodbye, snaked his hand under it. I floated home, tasting salt on my lips, feeling the imprint of his fingertips on my regulation St. Hilda's tights. I've been floating ever since. Now mornings when I should be training are spent lazing in bed, thinking about Stuart Laird McAlistair putting his hands all over me.

♦

Kate stops mid-bow and starts packing up. And I'm back to the real, the now, late for breakfast. I dart off before she can see me. I don't even go to the mess hall. I just get a coffee from the machine and drink it in my room. I hang the new suit over the back of my chair, for thin-spiration. But I can't help hating it.

And it's the draggingest day.

I think about Stu, and I think about food.

At lunch I snub the lasagna and pile on the salad. If I'm going to fit into that suit I'll have to ease up on carbs and sugar. But I'm a defunct dieter, bound to fail.

After lunch we have the new unit—wellness. We lounge on the beanbags and generally take an age to settle down. My empty stomach rumbles violently. Tash (coathanger, pretty, popular) makes a face. "Hey, She-man, have an energy bar." She snorts like a pig and laughs. In the next second, something flies through the air. An eraser hits the back of Tash's head.

"Ow!" She whirls around. It was Iris. I can tell by her tiny smile. Iris wants me to meet her eyes, but I won't do it. I hate it when my sister comes to my defense. Dr. Malik is standing patiently in front of a quote on the board—*I celebrate myself, and sing myself.* I groan inwardly. Since when is wellness even a word?

Kate

Monday, July 11

I wake up with my hands in the air, curved as if I'm holding my cello. I can't remember what I dreamed about when I lived in the country. The city, no doubt, but I don't have a clear recollection. I remember daydreams from then—staring at white, dry fields, wishing they were streets.

The Marlins move along the dorm hallway, up before dawn for swim practice. Jinx and Clem slide past almost silently in socks, floorboard-surfing the downward tilt outside the room I share with Iris. If you get up some speed, a smooth pair of socks will take you all the way to the sophomore bathroom.

We're on the third floor, so we have the unreliable showers with the pressure of mist. The junior and senior boarders are above us on the fourth floor, and the eighth and ninth graders are below us on the second. The mess, kitchen, boarder study rooms, lounge, and seventh graders are on the ground floor. It's as if the water's being sucked and heated in every direction except ours.

I've heard that the basement has an excellent shower, if you don't mind the cobwebs. Every morning, when I'm freezing in the sophomore bathroom, I decide it'd be worth pushing my way through all the forgotten things they keep down there—old suitcases and chairs and blackboards and costumes—to shower under a blast of water as hot as we had back at the farm. I'd happily get naked with the spiders for that.

Thoughts about the basement lead to thoughts about the portal—the door down there that's too swollen to shut, forgotten by everyone except the boarders; forgotten even by Old Joy, who spends her life in constant fear that one of us will break her rules and have sex.

I don't want to go through the portal for sex. Sex would be nice. I wouldn't mind a date for the formal, followed by sex, but that's not my most pressing need at the moment. It's not why I'm obsessed with the door in the basement.

Instead, I imagine myself walking silently across the cold grass of a shadowy world, toward the main gates. I climb over them at the low point and land on the street. From the street to a tram, from the tram to the city, and from there to Orion, this small club above a record store where Frances Carter plays; where Emilie Autumn, Zoë Keating, Anna Meredith, Amiina, and Wendy Sutter have all played. I need the portal because it could get me freedom at night without a pass, and the night is when the clubs are open, and the clubs are where the music is happening. And music, these days, is pretty much all I think about.

I try to be quiet in the morning, but it doesn't matter all that much. Iris sleeps through anything. She sleeps through me feeling around in the dark for toiletries, through me tripping over her laptop cord, stubbing my toe on her desk (fuck!), through me shining my phone around, looking for the door handle.

She dreams while I shower, while I come back and get dressed, while I take my cello, my laptop, everything I need for practice. She's still dreaming as the stale heat of the dorms gives way to crisp air, as I head into a morning so early it's dark; so dark the stars are out, and I can imagine, for a second, that I've escaped into the night.

The old pool is down the back of the grounds. Past the tennis courts, it's hidden by a huge box hedge that's perfect for cover. The gate is always open—there's no point locking it. One day they'll build something else here, but until then it's the best place to play. Empty of water, it's perfect for echoes.

I climb down the stairs into the shallow end, where I've left an old school chair. Joseph, the groundskeeper, gave it to me. He doesn't seem to question why a girl would get up before light to play her cello in a pool full of leaves. He's worked here a long time, I guess, and seen all types come and go.

My breaths are sharp wisps in the dark. This is the moment I love. When I'm alone, warm in my jacket, angling my face at the moon. I put on headphones and start my practice session the same way I always do—listening to Frances Carter and waiting for sunrise.

It's as if I were one person before Frances Carter walked into the auditorium in my third week at St. Hilda's, and then another person when she walked out.

She's lean, wiry, about 30. Wearing black that looked even

blacker against her red hair. Her face wasn't unsmiling or unfriendly. She had the same look I'd seen on my own face in photographs, when someone took a shot of me working on a math or science question, or a computer problem.

She set up—cello in her arms, laptop on the floor, which she used as an instrument controlled by a foot pedal. A pickup mic attached to her cello caught and threw sound. When she was ready, she looked at us with this quiet certainty.

Then there was a second before she started. A second before I knew you could combine my two loves—computer and cello. Before I knew I could use a computer to loop and layer and build sounds. Before I started listening to everything electronic and experimental I could get my hands on.

Before.

When a solid career in medicine seemed like the best thing in the world. When I didn't know that a cello had a throat and a heart. When my life was ordinary and I didn't mind because I didn't know.

Frances started her first song and Iris shifted in her seat like she was bored. I wondered how a person could ever be bored by the mixing of something ancient and new—human and machine—engineered to make honey.

Only a few of us were still in the auditorium when Frances left. The others, Iris included, moved out as soon as Mrs. Davies said they could. But I stayed, matching the pace of my packing to hers. Every movement was graceful and deliberate. I wondered how she came to be so full of choice.

"There's an audition," she said to those still waiting. "I've given the flyers to Mrs. Davies."

Then she was gone, and I was reading the flyer, reading about the Harpa International Music Academy in Iceland, imagining an unknown landscape, where classes would be held over the summer—our winter—in June next year. Frances Carter was offering three scholarships to the Harpa Summer School because someone had given her a scholarship when she was a sophomore. *I want to sponsor students in my area,* she'd written on the flyer, *so auditions are for young musicians using technology.*

A life changed in 30 minutes.

At the sign of first light, I take off my headphones and set up.

Frances Carter uses Ableton Live and Super-Looper on a MacBook Pro with a MOTU Ultralite audio interface, so I've bought the same. Add in the price of some pickup mics, and the whole setup cost me a little over $2,000—half my bank account.

When I told Iris about my dwindling savings and where most of it had gone, she cut me off mid-sentence. "Your parents have spent everything to send you here. Are you effing crazy?"

Probably. I'm definitely obsessed; of that, there's no doubt.

Curved corners catch and bounce sound. I bow long strokes, cello humming through my arms, my chest, my thighs. I lay down separate tracks this morning, experimenting with tone. There are sweet spots: places where I play and the sound bounces back at me. Echo spots. Later, I will take these lines of cello and mix them. Heighten, twist, shape, and color.

I'm getting better, but I'm not great. There's only so much I can learn alone. What I really need is to meet people playing this kind of music—people I can talk with, experiment with. Those people are at clubs like Orion, which is why I need to escape. The problem is I need backup. But Iris is pretty much my only friend in the city, and there's no way she'll sneak out with me.

It's something I have to do alone, but I can't quite find the courage.

I force myself to pack up at 7:30. Orchestra is at 8:00 in the new arts center, at the other side of the school. Plush and warm in winter, the acoustics are brilliant. And, best of all, it's near the new canteen, which sells real coffee.

I order an americano and take it over to a spot bathed in winter sun. It's one of my favorite times of the day, spoiled only by one thing.

"Hello, Kate."

It's a combined orchestra. We play with Basildon, the boys' school. We do most things with them—orchestra, plays, the school formal—since they're close by. There are seven other cellists in the orchestra. Iris is one of them. I sit next to her. There are five other people I wouldn't mind on the other side of me.

"Coffee's bad for your health."

But I get Oliver Bennet.

"So, some studies say, is a lack of quiet time," I tell him.

I'm a friendly person. At my old school back in Shallow Bay, I was considered pretty much the friendliest person in the school. But I have the urge to cut Oliver Bennet's cello strings one by one, and watch him watch me doing it, and this is why:

1. He thinks he plays better than me.

2. He does, sometimes, play better than me.

3. Oliver is obsessed with perfection. I heard him laughing when Frances Carter played.

4. He loves nothing more than to give me a lecture on the importance of technique.
5. Oliver, in short, is a boring, anally retentive, fuckwit.

Iris told me that Oliver's mum is a cellist in the Australian Chamber Orchestra. A child prodigy, she was playing Bach at six. Oliver's never mentioned that to me directly, but for the last six months, he's acted as though he knows everything and I know nothing.

Iris arrives as I finish my coffee and we all walk inside. Oliver goes through his setup routine—shifting his chair until it's in exactly the right spot, setting out his music so it's exactly in front of him, asking me to move a little to the right, and then asking if I'd like him to show me how to play double stops.

"No, thanks," I tell him, but he goes ahead with the instruction anyway.

"The double stops," he informs me, "are the most misunderstood device ever."

"That's fascinating," I say, and concentrate on fading his voice to background noise. Because this is my favorite part of orchestra—what happens while we're tuning. The steel shift of chairs. The whispers before notes. The third viola staring at the first violin while she thinks about sex. I can hear it in her eyes. It's a slow, slow slide. Blinking heat and the sweetness of C.

"You nearly have it," Oliver says, whispering some last instructions.

"Thanks," I tell him, as I think: *Go. Away. Fuck. Off.*

He keeps harping on it, though, in that stiff, repressed way of his, so I turn to him, and hold my hand up to stop him from talking. "I can play the double stops, Oliver. I choose to play the wrong notes."

He looks genuinely perplexed. "Who chooses to play the wrong notes?"

"Me. I do."

Mrs. Davies taps her baton, points her finger at me, and Oliver sees the tap and the point and looks satisfied.

"Experiment in your own time," he says, before we start to play.

I leave orchestra feeling stupid because Oliver has a small, small point. Orchestra is not the place to experiment. But when is the place to experiment? At the pool, sure. But experimenting alone only gets me so far.

Iris goes back to our dorm room to make sure she has her things, so I spend the time before class calling Ben, my best friend from back home.

He answers the phone with his foggy morning voice, and I hear a series of shuffles as he pushes himself up, fumbles for his glasses, and reaches for the cold cup of coffee on his bedside table. Ben can't get up before caffeine, and since he doesn't mind cold coffee, he makes himself a cup before he goes to sleep.

"Okay, I'm awake."

He's not. He never is until he's had a good couple of mouthfuls.

"Okay," he says after a few minutes. "Really awake now."

"I need to get out. I need to go to Orion. I need to hear music. I need to meet people like me, who are equally obsessed, or Iceland will never happen."

"Still too freaked out to use the portal without backup?"

"Still too freaked out to use the portal without backup."

"Rebellion cannot exist without the feeling that somewhere, in some way, you are justified."

"Orwell?"

"Camus," he says.

I never get Ben's references. He reads too widely. If I'm a mixture of computer and music, Ben is a mixture of book and plant.

"So, are you justified in breaking the school rules?" He takes another swig of coffee.

"I'll get back to you on that. What's news in your world?"

He talks about school and I hear my old life in his voice. I'm taken back to the farm, to the river, to the fruit trees. To my parents working crazy long days, buying water and feed and worrying about money, but telling me not to, telling me they have plenty to send me to St. Hilda's this year, and once I get the scholarship for junior and senior years, it won't be a worry.

"I'm concerned," Ben says, and I realize that I've drifted off. "Could it be possible—" Ben has a way of talking, a steady way, so that you can hear the dashes in his sentences. "What I mean to ask is—could it be possible—that the only thing people like about me—is you?"

He tries to say it as if it were a clinical, scientific observation.

"That is not possible. It's absolutely a hundred percent not possible."

"I've been collecting quite a bit of evidence to the contrary," he says. "No one really talks to me. I eat lunch alone."

I can see him in the part of the school we call The Back, staring over the fence into the dry grass of the out-of-bounds section. He's eating a cheese sandwich, and missing me.

"Twenty-seven percent of the universe is dark matter, and 68 percent of the universe is dark energy."

"The point?" he asks.

"Dark matter is essential. But it took some time to be known. Talk to people. You're funny. They'll talk back. Trust me. I'm smart. I know things."

A silent dash hangs in the air. "I'm a bit lonely without you," he says eventually.

"I'm a bit lonely without you," I say.

I want to talk more, but I have to go. The class is filing in for wellness, a new program designed to cure us of the urge to trash each other on social media. I love the internet, code, computers. I love that if I miss Ben, I can summon him into my room and talk to him over Skype. The internet is the most mind-bending invention in the last century and how do humans use it? They access porn and talk smack about each other.

I walk inside, and while I wait for Dr. Malik I put on my headphones and turn up Imogen Heap. There's a moment when her voice reaches a point so thick and high that it gets into my skin. It makes me feel like rebellion is possible. I'm cutting out at night, confident, walking into a club, cool-skinned in the face of possible expulsion.

But then class starts, and I put my music away. I go back to the old Kate. Reserved. Responsible. Am I justified in rebelling? Maybe. And if that's the answer, then probably not.

Ady

Monday, July 11

"Okay if I go shopping with Tash this week? We need to start looking for formal dresses."

My mother, cutting up fruit, points to her earbuds, and shakes her head. She is talking to her friend, Viv. "The reason you don't know her name is because she's the next big thing. She did Simon and Lucy's—you know, massive budget—it's stunning and *Vogue Living*'s doing a feature on it. You're welcome." My mother, the resident style know-it-all.

Breakfast at my house: We're a group of islands.

My father is on another call, standing at the middle set of French doors, looking out over the garden, my mother glancing toward him about every two seconds.

Charlie is head-deep in Brian Jacques, one elbow on the table, making his way through three Shredded Wheat biscuits in a pool of milk.

Clare is stirring oatmeal—Monday breakfast—and scrolling through world news headlines on Twitter.

I try to connect the islands. "Anyone have any ideas about the formal? I'm on the organizing committee."

"Here's an idea: Tell the brain trust to keep their tongues inside their mouths for photographs. They look like a posse of B-grade porn stars on Facebook." The brain trust is my friends. Clare's life is full of time-saving abbreviations. She slices a banana on her oatmeal, tops it with maple syrup, sits down, and opens the newspaper to the op-ed page. Senior year means keeping up with the state of the world every day, so no issues-based question on an English or history exam will ever catch you uninformed.

I'm eating toasted sourdough with peanut butter, and making a bagel for my lunch. Skills. "Is that better or worse than looking like A-grade porn stars?"

"You decide," says Clare.

"Don't say porn in front of a child," says Charlie, not looking up from his book. He's 10, and he plays the kid card like a champ.

"Good point, darling." My mother sits down next to Charlie and drops a kiss on the side of his head. They look so . . . Instagram-able, his hair streaky blond, hers sleek and dark. Genes divide up hard-core in this family: Clare is like our mother, blue eyes, dark brown hair; Charlie and I have our dad's blond hair and gray eyes.

My father is winding up his call, sounding very peppy. "No, great—totally. Absolutely. Soon, for sure. Cheers, buddy."

"Yes?" my mother asks him.

"No." My father walks out of the room.

My mother compresses her lips.

Clare gives me a knowing look, but I'm not quite sure what it is she knows.

"Mother, the formal dress—I need to start looking and thinking."

"Looking and thinking *only*. The credit cards need a rest."

Okay. This is new, and I don't like the sound of it. "Is there a particular reason why?"

My mother doesn't answer. She's hardly eaten any of her fruit and yogurt, but she stands up and follows my father out of the kitchen. I pick up the pace on lunch prep, eager to be out of the house before they start arguing, and try to remember exactly when he last worked.

Walking the three blocks from River Place, where I live, to St. Hilda's, where I learn, I'm chewing over last night's PSST post and worrying about Bec—a member of the brain trust—whose name was on their shitty list. Way to start the week. PSST is like a slime monster that feeds on lies and nastiness. Every time it lifts its arm to drag another victim down, it gets stronger.

I get to school just after Bec has arrived. She is tragically holding up a "Disorderly Friendship Foundation" brochure that someone has slipped into her locker. Three juniors are staring at her from the other side of the hallway, whispering. I give them the death stare and they slink off.

"I don't even have one . . ." she starts, a tear brimming in each eye.

"I know. You're just a skinny Minnie, Becs. It's not a crime." I give her a hug.

Lola arrives and throws her bag down. "Hey, at least you were top of the list."

That's enough to get the tears flowing. Trouble is, in our group

Bec is the peacemaker, the diplomat, the smoother; she's the one who knows exactly what to say at times like this.

Tash emerges from the door of our homeroom, right next to the lockers. It's out of character for her to have arrived at school before the rest of us. "Ady! Have you opened your locker?"

"Not yet."

Tash has a huge smile as I unlock it. We four have each other's combinations, naturally. I spy a square box, tied with the signature satin ribbon of *Délicieux*—the patisserie. Inside is one perfect coffee éclair—my favorite—and a note, *To sweet Ady, love Rupe X*

"Thank you, Tashie—you sneaky cupid." Tash and Rupert both come in on the Brighton train. Rupe goes to Basildon.

"He *adores* you, Ady," says Tash. "God knows why."

We share the perfect éclair in four luscious bites, with me getting the dark chocolate coffee bean, then cluster around Bec to give her some more love before first period.

How horrible for the girls on that list who do have eating disorders, to have PSST make a joke about your sickness. Jessie Ong was in the fricken hospital earlier this year.

Not. Funny.

The gravel path crunches underfoot as Bec, Lola, Tash, and I head for wellness; early bulbs are green, spiking from the cold earth, and the air is scented with Daphne. How can PSST even exist in our shiny, shiny world? It's not like nastiness is a new invention. It's just floated closer to the surface lately. Scum will do that. Mean stuff spreads so fast. One click. Post. Send. Share. Online bullying = sometimes-suicides, so all the private schools have strategies for dealing with it. At St. Hilda's, it's wellness classes. We greeted the idea with genuine enthusiasm. Why not? Everyone loves the chance to slack off.

The classes are being held in the Oak Parlor in the "old building," as we call it. Framed sepia photos show actual cows grazing on the riverbank, with the old building—then, a freshly built Victorian tower mansion—in the distance. These days, a handful of architect-designed hubs populate the sprawling, beautifully landscaped campus. And there are a few blocks of luxe suburbia between school and the river, including my street.

The old building smell reminds me of being in awe and in preschool. In recent years there's an added layer of let-me-out-of-here.

I trail a finger along the hand-blocked wallpaper, strictly forbidden, but I can't resist touching the delicately raised surface of the bronze-painted fleurs-de-lis.

What was once a formal sitting room, with its ceiling of some arcadia or other, and stained-glass windows, is today the land of wellness. We sit in the moss-green corduroy beanbags, which I will forever associate with meditation and sex ed, also held in this room. No friends allowed to sit together, so Dr. Malik separates me and Tash by swapping her with quiet boarder, Kate Turner, who is doing some strange finger-tapping on her leg and looking at the ground, so she doesn't notice Tash push her tongue behind her lower lip like a chimp. Wellness abounds.

Malik has the dubious honor of being the best-looking male teacher at school. Small pool, of course—a girls' school staff room. People think he looks like an older Dev Patel. You have to really squint to see it, in my opinion. But, then, I've got my own handsome boy.

Malik is happily babbling on: overview blah blah; identity blah blah; more things that unite us than divide us; when we find common ground, we find mutual respect; the better we know each other, the more we'll look out for each other. And various other all-very-well-in-theory principles that basically bullshit out in practice. The bonds of girl friendship can be tight to the point of strangulation, and no one's going to start skipping from group to group. Teachers don't get the most basic stuff sometimes.

"Okay, girls, I'm going to ask you to sort yourselves into groups of three according to thumb length," Malik says, as though that's a fun thing to do.

Lola gives me a solidarity eye-roll as we move about the room, hand to hand with girls we routinely ignore.

Tash is standing next to me and compares thumbs with swim-team girl Clem Banks, whose thumb is longer than hers, but Tash says, "Back off."

Clem Banks looks at her as though she will, as though she doesn't care either way, but then she stops and says, "You back off."

Tash isn't going anywhere.

"They look about the same to me," says Bec. "Maybe you'd be happier with another group, Clem?"

Dr. Malik senses the standoff. "Do you need to take a more careful look at your thumbs, girls?"

"Oh, fine." Tash stomps off and continues thumb-measuring with other people.

Kate Turner is already standing next to me; both of us have distinctly long thumbs.

So I end up with those two, Kate Turner and Clem Banks,

who is so scowly she's already got permanent frown lines. We are the longest-thumb group. Makes sense, when you think about it—a cellist's hands, a swimmer's hands, and a tall girl's hands. But so what? Malik tells us to note our groups for future reference. It reminds me of a kindergarten icebreaker, but at 16 we're frozen deeper than he knows.

So it's the same old. They can try stuff like this, and we'll go along with it, but nothing really changes. I zone out again as we resettle in our beanbags. Is it like this for everyone—that school and family are balloons that blow up and shrink? Sometimes school is everything, and I hardly notice what's going on at home. Other times, like now, family seems to be blowing up. Plus, there's the whole Rupert question.

Wellness feelies won't fix the real problems.

Whatever was happening at breakfast this morning is connected to last night's parental altercation. Traditionally, there's been a pattern in my family life: fight, fight, settle, fun; fight, fight, settle, fun. Lately, it's all *fight, fight,* very little *settle*, and even less *fun*.

I went into Clare's room. She was studying with earbuds in, as always. Mozart is her preferred study music. Classic dweeb. "Did you hear that?" I asked.

"*What?*" She removed one earbud, exasperated before I even started.

"Mum and Dad. Something about money."

She rolled her eyes, which light on her bulletin board. Picking up a pen, she crossed one more day off her calendar. Countdown until she escapes to university. The other thing on her bulletin board is a huge printout of her goal for the college entrance exams, the grade she figures will get her a full academic and residential scholarship to study medicine at the University of New South Wales in Sydney. She put the earbud back in. "Some of us have work to do."

She's turned herself into a study machine for senior year. She's more like a hard drive than a sister. I went looking for Charlie instead.

Charlie is the family's emotional barometer. When things get tense here, he buries himself deeper in his books, and spends more time at the Coopers', our neighbors over the back fence. Sure enough, when I checked his bedroom he wasn't there. But I did see Snozphant, his most precious stuffed toy, hiding under his pillow, even though he has declared himself "over" stuffed toys and officially retired them to the highest shelf in his closet.

Clare's ready to bail and Charlie is more like a Cooper than a Rosenthal these days, so that just leaves me to figure out what's happening. I'm going to need some after-school time in my closet. Just thinking about that space calms me down. Not that I'd say that out loud. It's more of a clothes archive than a closet, anyway: a room adjoining my bedroom, lined with shelves, drawers, and hanging racks, designed by me. My sewing and cutting table is under the window, and stretches to the middle of the room. I collect clothes. I dream up and make clothes. I refurbish clothes. I repurpose clothes. I love clothes—*truly* love them. I care for, nurture, praise, pat, wash and iron, and appreciate them. I celebrate them. And when I'm stressed, I smell my clothes. If you can tell me a more calming smell than washed and sunshine-dried cotton, I probably won't believe it. If you cannot understand the comfort of burying your face in kitten-soft cashmere, washed in eucalyptus wool mix, we will probably never be friends.

At the end of our first wellness class Malik tells us to write wellness journal entries whenever we want. We can show him or not. He encourages us to be truthful, to use the entries as an opportunity to take our emotional temperature. He adds that there'll be no judging of anything we share in wellness class discussions. Ha-ha. He doesn't know us very well.

Clem's Wellness Journal

Monday, July 11

Am I happy? Ish.

My identity: Clem Banks, 16. Medium-length wavy brown hair. Roundish face to go with roundish body. I have nice teeth and good eyesight (Iris has to wear a plate and glasses). I bite my nails. I hate my period. I'm a virgin. I'm shit at math, but okay at English.

Defining moments:

1. *Fifth grade: Swimming Carnival. I won every race. My teacher, Mr. Mullane, called me Flash for the next few weeks. Up until then I'd just been the dumb twin. It was like I'd been searching for something special about myself and then I found it.*

2. *Sixth grade: I was a fish and I loved it. I was fast and strong. Why would I care about lip gloss or sleepovers or boys, when every weekend there was the chance of glory? But, now that I think about it, that was the year that things started changing. Hormones were happening. My body started to feel like a betrayal. You can't hide hills and valleys in a swimsuit. And Iris was only too happy to point them out.*

3. *Seventh grade: Waiting for Dad to pick me up from the pool. I was sitting on the side, watching the water, when a boy and girl turned up. They weren't much*

> *older than me. They jumped into the deep end together and then proceeded to make out with abandon. They were so brazen, so inside their own bubble, and so oblivious to the little-old-lady swimmers with their flowery swimming caps and snorkels. And then, at one point, the boy looked at me. His girlfriend was kissing his neck or whatever and he looked at me. It was like he was saying, "Don't you want this?" And I hadn't really let myself think about it before, but there, at the pool, I did. People hooked up. Romance happened. It was a thing and it could happen to me. But not if I was a fish.*

Point of fact: my name comes from a song about a girl who drowned.

I feel like I'm drowning all the time.

Kate's Wellness Journal

Tuesday, July 12

Dear Journal,

I like the idea of this but I'm not calling it a wellness journal. That makes it sound like I'm in some kind of formal therapy, which I fully support if you need it, but I'd rather think of it as a kind of diary.

Am I happy with my identity?

If you'd asked me before I came to St. Hilda's, I would have said pretty much. Now I don't know. I don't know a lot of things since I moved to the city. My life plan's gone all out of whack.

It's not that I thought I knew everything before. There were plenty of things I didn't know (never really worked out how to make a website hit the top ranks of Google, never worked out how to beat the Facebook algorithm, I mostly wear jeans and T-shirts because I never worked out the fashion thing, I've never understood how people can just make up stories in English, and I have absolutely no idea why some girl hasn't fallen head over heels for Ben).

But I did have some things figured out. I thought I knew myself, at least. My life plan had been in place for a while. Study hard. Convince Mum and Dad to send me to St. Hilda's, where I would study even harder in tenth grade, take the scholarship exam for junior and senior year, work like crazy to get into medical school. Become a doctor. Pay Mum and Dad back. Look after them and the farm.

I celebrate myself, and sing myself.

It's as though, on the day that I heard Frances Carter, my self changed.

A part of me that I didn't know existed spoke for the first time.

It makes me wonder what else is there, waiting to appear.

Ady's Wellness Journal

Tuesday, July 12

Do others see the real me? Do I reveal myself to my peers? *Wow. I show a pretty edited version even to Tash, Bec, and Lola. Classic example—I would definitely not tell them I'm writing this, not in a million years.*

Malik said we should regularly take our "emotional temperature," check in on how we are feeling, so here goes . . . How am I feeling? I'm feeling as though "confused" and "restless" had a baby that's settled inside me like an alien. I have a sense that things are about to get messy, like I'm standing at the edge of a whirlpool, or the air pressure is suddenly wrong for my body. Is "dread" the right word for that? Calm before a storm? (Checked with Clare; she suggests: "impending doom," or simply "existential angst." She tells me, in a reassuring tone, that I have catastrophist tendencies. She may be right.) The color for the way I feel is bruise-yellow.

I'm going to let myself write down stuff here that I usually wouldn't.

So, my father has been sleeping in his study for the past week, maybe longer. And, related . . . ? Late one night, from the top of the stairs, I saw him bring—sneak—a cardboard carton into his study. On investigation—yes, I'm a snoop—I found that it had been well-hidden, and that it contained 12 bottles of vodka, each in its own box. There is always vodka out in the open here; it's not a forbidden substance. So, if there's public drinking and secret drinking, is that a new thing, or not? I feel like I should've mentioned it to my mother, but I haven't.

My mother has asked if we can "sort through" my wardrobe. Translation: She wants me to get rid of stuff. She doesn't understand what it all means to me. Charlie is her beloved baby. Clare is the dependable, overachieving first child. And I'm in the middle, overlooked and misunderstood. Lucky I have my gram. Style maven. My stash of fabulous fabrics is thanks to her good taste and chronic stockpiling. She's told me all about them—I can tell silk from polyester blend by listening to the sound it makes when I rub the cloth between my fingers. And I know how to set the sewing machine tension so it doesn't chew up sheer fabrics. She's always talked to me about the garden, too, naming all the plants and flowers, and about art and design and architecture, since I was little. We are kindred spirits. As in Anne of Green Gables.

Last night—unsettling dreams of houses with rooms and hallways I've never seen before. Summary: feeling not quite right about everything—have possibly sprung a wellness leak.

PSST

GUESS WHAT SLUT PUT ON A SHOW AT JONNO'S PARTY?

NICE PIC, HUH?

sufferingsuffragette: if a guy did that you'd applaud
hungryjackoff: I did applaud her #uptightbitch
Feminightmare: #neanderthal
hungryjackoff: #fuckinguptightbitch
b@rnieboy: you grls need a good fuck is all give me yr numbers
skateordie: wtf?? i apologize for these dickheads. they are not representative of my gender
b@rnieboy: because u r gay
skateordie: great comeback #predictableloser

load 74 more comments

Clem

Thursday, July 14

Things about St. Hilda's: It runs on fat checks and fake smiles. It's like those ladies you see in the moneyed suburbs, the ones who look perfect until you get up close and see how much work they've had done. This school has been around for a century; it's old but remodeled so there are plenty of sharp edges and shiny surfaces. Iris and I have always gone to public schools. At our last one, if anyone had a problem with you, they'd be up front and punch you at the bus stop. Here, everyone's angst ends up on PSST. It's not just St. Hildans; it's people from Sacred Heart and St. Joseph's, Basildon—pretty much any private school within a 10-mile radius. Parents want to know college entrance exam scores, but PSST will tell you who puts out, who's hot, who's not, a whole host of things I don't need to know.

Last week there was a post about the odds of getting laid after the formal. It's always the cool girls who get named—it doesn't seem to hurt their swagger. I'm starting to feel a bit panicked about the formal. I haven't got a dress yet. Or a date. I'm working up to asking Stu, but maybe he'd think it's just kids' stuff. Jinx isn't taking a date. She's part of the Feminist Collective and they're all going together as a group. She said she might not even dress up. "Why should I? Who are we even dressing up for?"

After dinner, I head over to Iris's for our designated Mum-and-Dad Skype. I have to remind myself about the things I'm supposed to say, the things they want to hear. What they won't want to hear: that every morning this week I've failed to make it to training. I tell Jinx I'll be there by 7:00, but I never make it.

When I get to Kate and Iris's room, Kate's just leaving. Her eyes skate past mine. "Hi," she says. I'm about to say something about hearing her play at the old pool, but she's gone too quickly.

Iris is in her usual position in front of her computer, headphones on.

She nods at me and lowers her headphones.

"Is it working?" I ask. I don't know why it's always so glitchy. Maybe the computer senses our reluctance. Then Mum's face appears—she's right up close.

"Hello, my darlings! Hello, hello!"

Mum and Dad have started doing this thing where they talk to me and Iris like we're adults, which basically means they tell us all their problems. I'd rather they didn't. I don't want to know that Mum's finding the expat scene intellectually vapid, or that Dad's in a quandary because he's had to take on more corporate clients and it feels unethical. I don't want to know how much St. Hilda's costs because implicit in that is how much Iris and I should be enjoying it. Lately I've been thinking it's all a plot. Dad didn't have to accept that job, the whole move was just to bring me and Iris closer together. As if!

"Tell me good things," Mum says. Dad's head nods next to hers.

So I tell them my wrist is fine and our new swimming uniforms are cool, and Iris tells them how one of her essays is going to be featured in *Hilda's Herald*. We both say how excellent school is, how grateful we are that they sent us here.

"It's the best," Iris says.

Mum looks teary. "You girls," she says, "We're so glad you're looking out for each other."

Off-screen, Iris flicks my thigh, like she used to at the dinner table when we were kids. I flick hers back and get a sliver of that old kinship feeling, but it doesn't last. It never lasts. I'm standing even before we hang up. Mum and Dad blow kisses and are gone.

"You're such a bullshitter," Iris says. "You're not swimming."

"So what? God. It smells in here, Iris. Don't you ever open a window?"

"I'm working."

"What on?" I reach across her quickly and before she can stop me I've clicked on her history bar. The last thing she googled was: *How do you know if a boy likes you?*

"What boy?" I laugh. "You don't know any boys."

"Shut up. It's for an essay."

"You're such a robot."

"Fuck off, Clem."

I put my palm to my heart. "Oh, Theo!"

Iris looks like she wants to kill me. Theo Ledwidge goes to Basildon; Iris knows him from Chess Club.

"Are you hot for Theo? Are you going ask him to the formal?"

She puts her headphones back on and turns to her screen. She carries on with her homework like I'm not even there. And then, after about a minute, she takes her headphones off again and turns to me, and there's a glint of triumph in her eyes.

"Actually, I have asked Theo to the formal. And he said yes." She smiles without showing her teeth. "Who are *you* going with?" She dismisses me with a well-aimed finger flick right in the soft cushion of my stomach. "Out."

Up until we were 12, Iris and I shared a bedroom. Shared everything. But that was the year that Elise Hardy invited just me to her party, and I went. And that was also the year that Dad had one of his research students staying with us and Iris got a crush on him. I knew because I read her diary, and then I showed her diary to Elise, but it all exploded because our teacher confiscated it. What Iris had written was just fantasy, but the teacher thought it was real, thought Dad's student was messing with Iris. So much embarrassment. Poor Iris. Mean Clem. She hasn't forgiven me for that, either.

Back in my room I lie on my bed, eyeing the Kit Kat on Jinx's bedside table. It's been there for over a week. How can she be so casual about chocolate? She's at a Feminist Collective meeting. She keeps telling me I should come, but I don't go for extracurriculars—swimming's enough. Besides, I don't know what kind of witchcraft they do in there.

I think about the formal. I can't believe Iris has a date. The thought depresses me so much that I feel I must appropriate the Kit Kat. While I'm enjoying it, I send a text to Stu.

miss u

I eat a finger, and wait, and then my phone pings back and it's a photo of Stu looking tired.

all wrk and no play . . .

Then: *Send nudes!*

He's added a wink emoji. It's a joke, but when I read it again, a hot and prickly feeling comes over me. I finish the Kit Kat, but there's no more from Stu. I decide to go to bed early. Getting changed into my PJs, I catch a side-on view of myself in the mirror. I look like a truck. How can Stu want a nude of that? Does he really like me? Does he think about me the way I think about him? I lie in bed and zoom in on his photo and stare and stare. I'm doing this when Jinx comes in. She rolls her eyes. "Girl! Go have a cold shower!"

Kate

Friday, July 15

I wake up to the sounds of a storm building—no rain yet, just a dry wildness—and my first thought is I need to be outside. I need to record the sounds, not to mix them with songs, but to re-create them on the cello.

I'm at the pool by 6:30, bundled up against the freezing weather with coat, scarf, and fingerless gloves, holding a mic to the sky, trying, unsuccessfully, to capture the force. It's pointless. The mic can pick up the crackle, but it can't pick up the atmosphere. It can't pick up the feeling I get as I stand under all this gray. Mics can't record nostalgia—how this morning reminds me of winter at the farm, standing under a buckling sky, hands out, face upturned.

I put down the mic and close my eyes, feel the sound I want to make with the cello.

"What are you doing?"

I know the voice belongs to Oliver before I turn. He stands there under his black umbrella—it's not even raining yet—and looks impatient. "Iris wants you. She sent me. To remind you that we have practice this morning. And you're late."

She's reminding me because, on Wednesday, I missed half of our tutoring session with Gregory. I told her I'd forgotten what day it was, but I knew it was Wednesday. I knew it was math and science hour. I knew I should be in the library with her and Gregory, working on calculus, but I'd just downloaded the new Tune-Yards album and I wanted to listen to it.

I pack up my computer, put it away carefully with the mics. My cello is already in its case, under shelter, protected from possible rain. I've never quite worked out how to walk fast with the cello. It's such a cumbersome thing. Another body. An attached friend. Fly with it, and you need an extra seat. Travel on trams and you need the same. My case is hard and it doesn't have wheels, but I have a way of hoisting it on my back and then collecting everything else I need to carry.

Oliver sees that I'm struggling and takes it from me. He swings it easily over his shoulder while still holding the umbrella above our heads. He's elegant. The thought arrives uninvited. I push it out, and speed up, but he widens his strides and keeps my pace.

While we move, he fills me in on what Iris has told him about me. How I've been forgetful lately—forgetting it was Wednesday, forgetting my graphics calculator, forgetting my pencil case. I hadn't realized that she was keeping such careful track.

"I've had other things on my mind," I say.

"Like?" he asks, as we reach the auditorium.

"Like none of your business," I say, taking back my cello. I check my watch and hold it out to him. "Not late. Early. See?"

We walk inside and Iris looks up from her music. "You found her then?"

"I wasn't lost."

"She'd forgotten," he says.

I'm not a forgetter. I remember everything. I remember in that first week, before I knew anything about Oliver, I saw an Orion sticker on his cello case and I thought maybe I'd misjudged him, that maybe, *maybe*, he might be a friend. Then I found out that he'd inherited the cello case from someone who didn't have a stick up his ass. I remember how he told me he had heard of Orion, but it wasn't the kind of place he'd go. I had the urge to take my bow and whack it, wood side, over his knuckles.

I have the same urge today.

"Did you remember that we've got the excursion this morning?" Iris asks. "To the Botanic Gardens?"

She gives me a smile when it's clear that I had forgotten. It's a kind smile, but I still don't want it. I'm preoccupied and obsessed, not stupid. "We get on the bus after homeroom," she says.

"A morning off school. Excellent," I say.

"Some people work hard for this opportunity," Oliver replies.

I lean on my cello and motion for him to continue. "Go on, Oliver. Tell me what you really want to say."

"Just that," he says. "Your technique's hit and miss, probably because you're not being classically trained—"

"I am being classically trained—"

"You were being classically trained. You dropped out of private lessons."

"How do you know I dropped out?"

"I listen to you play," he says, pausing just enough before he says the words to give them maximum impact.

Sarah Watford, the quiet flutist, snorts with laughter. She's staring at Oliver like he's some kind of god. What's godlike about him? My brain immediately supplies the answer that he's got incredibly serious dark blue eyes, navy eyes really, navy eyes that are as full of music as mine. Shut up brain. Shut completely up.

I'm not usually competitive with other people. I'm not even really competitive with myself. I get passionate about things and then I want to know as much as I can about them, so, usually, not counting the time I got obsessed with the ukulele, which still eludes me as an instrument, I get good at things.

I put in the effort.

I dropped out of private lessons because I knew Mum and Dad couldn't afford them. And because I wanted to work with the computer, which was something my cello teacher couldn't help me with.

The idea that someone would think music isn't important to me—when I've been practicing in the freezing cold, when all I think about is the Frances Carter audition, when I'm skipping math and science tutoring because I'm so serious about it, when I'm spending all my hard-earned cash on looping software and how-to guides and music—is infuriating.

Somewhere along the way, elegant Oliver's gotten the wrong idea about me.

Anal, not elegant. Anal Oliver. Repressed Oliver.

Most people have the wrong idea about me at St. Hilda's. Here I've been slotted into the category of quiet, studious geek. Friend of Iris Banks and the go-to-person for anyone at St. Hilda's who's got a computer-related problem or a website to be built.

This doesn't bother me.

But this—this view Oliver has—really bothers me.

And it's not about me secretly liking him, as Iris's eyebrows are suggesting right now. She's so obvious, wiggling them at me like our argument is a sign that there's something going on between us.

There's nothing going on between us, I think, as he helps Sarah tune her flute, his lips hovering over the mouthpiece, stopping to inform her that the flute has the highest voice in the woodwind family.

I do not want to kiss Oliver.

What I want is for him to shut up with his explanation to Sarah.

"Frances Carter doesn't play the stops." I interrupt him. "Did you hear her that day? She played what she wanted to play, how she wanted to play it, and it was brilliant."

"You're not Frances Carter," he says, and Sarah snorts again.

"I know I'm not Frances Carter."

"Wait . . . you're not thinking about auditioning?"

That's it. It takes me a long time to reach my limit, Oliver. A long time. But I have reached it. Well and truly at the limit now.

I pick up my bow.

I look at his knuckles and think about whacking.

But then I decide to do something else.

I pull my cello close, place my legs in exactly the right spots on either side, close my eyes and find the piece I want to play. I find it in my head. I remember notes like I remember mathematical formulas, like I remember where I'm meant to be on Wednesday nights. I see the piece hovering there in the dark under my closed lids.

I count to three.

My old music teacher used to say that "Sonata No. 3 in G Minor for Cello and Harpsichord" hit her like heartbreak every time. It hits me like that, too. Looped or not. In the sonata I hear dreams and conversations. I hear how much I want to win the place in Iceland. I hear longing in these notes. They go all the way to the past and forward to some future where I haven't yet arrived.

I finish playing and there's quiet all around me. Mrs. Davies and Iris are smiling. Grinning, actually. Sarah's flute is forgotten. Oliver is staring at me. It's the first time I've seen him speechless since we met.

"We'll have a little more of that, Kate," Mrs. Davies says.

"Nothing to say, Oliver?" I ask, before rehearsal begins. "You're uncharacteristically quiet."

He focuses on Mrs. Davies.

"That's what I thought."

I celebrate myself, and sing myself.

Oh, yes, I do.

I'm celebrating and singing myself all the way from the auditorium to the bus. Iris has gone back to the room for her travel sickness tablets, so I call Ben while I'm waiting for the rest of the sophomores to arrive.

"I'm celebrating and singing myself," I say when he picks up, before he's even had a chance to drink his coffee.

"I don't know what that means."

"It means that I showed Oliver that I'm a good musician."

"You're a great musician."

"I love you."

"I love you, too. In a completely platonic, stick a fork in my eye rather than date you kind of way. No offense."

"None taken. Have you spoken to anyone at school yet?" I ask.

"I had a brief conversation with a pigeon yesterday."

"I'm going out on a limb here and saying that doesn't count."

"It was quite a pigeon," he says.

"You and I both need to take a risk. I need to make something happen. You need to stop talking to pigeons instead of people."

"Plans of action?" he asks.

"Plans of action."

I make one for him. He makes one for me. We've been doing it forever because it's easier to do what you're told than to do something you tell yourself. Plans of action are the reason Ben joined the Wilderness Society and started writing to the environment minister every week to stop fracking, to close coal mines, and to at least *attempt* to save the forests. It's the reason he got on a bus and then a train, and went to help a pod of whales that had beached themselves on the Warrnambool coastline. Plans of action are the reason I lobbied Mum and Dad to send me to St. Hilda's, the reason I started up a website-building business to save money for Melbourne—they're the reason I'm here.

"You need to join the Chess Club. Iris is shy. Iris is in the Chess Club here. Every second Sunday. She says it's a good way to meet people," I say.

"Not possible. I don't even play chess."

"Then learn. Better yet, find someone, an actual person, to teach you."

The bus rolls in and I tell Ben to hurry and give me my plan of action. "I'm about to go on an excursion. No time to argue the finer points of my plan."

"Okay—you have to cut out on the excursion. Go to the record store and check out that club Orion you've been telling me about."

"Not possible. I don't break rules like that."

"Then learn," he says. "Better yet, find someone, an actual person, to teach you."

Plans of action are always followed.

This is the point of a plan of action.

Iris appears after I've hung up. She couldn't find her travel sickness tablets, so we sit at the front of the bus, right behind the driver. I would have thought the vibrations of the wheels would make the sickness worse; but Iris says no, all the space in front of her is good. "I can't talk, though. I need to sit quietly or I'll vomit."

I'm happy to be quiet.

I can feel the thrill of playing still in my hands. That thrill makes me entertain the thought that I might cut out on the excursion. I take my phone and look up Vinyl City on Google Maps while Ms. Yelland gives us the outline of the day. We start at the Herbarium. There'll be no chance to cut out during that. We're all together and we have to answer questions on it.

"You get an hour for lunch," Ms. Yelland says, holding onto the overhead rail and swaying slightly. She looks disheveled. I can see her racing for a coffee as soon as break starts and not checking on us until roll call on the bus back.

I can get to the record store and back in an hour.

"Can you open the window?" Iris asks.

The breeze pours over us and the sky along with it. I fill Iris in on the plan, and ask her to cover for me. "Will you do it?"

She keeps staring straight ahead. "Yes," she says after what seems like a long time. She doesn't offer to come with me. There's no way she'd risk her chance at the scholarship, which is based on behavior and grades.

So why am I even considering risking it myself?

I've been to the Herbarium once before with Ben and his parents. So, thanks to Ben, I already know about the history and the collection (1.5 million dried plant and fungi collections, botanical library, archives, art), so it's not a big deal that I can't completely concentrate.

I stand in the tropical greenhouse, staring at a titan arum from Indonesia, noting that it's the largest unbranched inflorescence in the world, while I go through the pros and cons of cutting, the possible consequences, the potential fallout. I'm not sure what happens when you do something like this and get caught, because I've never done anything like it in my life.

Iris isn't paying attention, either. She's trying to get me to read the latest PSST post. I act like I'm looking, but I couldn't care less who's giving who a blow job. It's not my business and it's not interesting.

What's interesting is Orion.

At the start of lunch, I watch Ms. Yelland and wait for the best moment. When she's lining up for coffee, I walk toward the road as fast as I can while still looking casual. I'm determined at first, but as I get closer, I feel more hesitant. All that traffic. All that everything on the other side. *Cross the road, Kate. Cross the road. On the count of 10, cross the fucking road.*

"You keep standing there, she'll catch you."

I turn to see Ady sitting on the ground, legs stretched out, back against a tree, watching with what I'd describe as bemused disinterest. She nods over my shoulder, at Ms. Yelland in the distance, and then tilts her head toward the road. "The light is green, Kate," she says.

I take it as a sign.

I go.

Oh my god, I'm going.

I get to the stop seconds before the tram arrives. I'm out of breath and ecstatic—euphoric—scared out of my mind—I can't believe I'm doing this. After months of waiting, I'm rolling along the city streets, rolling toward the record store, free of St. Hilda's, feeling crazy good. I stare at the time, willing the tram to go faster.

I get off at Collins Street and follow the dotted line on the map that leads to Vinyl City. It's in a regal old building, light brown brick that's golden in the sunlight. The Subway next door looks out of place; the present slapped next to the past.

Through a glass door on the right, I can see stairs. The sign on the glass says Orion and there's a hand-drawn arrow pointing up. Standing back, I see there's also an old sign made of light globes on the outside of the building. I imagine it lit up at night, the beckoning buzz.

Leaning against the front of the record store is a girl my age, maybe a little older, wearing a black dress underneath a deep blue 1950s overcoat with black-and-white-striped tights and black boots. Her hair's short short, and the same color as her dress. She's sipping a Big Gulp, staring at me. I remember that I'm dressed in the very distinctive St. Hilda's uniform. Without taking her lips from the straw she smiles. I smile back.

We walk inside.

The shop is narrow and long. Vinyl on one side; CDs on the other. It smells of cigarettes and dust, but most of all it smells of music. Blues and jazz, electronica and indie. Gig posters stapled to the walls fight for space. There's a huge picture of Dylan behind the counter—he's surveying the store, the god who decides who's in and who's out. The guy working at the register drifts around to Beck. I locate the sound coming from a turntable at the front.

I pick up some flyers for Orion, then gravitate to electronica. I'm flicking through the O section when the Big Gulp Girl appears next to me and starts flicking through the Ps. She holds up Portishead's *Dummy*, and I nod and hold up ohGr's *Welt* and she makes a motion with her hand to signal that they're kind of hard-core, and I make a sign back that I agree. We keep flicking through records. Every now and then she looks at one I'm holding or shows me something she found, talking in vinyl.

After a while, she heads to the counter, makes a purchase, smiles again at me on the way out, and she's gone. I follow her but I'm too late; she's about to get on a tram, a piece of fast-moving sky.

"Wait!" I yell, and start running. I feel crazy chasing after her, but she turns toward the sound of me, shields her eyes against the sun, and waits for me to jog over. "I'm Kate," I say when I arrive, slightly out of breath.

"Max," she says.

"Your tram," I say, pointing as it pulls out.

She dismisses it with a wave of her hand. "Interesting taste in music. Unusual for a St. Hilda's girl."

"Do you know many?" I ask.

"I like a woman in uniform. I know some Basildon guys, too."

I make a face.

"They're not all bad," she says.

We don't have time for a long conversation or a gradual lead-up. "I'm dying to go to that club," I tell her, and point at the Orion sign.

She grins. "I'm going next Friday. Open-mic night. Some of my friends are playing." She takes out her phone and waves for mine, keys in numbers, and hands it back to me. "You're a musician?"

"Cello," I tell her. "You?"

"Fan of music. Drama queen. I have a friend who plays cello. He'll be there Friday night. I'll introduce you." She looks at her watch. "I'm so late. See you Friday, Kate," she says, and only then do I look at my own watch. Time to run.

Clem

Friday, July 15

At the Botanic Gardens, everything is green and black and damp. Our guide takes us through the Herbarium and the native path and up to the Volcano, which is planted with every kind of succulent imaginable. Lainie keeps saying they look phallic or like baboon butts. Once she says it, I can't stop thinking it. We laugh and make stupid monkey noises, much to Iris's disgust.

For lunch we have free time to wander, gather intel, take photographs, whatever. I tell Lainie that I want to find the Temple of the Winds. It's this totally romantic-looking structure with columns and a domed roof. It sits at the top of the gardens and from it you can see the river and the city and all the way to the mountains.

We set off for it. Right from the start, Lainie's complaining and saying, "Can't we just get some fries?" We're walking alongside the lake when I notice a guy in the distance who looks like Stu. My heart stops for a second. It *is* Stu!

He's with a big group of picnickers; about 20 of them, some on camp chairs, some on rugs. I wonder if it's his family, but they look too disparate. There's a short, busty woman bossing people around, a guy in a cap who wobbles when he moves, and a really fat guy who doesn't stop talking. Stu's bending over a girl with a guitar—he's showing her a chord or something—and I feel mad envy.

Lainie's voice is gnatty in my ear. "Who are you looking at?"

I cup my hand to smell my breath, then tell Lainie I'll meet her at the cafeteria. "There's something I've gotta do."

When Stu sees me walking toward him, he does a double take. "It's you!"

"It's me." I glance down at my uniform. "Excursion."

Stu indicates the party behind him. "Colleagues and clients."

"Who's the skirt?" I ask, trying to be tough.

"You mean Millie?"

"She's got your guitar."

I'm an idiot. Only now realizing that most of the people in Stu's group look . . . different. I know there's a politically correct way to say what I'm thinking—"intellectually challenged" or "differently abled." Anyway, Millie is immersed in the guitar, plucking away on one string, but holding it like a baby.

"Work do. Christmas in July," Stu says. "Never say no to free food—that's my motto. I do care work. That guy there is Benny, and that's Daulton and that's Ed. They live at the Blue House, a group home. When I do the overnighters, those are the dudes I'm minding. You want to meet them?" And before I know it he's leading me over and introducing me to everyone. One guy tries to hide in his sweater, another is all up in my face with a barrage of soccer statistics, and Millie smiles at me like I'm amazing.

Stu takes my hand and a plate of half-eaten pavlova. "We're just going for a walk," he announces. The busty older woman gives him a look, but he just winks at her and half-marches me across the lawn until he's out of their view.

"Where are we going?"

Stu looks around, frowning. I'm about to suggest the Temple of the Winds when he says, "There." He leads me to a clutch of trees that has a hollow just big enough for two people and a pav.

Half an hour goes by in five seconds. We gorge on sugar, and kissing, and we roll around in the leaf litter. After a while, Stu sits up.

"This is no good," he says.

"It isn't?

"We need a place."

"Don't you have a house?"

He looks pained. "I live with my parents. It's temporary. They're retired. They never go out."

Stu picks up a branch that holds two seedpods, their smooth necks twisted together. He presents it to me. "Ah, the lovers." He has a light in his eyes and an edge to his voice. "What would happen if you got caught with me in your room?"

"Expulsion. A BIB is a major infraction."

"BIB?"

"Boy in Bed."

Stu's finger has found a hole in my tights and he's driving me to distraction. I start to babble, "There's a door. We call it the portal. It's in the basement. It doesn't lock."

A text from Lainie, *Where are you?*

"Shit!" I scramble to my feet, brush down my tunic and press myself into Stu for a final kiss. Then I bolt across the gardens, feet nearly sinking in all the soft green lawn.

I get back to the bus just in time.

Ms. Yelland eyeballs me. "So nice of you to join us, Clem."

"Sorry," I say, making my eyes big. "I got lost."

I sit, quietly shimmering, with the seedpods, the lovers, in my pocket, and my hand over it making a protective cage. We haven't gone far when I feel something at the back of my head. I whirl around. Adelaide—Ady—has plucked a twig from my hair. Tash says, "What *is* that?" Ady flicks the air. "Nits." She makes a face, her lips all drawn, reminding me of zombie dolls or fork marks in pastry. I give her a fake smile and she goes shadowy for a second. I think, *So what if you're beautiful. I've got Stu! Ha!* I think this all the way back to the groan of fifth period.

Ady

Friday, July 15

Bec is absently flicking up and closing the lid of her Tic Tac container as we wander back to the bus after lunch. She just ate a huge public sandwich that she didn't even want because of the PSST ana list crap.

"Ady, tune in," Tash is saying. "Get that." She's turning my shoulders, pointing me in the direction of a St. Hilda's–uniform–clad body tangling with a tall guy, not at all well hidden behind a bank of camellias. "What a slut."

Wow, the navy really stands out against the greeny. It's the swim-girl boarder, Clem Banks. Interesting. Since when do lap-training drudges do illicit boy rendezvous? "I could not be less interested." I catch Tash's fleeting smile of approval as I turn away. Being unimpressed is such a cheap win. Like being bored. But it's a default mode with my group.

On the bus back to school, Clem is sitting right in front of us.

I reach forward and pull a dry twig from her hair. A barbed

briar-rose stem. She twists around and glares at me. There are leaves and twigs all over the back of her blazer, as though the garden has tried to pull a schoolgirl into its pagan embrace and hold her there. She escaped, but when she turns and frowns at me, I see her scratch-kissed puffy mouth and her eyes still full of that place.

I'd love to dress someone as spring. Primavera. Rose red. Any old white shift, a gauzy fabric, a bit grubby and ripped, twined in creeper. Strewn with ivy leaves. And flowers. I would need . . . I look around. Kate Turner. Her dark hair, her pale skin, uncharacteristically pink-cheeked right now. Perfect. I would paint her face. Feathering fern fronds connecting her eyebrows to her hairline. Hair piled up and woven ratty with leaves and twigs and flower buds: a nest. She would be about to hatch, about to bloom. And the dress would be constructed so it looked like—like a garment in which to joyfully deflower. I declare this an active verb! Flower, deflower . . . An awakening motif. I'm twirling the twig, examining it, as I assemble the look in my mind's eye, itching to make some sketches; but it'll hold until later. Bare feet, tinted icy blue, walking away from winter . . .

Tash says, "What is that?"

I drop the twig. "Nits," I say. "Most likely." I pull another leaf from Clem's hair and flick it at Tash.

"Earwigs," says Tash.

"Compost," I say.

"Trash," says Tash.

And there we have it. Another satisfactory reduction of someone who doesn't count. We're good at this. We don't even have to try.

Have I ever been so lost and entangled in Rupert's arms as Clem was lost in her embrace just now? Pretty certainly not. Gotta say I'm finding the erect penis to be a distraction. It's like an insistent puppy. If it could talk, it would be saying something like: *Sex, sex, sex, ready right now, I want the sex, please, do you want the sex, now's a good sex time, sex, sex, sex, are we having sex now, let's go . . .* I'll have sex when the time is right, so it's not that I feel pressured, it's just that I'm not as into Rupe as he and his peen are into me.

In fact, I definitely seem to like Rupert more in theory than in practice. He never seems more attractive than when we are apart. That cannot be right.

"Dreaming of your dream boy?" Tash elbows me from my reverie.

Do I reveal myself to my peers? "You know it." I smile. It's the official smile of a girl who's going out with a dream boy. But it's not a smile like Clem Banks's private, lit-up smile when she ran up to the bus late, claiming that she'd gotten lost.

Ady's Wellness Journal

Friday, July 15

I'm spending my nights eavesdropping and anxious, interspersed with fake fun times with my friends online. Last night my mother was talking about coming to the end of the line with credit cards and maybe even having to sell our house. My father said that all he needed was a break and then everything would be okay. When he talks about a break, he means someone giving him a job—he directs TV commercials. He goes all over the world to do it, and wins awards. That set her off: Don't you realize, there are no more fucking breaks? You've burned all your bridges and we're this close to losing everything. Have you ever even stopped to think how much money you've spent frying your brain? Is she exaggerating to make her point, to get my father back on track? But if she means it, what comes next? Where would we live?

You can find out a lot if you sit at the top of the stairs and listen. I wonder how my father would answer the question: Do others see the real you? He is a cocaine addict and an alcoholic. It's a pretty big secret. Writing it out has made my hands shake and my heart beat so hard it might explode. When I first heard my mother talk about his problem with "coke," I was 10, Charlie's age, listening to a fight from the landing, and I thought she was talking about the drink. Why was she so angry? Also, I was confused because it's not a drink that we have at home. I thought he must have been drinking it at work. That's how silly I was.

Clare knows about it. Charlie doesn't. Mum's never spoken to me about it. And I've never told my friends. Addiction seems to go away, but it also seems to come back again. Have I made things worse by not telling my mother about the secret vodka? Is that a big thing or is it nothing?

One in 200 pregnant American women believe they are virgins. Most of the world believes in a god. I've been thinking that things were more or less okay at home, despite the fights. I thought the main problem was his lack of work. True stories. So—delusion is obviously a thing. How else is it that my world is on a steep tilt so suddenly? I've been zipping around in my own little delusion bubble. Now, it seems that we are on the edge of a cliff. If fight, fight, settle, fun isn't the pattern anymore, what takes its place?

I'm still running some of the lines from last night. I wish I hadn't heard them. When the two people who made you are pitching hate bombs at each other, you can't help but wonder which bits of who you've got swimming around in the DNA soup, ready to let someone down when the time comes.

Kate's Wellness Journal

Friday, July 15

Dear Journal,

I'm writing this in the boarder bathroom. It's midnight, and the moon is shining on the tiles, water dripping from the taps. It's actually quite nice in here when there aren't ten girls waiting in line at the showers and another five at the mirrors.

I can't sleep—too restless. I keep thinking about Max and the record store, about Orion and the open mic, and how I can meet her there Friday night.

Option one—the portal. Unlikely, as I just tried to walk down into the basement and was scared of the dark. I couldn't find the light and my phone gave off only the dimmest glow. I could take a flashlight, and I will if I have to, but if I go via the portal there's the problem of cover.

Iris said she'd cover for me and lie to Old Joy if I needed her to, but if there's a bed check, then there's nothing much Iris can say. She could stall for a while, tell Old Joy I'm in the bathroom, but if Old Joy checked—and she would—I'm busted.

Option two—tell the truth to Mum and Dad and ask for permission. But that means they'd have to agree to me going to an over-18 club with a stranger to listen to music. Mum and Dad are pretty relaxed, but that's definitely not happening.

So that leaves option three—get a pass for dinner at a friend's place and go with them to the club. This is definitely the best option.

If only I had a friend.

Kate

Saturday, July 16

I wake up tired. I sat in the bathroom for a long time last night, listening to music and thinking through my escape options. I've agreed to shop for formal dresses with Iris and Clem this morning, but I'm not in the mood for shopping—I never am. I mainly find stuff online. I know my size. I know the jeans and T-shirts I like. It's easier when they arrive at my door in a package. I hate shopping at the best of times, and I have a feeling that today won't be one of those.

I have to be there for Iris's sake, though. The only reason Clem and Iris are going on the same shopping expedition is because they have to share their parents' credit card, according to Iris. I'll be the referee so they don't tear each other's throats out.

"You need a date for the formal," Iris says while we wait for Clem to arrive. "I've got one. At least I think I've got one."

This is BIG news.

"Who?" I ask, and it tumbles out of her that it's Theo

Ledwidge. I don't know him, but she says he's gorgeous and she met him at Chess Club and it just happened. She says that last part as if it's a miracle.

"You need to hurry up and find someone so we can all go together."

Oliver immediately pops into my head. I picture him in a tux and bow tie with fantastically neat hair. We're dancing and he's telling me I'm not doing it right.

Not Oliver, I tell myself, freaked out by my brain going rogue and suggesting him. I put it down to lack of sleep and the prospect of shopping. What I'm looking for in a date, I've just decided, is someone whose most obvious attribute is that he is *not* Oliver. That's what I'm looking for in a guy: not-Oliverness.

Clem knocks on our door—kicks at it, really—and saves me from further date discussion with Iris. When I open it, she yells at Iris that she wants to be in charge of the card.

"Mum and Dad put me in charge of the card," Iris says, and Clem tells her to hurry up, that her friends are waiting, then kicks the door shut.

We head to High Street, because Clem said that's where the dresses are. Iris wanted the city, but she won the credit card battle, so I quietly suggested she give in on this one so we could avoid a raging fight at the tram stop.

Clem sat with her friends on the tram, and now she's flicking through dresses in the short-and-sexy aisle, while Iris browses in the not-so-short-and-sexy aisle. Clem snipes at Iris across the shop—"You're in the old woman aisle." Iris snipes back—"At least I'm not a slut."

A girl near us flinches.

Clem and Iris are fraternal twins, not identical, but they're recognizable as sisters. Clem is shorter and has the kind of shoulders shaped by the pool. Iris has the slightly hunched look that comes from sitting at a computer all weekend. Same brown hair, though Iris's is longer. Same fierce mouth.

It's not really my kind of shop. Racks full of incredibly expensive clothes, all hanging under the cool gaze of a girl straight out of a fashion magazine. Her eyes are coated in dark green, and they make me think of a beautiful snake. She's tolerating us. *Buy or get the fuck out of my store*, her green eyes say. *And don't touch the clothes any more than you have to.*

If I had a type of shop, I think it would be one that sells clothes like Max wears. Retro, original, stylishly haphazard. She looks like she's thrown on a collection of things and they've assembled themselves into effortlessly cool. Since that never happens for me, I settle for nondescript and easy to match.

Iris pushes me to try on a dress, though, and I give in. I grab one off the rack—deep blue, silk, short with flowing sleeves. Completely impractical for playing the cello. Too tight around the legs and I'd end up bowing the sleeves.

There's only one dressing room free—the big one—and we all go in together and move to our corners. Iris and Clem have their backs to each other, pressed into their corners, undressing without showing skin. I know Iris and Clem fight, but I assumed there'd be an intimacy.

At Shallow Bay High, the Tripodi twins were in our class. They only seemed completely there when they were in a room together. I asked them once what it was like. "I'm completely my own person," June told me, "but somehow I'm Joanna, too." With Clem and Iris, it's as though the thought that they might be the same person sets them scrabbling against each other for freedom.

When Clem and Iris are dressed, I'm the one who zips them both up. They turn around, and the first thing they see is the other, and then their eyes shift quickly to their own reflections.

Clem's dress is red and short, her stocky swimmer's legs on display. She looks amazing. Iris is in a black dress that ties around her neck, 1960s-style, and goes all the way to the floor. She looks like a gothic mermaid, and I wonder if I've misjudged her level of rebellion. I need to play her some Mazzy Star. Maybe The Cure. I can see her plinking around to "Fade into You" and "The Love Cats."

"Okay?" she asks, and I say yes at the same time that Clem makes a snorting sound. I'd say it was bitchy, but Iris immediately fires back: "You look huge. Turn around and check out your ass."

Clem does, and I wonder if they were close once. If, at some time, Iris's opinion mattered.

There's quiet for a bit, while they assess themselves, assess each other.

"Will Theo like it, do you think?" Iris asks.

"How much did you pay him to take you?" Clem asks. "Out of curiosity."

"At least I have a date," Iris says.

There is an intimacy between them, I realize, but it's a terrible kind, where they know what to say to hurt each other and don't hesitate to say it. You'd never talk that way to a friend.

"I look like a mutant butterfly," I say as a distraction, waving at my outfit. "There's something bizarre going on with the sleeves and the dress is way too short for my legs."

"You have great legs," Clem and Iris say in unison.

We continue shopping.

Iris goes into the dressing room to try on another dress, and I wander along the aisles, pretending to look at clothes, but not really.

Clem walks over and holds a dress up against me. "You'd look good in this."

"You didn't look fat in the red dress."

"I did a bit, but I don't care. Thanks, though."

It occurs to me that Clem is someone who might know how to get out at night. She's the polar opposite of Iris. Street smart and only angry when it comes to her sister, really.

She looks through the rack again, checking that she hasn't missed a bargain. I flick through next to her. "Have you ever gone out through the portal?" I ask, and she says no, but it's easy. "You just go down there, push and—voilà! You're free."

"But then what?"

"But then what *what*? You're free."

"But what happens if you get caught?"

"You get suspended. So make sure it's worth it."

Iris comes out in a shorter black dress, ending the conversation.

"Morticia," Clem says, and then decides she can't stand it anymore. She puts out her hand and demands the card. There's some power play, but Clem wins.

She runs out of the shop yelling that she'll be back in a minute. After Iris has changed, we leave and wait for her on the street.

Clem jogs back eventually and gives Iris the card. "I took money out at the ATM."

"How much?" Iris asks.

"Not your business." She gives me what feels like an apologetic smile and says, "Good luck with the portal," then heads across the road to another shop.

Iris doesn't talk to me all that much after Clem goes. I can't figure out if she's hurt by Clem's comment or mad at me. It feels like both.

Five shops later, she finally finds a dress. It's black, but suits her even more than the others. Iris has red tones in her hair and the dress makes them obvious. She takes off her glasses and studies herself. "I'm wearing contacts on the night. And I'm getting SNS nails. You should book an appointment with me."

It's an offer of peace, and I take it.

Iris and I seem to have a lot in common—math, science, a deep love for *Arrested Development*, peanut butter, and all things technical. But proximity made us friends. I don't think we would have gravitated to each other naturally.

I don't mean that she's not a good person. On the first night, when I was homesick, she came over to my bed and sat next to me while I told her about the farm. I needed to explain to someone how I missed the animals, the river, all that space, but how, at the same time, I was desperate to come to the city. I needed someone to understand that I could want two completely different things at the same time.

She listened, but she didn't get it; in Iris's mind, we're one thing or the other. Still, she tried to make me feel better. She told me to open the calendar on my computer, and mark the holidays so I could see them coming up. I felt so grateful to her that I invited her to visit the farm on the long weekend in August.

Maybe the reason that she and Clem fight so much is that Clem is all things happening at the same time. Iris thinks about everything she says, plans her entire day. Clem sock-surfs down the hallway, collides with the wall, and laughs hysterically. I think back to her in that dress today—the wild red next to Iris's sedate black. I see Clem's mouth, grinning, next to Iris's cautious smile. It's as though in the womb one person was divided. Iris and Clem—two halves of the same person—looking at each other and seeing themselves, seeing a flat chest or fat stomach, when they should see something beautiful.

Kate's Wellness Journal

Saturday, July 16

Dear Journal,

Iris told me about Theo tonight. They met at Chess Club, and they still meet there every second Sunday. These are the things she likes about him:

He listens to her.

He doesn't like Clem better than her (apparently guys usually do).

He has good hands—wide and not hairy at the knuckles, very important.

He's smart (great chess player).

He's good at sports, too (plays tennis).

He's gorgeous (though looks are not a deal breaker, she says).

These are good reasons to like someone, and I'm happy for her. We spent tonight lying on our beds, eating salt-and-vinegar chips, and talking about guys. Iris wanted to know who I've gone out with before.

Have I kissed someone? (Yes.)

How many people have I kissed? (Three—Jeremy, Ryan, Joseph.)

Was it good? (Yes, yes, and yes.)

Have I had sex? (Close, but no.)

How close? (Pretty close.)

Why'd I stop? (I felt like it.)

Did he care that I stopped? (I didn't care if he cared. I wanted to stop.)

Do I like Oliver even a little? (Absolutely not.)

Who do I dream about before I fall asleep? (Not who, what.)

I dream about Orion, about getting there, being there. I dream about walking up the stairs, the music, and the dark. Seeing Max, meeting her friends. They're not crammed at the front, they're leaning against the back wall, music washing over them. There's a guy—not Oliver—standing next to me, talking about the new Jónsi album. Most of all, I dream of sound. Tonight, headphones on, I listen to the storm I tried to record Friday. I thread through lines of cello, and, I hate to admit it, but Oliver's right. My technique is slipping and it makes a difference. His voice is on the recording—asking me what I'm doing.

He answers himself, which I hear now, but I didn't hear then.

"You're recording the storm."

There's no mockery in his voice. I listen to it twice over to make sure of the tone. I can't be certain because of the wind and the rain, but I'm pretty sure it's excitement.

WEEK 2

SHOW-AND-TELL

Wellness

Monday, July 18
Dr. Peter Malik

Week 2: Identity, Part II

Getting to know you . . .

This week we revisit a fun activity from elementary school: show-and-tell.

Provocation

A wonderful fact to reflect upon, that every human creature is constituted to be that profound secret and mystery to every other.

—Charles Dickens, *A Tale of Two Cities*

Your closest friends were once unknown to you.

—Anonymous

In order for us to get to know each other we need to employ respect and trust.

We respect the confidences that are shared in wellness classes. We trust our classmates with some information about ourselves.

Helpful dispositions to bring to the activity: curiosity, openness, interest in others, suspension of judgment, suspension of preconceived ideas.

Each of us has certain touchstone items that say something about who we are.

Points for Discussion/Reflection

Each of us is an individual as well as a member of various groups—family, community, school, friendship. Our identity is developed through a combination of our personality, our beliefs and values, our cultural background, our opportunities and privilege, our experiences and actions, our defining moments.

- What is the intersection of objects and memory?
- How might sharing a memory help others understand who we are?
- How well do we really know each other?
- Are there classmates we have labeled and dismissed?
- How might we change our thinking about others?

Task

Share your thoughts and feelings about your item. Let us get to know you better through this sharing.

WELLNESS WORKSHEET ST. HILDA'S MALIKDRP@STHILDAS.VIC.EDU.AUS

Sender: susanbeazley@sthildas.edu.au

To: clementinebanks@acaciahouse.com.au

Date: Monday, July 18

Dear Clem,

Have you received my messages? Is there a reason you're not coming to training? Is your wrist still giving you trouble? Training's just as much for the mind as for the body. You don't want your teammates to lose confidence in you. I trust that Jinx has been filling you in regarding the Canberra trip (please remind your parents that we need signatures on the attached form).

The Marlins will be putting on a swim showcase at the Winter Fair as part of the celebrations for the official opening of the new aquatic center. The squad will swim a continuous loop for an hour. There is a key available for squad members wishing to train outside regular hours.

If you need to talk, my door is always open.

Kind regards,

Coach Beazley (Beaz ☺)

Ady

Monday, July 18

Bec and I walk to wellness one step behind Tash and Lola. I'm looking forward to another slack class. I picture myself walking through the front door at home after school today and finding the guts to ask it out loud: Can someone tell me what's actually happening around here and what happens next?

Malik made us bring something that's important or special for week 2 of this fruitless pop psychology exercise that is wellness class. Fruitless pop psychology is Clare's take on it; she's harsh, but often right.

Lola goes first. She cradles her dog Pepé's ashes and starts to cry before she gets a single word out. (Dear little Pep! I'm welling up, too.) Bec jumps up and gives her a hug. Malik asks Bec to sit down, which is a bit anti-wellness if you ask me. (Because Lola wants to be an actor, she does seize any opportunity to cry on cue, and Bec's mainly hugging to enhance the class disruption, but Malik doesn't know that.) Lola takes some deep breaths, and

Malik gives her a nod of encouragement. "This urn holds the ashes of our darling little Pepé. We had to have her put down last year . . ." She dissolves into another flood of tears. She does genuinely feel sad about Pep, but she is also honing her crying skills like mad.

"Thank you, Lola. We're honored that you shared such a heartfelt memory with us today through this precious object."

Tash goes next, showing her first haircut curls, preserved by her mother, proving that she was once a natural blonde.

"Things from our childhood are often particularly potent emblems of who we are," Malik says. "Our sense of self springs from these years. Interesting aside: Victorian mourning jewelry uses woven hair as a decorative element in commemoration of someone who's died." That elicits a few heartfelt ee-ews.

I settle deeper into the beanbag's hug and watch away-with-the-pixies Kate untangle a necklace that's special to her for reasons I don't tune in to. I finish dreaming up her Primavera costume as she sits in a pool of sunshine, streaming through the stained-glass windows, flooded with new colors.

My show-and-tell is so super special that my mother would have a thousand kittens if she knew I'd taken it out of the house. It's a silver bonbon spoon with a vine pattern. It belonged to my great-grandmother, my gram's mother.

"Well, I've brought along a spoon today." It takes me quite a while to struggle out of the beanbag into a standing position. I walk to the front of the group and hold up the spoon, feeling suddenly stupid for bringing something like this to class, and then not wanting to pass it around.

"Something about me is that I love eating, and we eat with

spoons, so spoons are significant and important to me." A couple of people are amused. With a perfectly straight tone of voice, I'm sending up the activity without even trying. Malik's serious, respectful look makes me want to scramble toward a conclusion, so I can sit down. "This was my great-grandmother's. She lived in Vienna. And she loved pretty things. Like I do."

My great-grandmother lived a beautiful life in a beautiful house in Vienna, until being Jewish meant being persecuted. She and her family lost their beautiful life and lost each other. Only she survived, and all she ended up with was a handful of things that could be stitched into the hem of a jacket. So I'm only sharing about 2 percent of the story. And if my mother really does face losing, say, her house, there's probably trauma memory in her DNA that makes it more horrible than it might otherwise be.

"I'd also like to share that I'm a fan of Tiffany." I put a finger to the silver bean on a silver chain that I wear every day. "And, coinkydinky, this spoon is by Tiffany, too. So even though my great-grandmother and I never met, I'm pretty sure we would've gotten along. At home, we use this spoon for jam. The end."

When Malik tells us that sharing significant things will help us to get to know each other, he leaves out the part about it making us more vulnerable, and the part about people, such as me, not usually exposing themselves that way.

I realize that I've never told Rupert any family stuff, past or present, which makes my brain buzz back around the should-I-end-things-with-Rupert-or-will-things-get-better question. It doesn't seem fair to stay in what is feeling like a one-way relationship. But I obviously don't want to break up before the formal. Why can't I get properly into Rupert? It's annoying when the perfect boy turns out to be all wrong. Why is life so unsimple? Maybe if we had more in common . . . He's super sporty, which I find super dull. I'm sure someone out there wants to hear all about the records he breaks when he runs, and the goals he kicks when he plays soccer, but not me.

While I wonder about the kindest way to dump Rupert when the time comes, mind-directing various heart-wrenching scenarios—he's a mess, I'm dry-eyed but gentle; I'm crying, and he's comforting *me*, etc.—girl after girl after girl coughs up an acceptable fur ball. Swim-girl Clem shows off a medal. Iris Banks, another boarder, holds up a photo of herself with a girl, both aged about eight, dressed as Thing One and Thing Two. Turns out the other girl is Clem. I keep forgetting those two are twins. They could not look more different from each other if they tried. I've never seen them speak or even acknowledge each other's existence until now. Clem is giving Iris the evil eye; I guess Iris didn't clear her show-and-tell object with her twinnie.

As we leave wellness class, Ms. Zahir, who is our head of IT, comes to confer with Kate Turner about an IT thing. I realize that I've seen the apparently vague musician being consulted by teachers about stuff like this before. She obviously has computer superpowers, as well as her music thing. I'm *curious* and *interested*, as instructed by Malik.

Kate looks at Zahir's laptop screen and starts tapping the keys with quiet concentration, appearing to simultaneously diagnose and remedy whatever the problem is, earning a relieved thank-you from Zahir and some puppy-love fangirling from Iris Banks.

Oh, Malik, I am, from now on, going to be totally all over this understanding-people-at-a-deeper-level shit.

Text to Tash: *I will respect your confidences about what you think you might want to wear to the formal if you feel like sharing after school today.*

Text from Tash to me: *I will trust you with that confidence and respect your confidences re formal dress thoughts, too. We. Need. To. Shop.*

Text to Tash: *We can probs be our best selves with hot chocolates at Figgy's.*

Text from Tash to me: *Deal for real.*

Clem

Monday, July 18

Our show-and-tell wellness class is not very telling. No one wants to reveal themselves—can't Malik see that?

Jinx forgot about the assignment, but she's been wearing her Marlins bomber jacket since she got it, so she just raves about that, then has a rant about disposable fashion and how all the shitty fibers of cheap clothes are polluting the ocean via washing machines . . .

If I was going to show something that was meaningful to me right now, I'd show the seedpods, or my phone. (No phones! Wellness is a tech-free zone.) But in the end I brought in my medal from Nationals. I sit with it squat in my hand. I could just as easily pitch it out the open window. I don't know why, but it doesn't feel like anything.

Kate has her laptop with her. For a minute I think she's going to play some of that crazy music, but she just talks about her necklace, trailing her pinkie along it.

Iris stands up. She's brought in a photo of the two of us from third grade, dressed up as Thing One and Thing Two for Book Week. I can't believe she's being so open. I don't want people to know about us—any of it. The photo travels from hand to hand to the soundtrack of snickers and Iris stammering about how, when we were little, even though we are fraternal, she somehow managed to convince herself that we were identical. I hear myself say, "That photo's a fake! I'm serious. That never happened. Photoshop much?"

And people laugh, but it's weird laughter, like when everyone knows something's wrong, but no one wants to say it. I slump in my beanbag. I imagine myself sinking until the material closes over my head. Maybe I can just stay here forever.

I feel fraught today. I feel guilty about the email from Beaz. Why don't I just go to training? But, but—my hair is the longest it's ever been, and I smell like a normal girl, not chlorinated. My skin feels soft. My diet has gone to hell. I can't seem to stop eating.

Later I'm in my room and I hear footsteps, and see a shadow at the door. Jinx looks at me and I look at her, but we don't get up. Whoever it is slides something under the crack. It's the photo of me and Iris—she's colored my face in with Wite-Out. I chuck it over to Jinx and she shakes her head and starts to pick the Wite-Out off.

"What the hell happened to you two anyway?"

"Nothing." I sigh. It's too much to go into and too hard to explain, because there's not one big reason but a thousand little ones. "We're just . . . different."

"You're crazy," Jinx says. "I miss my family more than anything."

She goes all pensive, puts her headphones on, and I know she's listening to music from home. I turn away from her and focus on sleep. I don't know why I feel how I feel or do what I do. Maybe it's just a twin thing.

WEEK 3

FRIENDSHIP

Wellness

Monday, July 25
Dr. Peter Malik

Week 3: Friendship

Look outside your friendship group

Provocation

Without friends the world is but a wilderness.
—Francis Bacon

Points for Discussion/Reflection

Each of us is an individual as well as a member of various groups—family, community, school, friendship. Our identity is developed through a combination of our personality, our beliefs and values, our cultural background, our opportunities and privilege, our experiences and actions, our defining moments.

- Who are your friends?
- How arbitrary or serendipitous might the start of a new friendship be?
- Opposites attract, so to what extent is it necessary to have things in common with people to maintain a friendship?
- How mobile are friendship groups at school? Are people open to making new friends?
- What are some of the things that make friendships work?
- Can broken friendships be repaired?

- What is a toxic friendship? Can friendships be good or bad for our self-esteem?
- Is it okay for friendships to end? How do we manage that?
- How can we monitor our friendships and check that they are healthy?

Task 1

Organize a social outing with your thumb-compatible comrades from week 1.

Make note of a couple of things you find out about them.

Task 2

Make a journal note to organize a second social outing with this same group in a month.

Clem's Wellness Journal

Tuesday, July 26

Who are your friends?

"Friends" is a bit of an overstatement. The girls I know the best are my squad mates—but can you really know anyone after six months?

Iris said I was lucky—I landed four friends in the first week and all because of swimming. She said it took ages for her and Kate to even say anything to each other without apologizing first. But I'm realizing that if I don't swim, I don't really have any friends, which makes me wonder if they were ever really my friends in the first place.

I like Jinx. I'd call Jinx a friend. She's funny, proud, ambitious. But she makes me feel lazy. Lainie is okay. I don't really know her, though. I just know about her (thanks to PSST everyone does). Roo and I only talk swimming—so we haven't really talked in weeks. Maggie smiles knives at me every time.

My other friends, my old friends, have all faded away. At first it was so hard to arrange to see them, and now that I've got the hang of St. Hilda's, they're suddenly impossible to find.

So I don't know about Malik's idea of "looking outside our friendship groups." I have nothing in common with Ady Rosenthal—I'm sure she doesn't think much of me. And as for Kate—well, she's Iris's. The only good thing about this "social outing" is that I can use it to see Stu. His studio is in Richmond and he's there most Fridays from 3:00 until 5:00. I'm going to show up and see if our paths cross. I know I could just call him, but I feel like I'm always the one doing the pursuing. This way, at least it will look like an accident.

Only thing is, do I tell Kate and Ady?

Ady's Wellness Journal

Wednesday, July 27

How can we monitor our friendships and check that they are healthy? Good question, Malik. It's never really crossed my mind to do that. Where would I even start?

Short entry, half because cbf, half because if I really try to figure out the whole friendship enchilada, that's going to take some time—time that could be better spent sewing or drawing.

Later . . . an excellent friendship thought. Tash was the one who gave me the idea of what I want to do forever and ever, and I'm hugging it to myself like the truly great thing it is. We were at a party at Griffo's house and I was wearing a new dress, one I made myself. I love it to a dangerous degree. I got an old merino wool dress of my gram's with a fabulous, boxy, 1960s shape. I cut six squares out of it, back and front, and replaced them with sheer silk organza in the identical color—a vivid acid green. And I've made the negative garment, too. It's a silk organza dress, with the square patches of wool sewn into it. Positive and negative. If only I had a friend who'd wear the neg while I wore the pos. Tash is not into that sort of garment; she's strictly a label girl. Two—now transparent—squares are at breast-level. I wish I had the guts . . . but I wore a bra under it. Even so, it felt like a fetish garment homage. That's fine by me. I'm a mad Leigh Bowery fan. Early Vivienne Westwood, can't get enough. But Tash said, "Cool frock, hon—but aren't you getting a bit . . ." she tilted her pretty head ". . . costume party?"

Costume. COSTUME. That is me. Smack my forehead. It's been sitting inside there all the time. I thought I liked old clothes. I thought I liked making stuff. I thought I was into fashion, looking different. But it's bigger than that. I'm going to be (I am) a costume designer. Stage and film costumes—and maybe a set designer, too. It was the most enormous flash of lightning revelation inspiration recognition. But I swallowed my smile and said, "Calm down, Tashie, it's just a party frock. This is a party, right? Or if it doesn't turn into one soon, we're out of here."

"Things to do," Tash said.

"People to see," I said.

We split and walked our separate ways through the hot, jammed bodies, looking for the point of the night. Such as it was. Our curfewed, baby-faced, don't-be-late, call-me, home-by-midnight night.

Bestie Tash, sweetie Bec, funny Lola, and me. How much do we really have in common these days? Will they understand why when I break up with Rupert? Will they even believe me if I tell them about my father?

Kate

Thursday, July 28

At the pool this morning before orchestra, I call Ben. We're on speakerphone, our voices echoing around my secret well, and I'm listing for him all the pros of going to Orion tomorrow night. The only con is getting caught.

"The signs all week have been telling me to take a chance."

"You believe in computer code, not signs."

"I'm changing in ways I cannot explain or entirely understand," I say, peeling back the wrapper on my breakfast bar and licking at the honey that's trapped on it.

"Tell me the signs then," he says, and I go through them.

"There are five so far. One: In wellness class this week, everyone seemed to be showing something that meant nothing. No one was giving anything real away. It felt pointless.

"Sign two: I was working in the computer room at lunch on Tuesday, running some tests for Ms. Zahir, when she said I was wasted in science and I should really work in IT. It's a small sign, but I'm listing all of them.

"Three: I've dreamed about the portal four nights this week. In all but one, I've escaped and returned *undetected*.

"Four: I finally finished a piece yesterday. Wait. I'll play it for you."

I balance the cello between my knees, rest the body against my chest, the neck and scroll against the left side of my head. I go through the routine I learned long ago, conscious of technique. I relax my wrist, drop my fingers into place, and, with my foot, hit the pedal that's connected to the computer to start the backing track.

It's not an original composition. Last night I recorded myself playing "Sonata No. 3 in G Minor for Cello and Harpsichord," the one I performed before the start of orchestra last week.

I looped the recording of myself, over and over, and then mixed in the sounds I captured from the storm. I wove through a recording that I found online—a soft, *soft*, heartbeat. When I'd finished, there was something missing so I added in Oliver's question and reply—*What are you doing? You're recording the storm.*

I don't close my eyes this time. I play looking at the smooth blue walls, imagining that I can see the sound bouncing back at me. I think about my old teacher telling me that she felt like the interpreter for her cello, that it had a voice and she was the one who could set it free. My cello's voice today is thick and rich. The word *cavern* floats through my mind and drifts out again.

When I stop, the air feels static with song, and I have this thought that years from now I will have left the ghosts of music in the pool. I am becoming a different Kate, and I love it.

"I'm speechless," Ben says. "Or I was. I was speechless. That never happens to me."

"Is that a good thing, or are you speechless because it's bad?"

"It's good," he says.

"Hey, did you join the Chess Club?" I ask.

"I did, in fact, and it went as expected. I humiliated myself because I can't play chess."

"Did you meet anyone?"

"Also as expected. I met a lot of people who can play chess. I have decided to put myself into suspended animation until you come home for the long weekend."

"I don't think that's a great solution."

"No, but since your solution was the Chess Club, and you've decided that you believe in signs, I'm no longer listening to you."

"These are all fair points."

"What's the fifth sign?" he asks.

"Oliver," I say. "Whenever I think about not going to Orion, I think about how repressed he is. Every practice last week he tried to teach me something, or he told me I really should take some more classical lessons, or he asked me not to drink my coffee near his cello, and did I know that caffeine is bad for cellos? Every time he says something like that I ask myself: Do I really want to be as anally retentive as Oliver? Do I really want to be as repressed?" I'm thinking too much about Oliver, which annoys and interests me. But I can tell Ben anything. He doesn't assume or tease.

I hear a cough and turn around.

"Hello," Oliver says.

"Is that Oliver?" Ben asks.

"It's Oliver," Oliver says.

"Don't hang up," Ben says, before I hang up.

He's standing on the side of the pool, staring curiously into the deep end where I'm sitting with my cello and my computer, at the pickup mic, and the cords.

"How long have you been here?"

"Long enough," he says, leaving me wondering what the end of that sentence is. Long enough to hear that I think he's anally retentive? Long enough to know that I'm thinking about him? Long enough to hear me play?

"I like the acoustics," I say, in answer to his unspoken question of why I'm playing in an empty pool. The other day I was on the side of it, so he hasn't seen me in here before.

"The leaves don't deaden the sound?"

"A bit. I like it."

He nods and points at the computer. "It's you on the track?"

"Why are you here?" I ask.

"You're late again. I've been waiting. We're all waiting."

He turns abruptly and walks toward orchestra. There's something in the straightness of his back that gives me the solution. I don't need to look for signs. I might not be repressed like Oliver, but I am as determined. Ben's right. I'm not a signs person. I assess the problem and find the solution. When someone brings me their computer and they're crying because it's midnight and they've lost their assignment that's due the next day, I stay calm and go through the problem logically.

I don't need to take a risk to go to Orion. Risks are not really my thing. I need to find someone who will lie for me so that I can get a pass. I go through all the people I've helped with computer problems in the last few weeks, but there have only been boarders, really.

Wellness.

When the thought comes, it's obvious.

It's not without danger. Ady Rosenthal is intimidating, to put it mildly. But there's something about her . . . I think back to class, see her lounging, listening, dreaming at times. I think about her at the Botanic Gardens, telling me to go: *The light is green, Kate.*

The light is green. The sixth sign, if I want to believe in signs.

I can tell Old Joy that I'm going to Ady's house after our wellness class to catch up. I just need Ady to tell a small lie for me. And Orion is a go.

PSST

ONE-PARTY WHORES, DESPERATE DATES,

FUCK-BUDDY BY MIDNIGHT . . .

Because we're here for a good time not a "relationship"

1. Hallie Saxby
2. Rachel Dunlop
3. Cat Bongiorno
4. Jess Bishop
5. Olivia Currie
6. Samira Prentice
7. Jodi Bennett
8. Grace Reddy
9. Sophie Christou
10. Tamsin Llewellyn

Ericsonic: Good list here, I can confirm 3, 7, and 8 from personal experience, easy hookups, no follow-up calls required
Catbong: lmao Ericsonic, that was not sex, that was you falling asleep next to me on a sofa drooling. Must have been a great dream.
sufferingsuffragette: More heinous idiocy. It's possible that none of these girls wants to encounter you more than once. Did that occur to you?
Ericsonic: dumb slut
Feminightmare: I think you really do mean relationship, not "relationship." Dipshit.
Bizjiz: I might work my way through this lot, thanx for deets—anyone got addresses for these sluts?
j0yful0ne2: if anyone publishes addresses here I will report this site to the police
PSST ADMIN:
Please forward contact info via DM only

b@rnieboy: yr not 2 happy j0yful0ne2—did you get left off the list? Or are you on it?

j0yful0ne2: I object to the list regardless of who's on it

PSST ADMIN:
Objection noted, now fuck off

load 137 more comments

Clem

Friday, July 29

Jinx,

I'm doing that first date for wellness tonight with Ady & Kate. Not sure how late it will go. If I'm not back by curfew can you cover for me? I'll use the portal.

Love ya,

Clem

I take the tram to Richmond, dressed as sexily as I can manage: tight jeans, low-cut top, lots of makeup. I bought a copy of *Fuss* for their smoky-eyes tutorial, and now I'm reading an article called *How to Hook Up: "OMG mind-blowing oral sex."*

Suggestion: Guys love it when a woman uses her mouth and hands on their package at the same time.

I try to imagine doing this stuff with Stu. Just reading about it makes me feel so embarrassed.

Suggestion: Don't ignore his balls.

I giggle and look up. There's a guy in a suit staring at me. I purse my lips and stare straight back until he gets uncomfortable.

Suggestion: Be enthusiastic! Never treat a blow job like it's a job.

When I arrive at the café, Ady and Kate are already there, sitting out front having what looks like a pretty tepid conversation. I don't apologize for being late. I just angle my chair so I have a better view of Rockland Studios. It's 4:32. Kate and Ady are both staring at me, and I take this as further proof that I look good.

I edge my chair a little further away from them.

"So, how are we supposed to do this? Should we play 20 questions?"

"We only need to know two things," Kate points out.

I stare at the studio door as if I can make it open through mental force and see Stu inside. I only know what the inside of a studio looks like because of TV. I'm picturing a gnarly-looking dude behind a panel of buttons, and Stu saying, "More foldback. More bass."

The waiter is waiting. I order a latte. Kate asks for tea and Ady surprises me by ordering cake. I don't imagine girls like her get to be girls like her by eating cake. Maybe she pukes it after. I pretend to take a note for Malik. *Kate drinks tea and Adelaide likes cake.*

I could talk about swimming, the Canberra trip, Beaz's hopes and dreams for next season, but it feels false. Ady's cake comes with whipped cream—she does not approve, actually sends it back. Kate sips her tea; she looks as if she's on the verge of saying something interesting, but the words don't happen. So I see if I can coax some.

"I heard you play the other morning. At the old pool. You're really good. I mean, I've never heard music like that before."

"Thanks." Kate sits up, her eyes bright. "It's something new I've been—"

"Wait—" The studio door has opened. Stu is walking out. He's wearing jeans and a khaki jacket. He's with an older guy who has so much hair he looks more wolf than man.

"—working on . . ." Kate's still talking, but I'm up and teetering on the curb. I call out to Stu through my cupped megaphone hands. He looks surprised and happy to see me. He hollers back, gestures that he's going to go to the lights. I return to perch on my chair.

"Guy you like?" Ady says.

I dig out $5 and leave, saying over my shoulder, "Thanks, it's been real."

Am I walking toward Stu or am I flying? It's all I can do not to break into a run.

"Magic girl," Stu says. "I think about you, and there you are."

"You were thinking about me?"

"I was. Bad thoughts. Wrong thoughts."

"Dude." The hairy guy says, shaking his head.

"This is Clem," Stu tells him. I'm willing him to say, my girlfriend, but he doesn't say it.

"What are you doing here?"

"Oh, just a thing for school."

"A thing for school." He nods, super serious, then his face

relaxes. I love his smile. It makes me go weak. The hairy guy lets out an old-man groan. "Are we getting a drink?"

Stu angles his head, inviting me. We're outside what looks like the last unrenovated pub in Melbourne. It's not the kind of place that has a menu or even entertainment.

The hairy guy goes in and the smell of beer wafts out. Stu holds the door open for me. I hesitate. An unexpected doubt has arrived. What if I'm walking into something more than I can handle? I cast a glance back to Kate and Ady, but they're not waving their arms dramatically or holding up any red flags. No siren sounds. No one MacGyver-rolls me to safety.

Stu clears his throat, and I go in, right foot first.

Ady

Friday, July 29

Clem has definitely not dressed like that for coffee with me and Kate.

She sits down in a drift of perfume, with her silver shoes and visible breastage. All wrong. She's good-looking in her usual careless no makeup state, and she could look great in full glam, but all she's managed to put together is a desperate *eat me, drink me* thing.

"What are you staring at?" she says.

"Just wondering why you didn't use a mirror to put on your makeup." Too mean. It's not like you'd have much time for playing with makeup on the swim team. But so what? Girls like her, girls on the outer, dismiss me as a rich bitch and hate me on principle.

She gives me a narrow-eyed look of pure irritation, but doesn't bite. She is barely present. We grind our way through the most tedious, stilted exchange to tick the box on this idiotic social outing as the thumb-size group that should get to know each other, according to Malik's bizarre dream of arbitrary and random friendship sparks.

Clem spends the whole time looking around us and through us, until she spots him on the other side of the road. By now I've sent back the inedible cake, and Kate has drunk a pot of tea and been to the bathroom, which she said is manky and best avoided.

Clem throws down five bucks and virtually sprints toward her dude. A protective pang for her springs from nowhere. I want to say, *Be cool, don't show him you care this much*—but why? Who decided that wearing your heart on your sleeve is the big love crime? It's the upper hand, power play school of dating. Second nature to me and my friends. Maybe that's my problem. If I could just crack open my rib cage and let that heart out for a walk down my sleeve. . .

So now it's just the two of us.

Me and Kate.

Kate and me.

She's balancing on the edge of her seat as though she's got a big announcement. I don't need further communication. Let this ordeal be over. Let me mindfully notice odd others from a safe distance.

Clem, a twin, loves jacket guy. Clem is duplicitous. Kate, of delicate complexion, likes Earl Grey tea. Kate enjoys playing cello. Fini.

"I told my head of house that you invited me to dinner at your place," says Kate.

I wasn't expecting *that*. "Why?"

"I'm going to a club. But you can't write that on your pass-out request form. We're basically prisoners." She looks apologetic. "It's just—once I had permission for our coffee encounter, lying about dinner with your family was my best shot to stay out."

Kate Turner's going to a club? This is like M&Ms suddenly becoming salt-and-vinegar chips. Quiet musician breaks the rules to walk on the wild side. She looks anxious, and where is the harm? Sure, I could squash her like an ant, but why bother? What has she ever done to me?

"Fine. Whatever. I won't blow your cover."

We leave the café and walk along together for a bit, and I'm wondering exactly when she's going to peel off and leave me alone.

"Anything else I can do for you?" It was rhetorical with a hint of snark; I wasn't expecting her to take me up on the offer.

"I'm not meeting my—person—there 'til later, and I need somewhere to be for a bit, so I thought maybe . . . I wouldn't get in the way."

So, she not only wants to pretend to come to my place, she wants to come to my place for real?

"Okay, but I'm planning to walk home along the river path. It takes half an hour from here."

She looks relieved, smiles, and puts her headphones on.

Kate gives the house an admiring look and I feel a pang of anxiety. *Don't sell it, let me keep living here, this is my home*. I lead the way along the tangled garden path, in through the back door, and head straight for the stairs. I instinctively try to distract Kate from the sound of my parents arguing by saying the first thing that comes into my head. I offer to help her get ready: she cannot wear what she's got on, which is basically stage blacks. Way to be inconspicuous.

"I do this all the time, so don't be offended . . ." I say, opening the door to my bedroom and leading her through to my walk-in closet. "Think of it as a clothes library—it's the only way I can justify having all this stuff."

Kate gives a wow whistle as she takes in the extent of it. Cool response. I've only ever seen or heard that in films. Having superior whistling skills must be a subset of being musical.

I flip through a few options and—perfect! A high-buttoned, ankle-length, silk-velvet, gored coat-dress. A thrift-shop find that I couldn't resist, but have never worn.

She nods as I hold it up. She turns and slips her arms in. Transformation. The antique gold color glows against her fair skin. Perfecto. Now she's dressed for a night out. Now her black boots look deliberate and ironic. Clothes, I love you.

She runs her finger along the nap of the velvet. "Wild fabric."

"Yeah. Suits you."

We mess around with some hair and makeup until our stomachs start rumbling, so I go down to the kitchen to see what's on offer. There's no smell of cooking, and no sign of Charlie or Clare. A door slams from the direction of the argument. I grab some leftover frittata, a chocolate brownie, two apples, and a bottle of sparkling water from the fridge, and run back upstairs.

Just before I close my door, my mother's voice floats up; she's calling my father "a complete world-class bastard loser" at high volume. Welcome to my family. Kate blushes—embarrassed for me, no doubt. Country parents are perhaps more polite to each other.

"You're probably already going out," she says. "But this club—Orion—is supposed to be good; it's a new music venue."

Am I laughing in disbelief and saying, *No, thanks?* Don't seem to be. Am I really about to ditch my plans and go to a club I've never heard of with a boarder I don't know at all? Apparently.

I have the strong feeling that city-clubbing is not a regular thing for Kate. "Have you got ID?"

She opens her wallet and shows me. "It's my cousin's old learner's permit."

They look similar enough for it to work.

"Country pubs can be pretty strict," she says.

Mine is a high-quality fake, organized by Tash's older brother. I've never been questioned.

Strangely, this is exactly what Malik was talking about in class—making friends outside your friendship group. If you want to *get to know someone new* (which I didn't think I did), he said, *take down some barriers* (or let your screaming parents take them down for you, whether you like it or not) and *let them into your world* (well, Kate asked herself, but I did say yes). I didn't intend to take down the whole family privacy barrier; it more or less fell over in front of Kate.

It feels like this night is constructing itself around me—I'm reacting, not planning. But perhaps that's okay. It's like I'm a tram taking an impossible left turn off the tracks and onto the road.

"I'm going to that party," I yell on the way out. "Won't be late." It's already in my mother's datebook that I'm going out to a sweet 16 tonight, back by midnight. I check the change bowl, usually good for the odd ten or twenty bucks. Empty. "I won't bother introducing you to the train-wreck parents. You've had more than enough exposure to them for one night. Better if they think I'm doing what I said."

Kate looks relieved. Good instinct.

Clem

Friday, July 29

It's late. We've been in the pub for four hours. No one's said anything about eating dinner. I've had three beers and 14 peanuts. I've never been anywhere like this—it's like a warren with beer-sopped towels along the bar, photos and curios between the bottles like what you'd find in a thrift shop, a scrum of old dudes and ladies sitting at formica tables with beers, and a for-real TV in a wood veneer case showing soccer.

The bargirl has tattoos and dyed black hair. She's wearing a bra-top and high-waisted black skinny jeans. She's been smiling at Stu since we came in. During a break, she takes it upon herself to lounge in his lap.

"Hey, handsome. How come I never see you anymore?"

"You're seeing me now," Stu says.

They chuckle. I nearly choke on my peanut.

The bargirl pushes Stu's hair away from his eyes and adds, "Hi, Danny," to the hairy guy. Then she looks at me. "Who's this?"

"This is Clem," Stu tells her.

"Right." She looks at me for so long it's uncomfortable.

Stu clamps his arm around my shoulder and squeezes me toward him—a bit rough, but the contact is still thrilling.

The bargirl says, "Look out, honey. He'll ruin you."

"Someone has to," Danny murmurs. He laughs. Stu laughs. I laugh. (What am I laughing at?) The bargirl moves away.

I feel really young. *Really* young. I don't know what anyone's talking about. I don't know what it is I'm saying that Stu and Danny think is so funny. Whenever Stu goes to the bar, there are terrible, torturous seconds alone with Danny. He picks his teeth with a guitar pick and looks at me and never says a word. When Stu comes back, the air changes again, and I forget Danny and drink my beer, which tastes like dead-flower water.

I listen to Stu and Danny talk about bands I've never heard of and look around at the faces of the customers—their skin is lined like hard land. They're scary, but Stu and Danny just talk and joke like having starburst veins and exploding noses from too much booze is normal. Every now and then, Stu looks at me, as if to ask me if I'm okay, but he doesn't actually ask it.

At about 10:00, Danny finally leaves. But then it feels strange to be alone with Stu. He looks bleary, pissed. I'm not exactly sober. I feel sloppy, heavy; I can't think of anything to talk about. His hands are on my thighs. He's probably thinking about how fat they are.

"Let's go outside," he says. "It's stuffy in here."

He takes my hand and leads me out the front of the pub, where the Friday night traffic is crawling along, and down an alley where empty kegs are stacked, silver as the night is silvery.

He pushes me up against the wall. We kiss and people leaving the pub walk right past us. One guy, drunk, kicks over a barrel and it crashes on the sidewalk, breaking the spell. "I'd better go," I say, my tongue feeling all thick now that I'm using it for words and not kisses.

On the tram I feel like I'm phosphorescent.

Stuart Laird McAlistair. I whisper it, affecting the accent, rolling the brogue.

All the way back to school I am amped, electric. It's only in the dark of the grounds that I get nervous. What if Ady and Kate have told? Why did I take such a risk?

But everything is working. The portal, the empty hallway, no cavalry.

Jinx is still up, doing crunches, listening to a podcast.

"I told Old Joy you were in the shower. She was going to come back, but she never did. How was it?"

"It was okay. They're okay, I guess."

"Jeez, Clem, you smell like a hundred beers."

"I had one. Please! Don't be a cop."

I'm so edgy. Sleep is out of the question. And I don't want to answer Jinx's questions so I get out Malik's sheet to write about my "date" with Kate and Ady and complete the lie. I make it all up, laying on the superlatives. By the time I've finished I've almost convinced myself that we're best buddies. Ady is classy and generous and stylish. Kate is calm and talented and honest. I don't write the one thing I hope: that they can keep a secret.

Ady

Friday, July 29

We're walking up stairs, then more stairs, and more stairs. And here, tucked into some low-rent office space, high up in this lovely decrepit building, is the club. Hot music swells into the innocent hallway as we push through a door and find ourselves at the back of a line.

The music is like Flume meets Violent Soho. What am I doing here?

Kate looks incredible—with really just a few tweaks. Hair piled up high with lots of fake flowers stuck into it. Pale ghost works for her, and nothing says that like black-crimson lips. The line is short. Naturally we get stamped and waved on in. Even grungy places love stylish girls. It ain't right, but it's a help when you're underage.

I have enough dollars for one drink, and I cross my fingers that there's enough credit on my transit card to get back home.

Kate has to leave in time to make her 11:00 p.m. curfew, and I've said I'll go when she does.

On the one hand, what am I doing here? On the other hand, this isn't the sort of place I usually hang out, so it makes for a change. And you know what they say about change. I check my phone. The screen is a long list of people I can't be bothered calling back, Rupert the most persistent.

I text him in case he gets worried and tells my parents that I'm not answering my phone. Text that I've detoured and won't make it to Sam's. I say sorry. I don't say: *I'm a bit over your self-involved conversation and my perfunctory hand jobs.* It wouldn't exactly be appropriate material for a text. I add to the sorry: *Talk tomorrow, manbabe x.*

Kate already seems mesmerized by the music being made by the two girl/two dude outfit onstage. She's moving her head to their strange syncopations. It's arty electronica meets strange noises, and I'm not particularly into it. I glance around and hold eye contact with the cute boy mixing sound; it gives me a little twing in the pants. Mmmm. Maybe. Another message from the universe about the wrongness of Rupert. For me. Not in general.

I ask Kate if I can get her a drink. "My treat," she says, absently handing me her wallet, not taking her eyes off the stage. Boarders are always cashed up. What do they have to spend money on, apart from chocolate and makeup? I'm often drinks monitor because I look older and intimidating when required. Seeing as Kate is paying, I get us both vodka tonics and tip the bar guy. He'll be good for a free drink later.

Kate is way on the other side of the floor when I deliver the drinks. She's found her people, but doesn't seem super relaxed. She knocks the drink back quickly, breaking briefly from an intense-looking conversation with a guy and introducing me to a girl called Max.

I get my second twing for the night. Max is beautiful in my ideal androgynous way. Tall—my height—with short, flicky black hair, ballet back, square shoulders, killer '60s cocktail dress, and a cautious smile. I smile back, reckless.

"Who are you here to see?" she asks.

"No one in particular."

"I mainly want to see Milton Glass, but they're not on 'til 11:00." Max is checking out my dress. "Family, thrift shop, vintage . . . ?"

"Family."

"Love it."

"Love yours."

"Thrift shop."

"What's your favorite?"

"Red Cross on—"

"Bridge Road," we say at the same time.

"I'm also addicted to Vixen," I say.

"Back room," she agrees. "Amazing."

"It's the best." It's where they put stuff that hasn't been sorted, cleaned, or mended. A treasure trove. Only available to people they like. I think that door gets opened based on whether they approve of what you're wearing.

I glance over at Kate—she's checking her watch as she continues her argument: Cinderella time soon.

A new band goes onstage, making a different bunch of challenging noises. One of their members is the guy Kate was talking to.

Max leans in close. "This is the Sherlocks, friends of mine. Dance?" One dimple appears when her smile widens. I follow her onto the floor and start moving; it feels like my joints need oiling and I don't know the music, but soon enough we're jumping and laughing.

The sets are short; the next act starts with a slow song, a girl singing and playing cello. Max keeps dancing as people drift off the floor. She moves unselfconsciously. It makes me think that the way I'm used to dancing at parties is much more about performing to be watched than it is about the music.

After another piece is played, my bartender gives me a nod; he's poured some tequila shots. Max and I converge and down them in a coordinated gulp. Kate joins us. Max licks the inside of her shot glass, picks up a lime wedge, eats it, and says, "Tall Tales Tacos should be downstairs by now—let's get one." Bartender boy smiles goodbye. Jesus, he's cute, too—three twings—it's like I want to have theoretical sex with the whole world tonight, except Rupert.

Down, down, down the stairs, passing lots more people heading up now. The three of us each fang down a taco—Kate pays. And those two talk music-tech while I watch Max. I could have taken more of that, but we have to hurry for Kate's curfew.

"Let's do this again," says Max, turning to head back inside.

I imagine her saying that after doing lots more things together. *Let's do this again.*

Like the responsible stylist I am, I have a travel pack of face wipes. Three wipes later, by the time the tram arrives at the stop outside school, Kate is shiny-faced, flowers out, bun down, velvet coat-dress swapped for her black puffy jacket, and looking just about as innocent as usual.

What I won't be telling Malik about the *Look outside your friendship group* experience: It wasn't what I expected.

Kate is interesting and I like her. All that apparent vagueness—she has a whole secret universe in her head. She's so into this cool-weird music scene, and seems to know heaps about it. If she doesn't get out much, how does she know it all? She must live online. She maybe likes or maybe dislikes the Sherlock boy; there's some friction there that could go either way. She is brave. She penetrated the rich-bitch facade. She bought me a drink and a taco. She saw nasty stuff on the domestic front, and it didn't faze her. She introduced me to the first someone in ages I've felt has obsession potential.

Clem is interesting and I don't exactly like her, but I can see that she's more than just a swim-girl. She's so into jacket guy. I want to know what it feels like to need someone that much. She seems shameless, or maybe it's fearless. She literally chased him. I've always been chased. Maybe if you win that many races you think everything is there for the taking. Or maybe she just wants time as a regular girl as well as a jock. People shouldn't have to choose between modes.

The Clem and Kate assignment definitely wasn't what I was expecting on any count.

More unexpected things when I get home. Tiptoeing past my parents' closed bedroom door, I hear my father crying against the background of my mother's urgent murmuring. I try to feel optimistic—at least he's back in their bedroom, not sleeping downstairs—but the sound of him crying is something I've never heard before and it is unimaginably terrible.

Kate

Friday, July 29

Ady cruises through the door without being asked for ID and I cruise through in her wake. I feel like I'm walking into a new life. I catch sight of myself in the mirror—the same me but different. Me with voltage.

Ady stares a path through the crowd for us, forcing space with her eyes. I try to forget the voices of her parents, her mum yelling at her dad, the sound filtering up as Ady stuck flowers in my hair.

"Drink?" she asks, and I give her my wallet. It's the least I can do. I still can't believe she lied for me. Ady Rosenthal—Queen Bitch, according to school folklore—let me into her home, lent me her clothes, came with me to a club.

The place is exactly how I imagined. Spinning lights and sound. The stage has as many laptops on it as instruments, and I'm so focused on working out how they're making the sound that I don't notice Max until she's standing in front of me, waving and yelling, "Hey. Space girl. I want you to meet someone."

She takes me by the hand, and pulls me through the crowd. I worry briefly about Ady, but then I remember that she can take care of herself. I let Max lead me. She turns and grins every so often, and then turns forward again, her eyes searching through the crowd. I'm imagining who I might meet—a musician like me, a guy, a good-looking guy maybe—and then we stop moving and Max says, "Here he is. Oliver, meet Kate; Kate, meet Oliver. Best cellist I know."

He's standing in front me, out of school uniform for the first time, wearing a Radiohead T-shirt and black jeans. He hasn't shaved, and in the light blinking over us from the stage, I see that Oliver has a faint jaw shadow. He's leaning on Max's shoulder, looking at home.

"Oliver? Oliver is playing at the open mic?"

"You two know each other?" Max asks.

"Not that well," I say at the same time that Oliver says, "Pretty well."

"It took me a year to warm to him," Max admits to me.

Ady pushes her way through the crowd and hands me a drink. "There's a bit of voddy in there," she says, and looks surprised when I drink it. Quick. I'm tempted to take hers and down it, too.

"Why does she keep saying your name?" Max asks Oliver, and Oliver, who's clearly enjoying my confusion, smiles and says, "I really couldn't tell you."

Ady nudges me, and looks over at Max. I make the introductions and the two of them start talking immediately, moving off to the side a little, which leaves Oliver and me. "Are you going to say my name again?" he asks. "I like it when you say my name."

"Anally retentive, fuckwit Oliver."

"Thank you."

"Happy to please," I say.

The crowd pushes us apart, and then we come back together again. "You said you never come here. You said the sticker wasn't yours. You lied to me."

"I chose not to reveal a part of my life. And in my defense, you had just told me to shut up immediately before you asked the question. You're always making me out to be conservative or boring and I'm not interested in convincing you of my worth. I'm here because it's a place to play, not because it impresses Kate Turner."

It's not like I don't know I've been uncharacteristically mean to Oliver. "You're always lecturing. It drives me insane."

"You're just as obsessed with music as me," he says. "Maybe more."

"But I don't lecture you about it."

"Yeah," he says. "You do."

He frowns at his drink. "You look different," he says after a while.

I feel self-conscious all of a sudden. As if Ady's put a costume on me and only Oliver can see that.

"So how do you know Max?" he asks.

"I met her at the record store downstairs. I was cutting class."

"Rebel Kate," he says, and, in a short space of time, I feel like the universe has flipped and it's Oliver who's the alternative one and I haven't been looking at him with the right eyes.

"How do *you* know Max?" I ask.

"Met in elementary school. We were at St. Martin's together. It's a youth drama center."

"I know what it is." I don't, actually. "I'm acting weird," I say.

"Maybe it's the lipstick," he says.

The band stops and the MC calls for the Sherlocks. "That's me," Oliver says, and moves onstage to take his position. It's been a long time since I've been hit with as much surprise as I feel right now. One of Ben's quotes floats through my head—"the precision of naming takes away the uniqueness of seeing." Oliver has been Oliver so long it's hard to see him as anything else.

The singer, a girl with long red hair and a bright green dress, turns and smiles at him. He smiles back and I'm hit with envy that's not all about that fact that he's onstage and I'm not. Oliver is very serious up there, and the serious is seriously attractive. Onstage with him is a keyboardist and a drummer/percussionist, a violin player, and a girl on bass guitar.

The singer counts them in with a soft, low voice, that's a little Björk, a little Cowboy Junkies. Oliver's good. He's concentrating the way he does in orchestra, one eye slightly closed, total focus. But somehow, sitting behind a rock band, his cello plugged into a microphone, playing sounds that ache, he's mesmerizing.

They're playing "Jane Says," sampling WTF and Know-how, and, every so often, a thread of what I'm pretty sure is Chopin runs through. Oliver's working the tech onstage, his foot on a pedal attached to the laptop. He's using a laptop? Every now and then he extracts himself from the cello and plays a line of trumpet.

He looks up after the set's finished, the concentration clearing from his face, and waves at me. Smart ass. After three more songs, he climbs back down from the stage.

"So, what'd you think?" he asks.

"It was okay," I tell him.

"Such high praise from someone like you means a lot."

"It was good. I'm surprised."

"Again with the praise."

"You just don't seem . . ."

"Interesting?"

"Like you'd play in a band."

"You met me in a band."

"A band like that."

He's about to say something else when a girl walks past him and his eyes follow her onto the stage. "Watch this," he says.

She's our age, maybe a year older, and she sits up there with such confidence. She has her computer, like Frances Carter. She bows this harshness from her cello, playing it like a guitar. Her voice is sweet, though, and the mix is astounding. I don't move. I don't breathe.

He stays there next to me, not saying anything, and I wish he'd go. Because hovering between us is how I sound in the pool and how this player sounds and how I am nowhere near her standard. I am desperate to play like her.

I stay here, transfixed, until her set ends, and then I go to find Ady.

She's at the bar with Max doing tequila shots. I join them for a while, and then we go outside and try to soak up the alcohol with a taco. Oliver walks over. He kisses Max on the cheek, nods at Ady, and holds his hand out to me in a strangely formal way. "I didn't mean to offend you," he says.

"You didn't," I say, my cheeks cold but my face weirdly hot.

"He's not as arrogant as he seems," Max says. "He's awkward."

I try not to think about him on the way home. The lights go past. I open the tram window and cup my hand at the air, trying to catch it for later, so it's what I take home from the night, not how Oliver made me feel.

Ady takes out some face wipes and before I get off the tram, she removes my makeup and takes the flowers out of my hair.

I feel like I've been pushed from a dream.

Iris is awake when I get to our room. She's sitting up in bed, glasses on, reading. I open our window. "I'm cold," she says, and I close it a little as a compromise.

"So?" she asks.

I hadn't gone into detail with Iris about my plan. I lied, actually. I knew she wouldn't like it that I was planning on using my wellness outing with Ady and Clem to escape—she hates Clem, and she's not fond of Ady—so I told her Mum and Dad had given me the pass.

But now I'm too tired to lie. I sit on my bed and come clean with her.

"You asked *Ady*?" she says.

"She's actually okay." More than okay. "I like her. You would, too, if you got to know her."

"I wouldn't," Iris says, and pauses as if she's thinking about whether or not to tell me something, then decides to go ahead. "Gregory's worried about you falling behind. He asked me to give you some extra help."

I think about Iris and Gregory talking about me in the tutoring sessions I've been skipping and turn over to face the wall, acting like I'm asleep. "I'm not falling behind in math or science."

"You don't concentrate in class."

"I'm getting good marks."

"You don't get perfect marks anymore."

"I don't need perfect marks."

You do if you want the scholarship, I can hear her thinking, but she doesn't say it.

I lie awake, thinking about the club, about the Sherlocks, about Oliver, about that girl onstage, applauded by the audience but lost in her music, lost somewhere inside herself.

Before I moved to the city, the scholarship meant everything to me because it was the way to the future. I didn't want to be a doctor. I wanted to be in the city. The only reason I want that scholarship is that it keeps me from having to go home. How much does staying in the city mean to me? Everything.

Kate's Wellness Journal

Friday, July 29

Dear Journal,

What things did I find out about Ady and Clem, my thumb-compatible companions? Ady has a home life I can't fully imagine and don't want to. It's not like my parents don't fight, but they're squabbling over who'll make the coffee in the morning or who has control of the remote. Small things. Forgettable things.

Ady's house is empty of home sounds. No cooking or talking or TV. When her mum swore at her dad on our way down the hall, I tried not to look shocked, but I'd never heard parents speak to each other like that before.

Ady heard, I'm sure, but I knew from the way she closed the door of her room and smiled as if nothing had happened, that I shouldn't say anything.

I can see where the edge in Ady comes from, but I like that edge. It's not bitchiness, like people say. It's an unwillingness to put up with high school bullshit. Or bullshit in general.

And Clem? She's in love. Or lust. Either way she can't control it and that I understand.

Other thoughts I am thinking . . .

Oliver.

Oliver is many other thoughts to think.

I don't like to admit it, but he was mighty attractive up there tonight. Annoying. But attractive.

I've looked up St. Martin's and seen a picture of him on the website, one arm slung around Max and the other around his cello. He's got an easy smile on his face, which is different from every single smile he's ever given me.

I'm listening to myself play as I type this. I don't compare to that girl onstage. She must have been experimenting with music and sound for years. I'm just getting started, which is why I need to go to Iceland.

Iris is telling me to turn off the light. I only have my small lamp on, so I know she's still annoyed. It's late, though, so I will turn off the light.

But I won't sleep.

I can't.

Clem

Sunday, July 31

I suppose the selfies really started in earnest after the gardens. Just the usual stuff, making faces, posing like stone-cold killers—I've got quite the collection: the many moods of Stu. But the photos he sends this morning feel like a game changer.

In the first one, Stu is staring into the camera, lips pursed. Ten seconds later he sends one with his shirt off—just his chest, but I feel weird looking at it, because nudes! His skin looks pale and smooth and not carpet-man hairy, but hairy enough to remind me that he's a man and not a boy. Then my phone pings again and I am almost too scared to look. This one is just of his lower half—he's wearing red jocks, like a shot for an underwear company. But he's stuffed something down the front of them so it looks like he has a mammoth package. I'm lying on my bed, giggling, while Jinx is packing her stuff for the pool. I hold the phone out for her to see, but she ignores it.

"What's up with you, Clem? Are you ever going to train again? Come today. It's Sunday. It'll just be us."

I shrug.

"Are you sending him photos as well?"

"Yeah, of course!"

Jinx looks conflicted.

"Come on," she tries again. "I can show you the stuff for the routine."

"What routine?"

"The Marlins! Winter Fair! Don't you care?"

"Yeah . . . just . . ." I enlarge the photo, trying to work out what Stu's stuffed down his pants. Sweat socks, maybe?

Jinx snaps her towel at me. My phone lands on the carpet with a soft thud.

"You'd better not have broken it."

"I'm sure your precious phone is fine."

"Can you please leave? I have some pictures to take."

Jinx stares at me for long seconds. "You know, you're getting to be really boring." She picks up her bags and leaves.

I text Stu: *Thanks for the happy snap.*

Who is this?

Very funny.

Hey. What are you doing later?

Not much.

You know the laundromat near the corner of Glenferrie and Malvern Rds?

No. But I can find it.

Meet me for breakfast around 10:30.

I don't have a pass, but I know that Iris has chess at 10:00. She used to ask me to come with her. I'd laugh: *Me? Chess? No!* Now I poke my head around her door. "Where's chess today?"

"Sacred Heart."

Perfect! Sacred Heart is a tram-ride away from Stu.

"Why?" Iris wants to know.

"No reason."

I run downstairs and check in with Old Joy to see if it's okay if I go along as a cheerleader. And then I spend the next 15 minutes selecting then rejecting items from my wardrobe. It's like all I have is tracksuits or school uniforms. I end up wearing what I wore on Friday. I lay off the makeup this time, remembering Ady's comment.

When Iris sees me down in the foyer, she looks wary.

I rip out a cheer move. "Gooooo, St. Hilda's!"

Iris isn't buying. "Since when do you want to be my chess cheerleader?"

"Since today."

"What are you wearing?"

I look down at my chesty top. "Clothes."

"You might want to cover up."

"Don't slut-shame me."

"You sound like Jinx," Iris says.

"You should take a leaf out of my book: Distract the opposition."

Iris makes a face.

Me, Iris, three surplus chess nerds, and their tutor, Mr. Miles, go in the minivan to Sacred Heart's leafy campus. Inside the

Barrington building, the chess players are playing in earnest, hitting clocks and smiling smugly at each other, creasing their brows and angsting their pants. Theo's standing on the other side of the hall. Iris waves to him and he nods back, but he doesn't make any effort to come over.

"Theo's keeping a low profile," I say.

Iris bites her lip. She shows me where to sit, but as soon as she moves off, I light out of there. Mr. Miles will be too focused on the team to note my absence. As long as I'm back by 1:00, there won't be a problem.

The laundromat is empty, except for Stu. He's sitting at the table in front of a brown paper bag and the local newspaper. He has two laundry bags behind him, emptied, and I see two of the larger machines are mid-cycle.

He stands up. "Welcome to my office. You look fetching."

He takes my hand and kisses me, then dips me, making me shriek and almost fall. He waltzes me over to the machines and we continue to kiss and it's getting quite heated. From the corner of my eye I can see ordinary people walking past, going about their day; surely someone will come in here soon.

Someone does. Stu and I go sit at the table. I look in the paper bag.

"What's for breakfast?"

"Egg-and-bacon sandwiches."

We eat, smiling at each other, playing footsies.

"You come here often?" I ask.

"Blue House washing. Sorting the sheets from the tea towels and whatnot."

"Sexy."

"You are." Stu grins.

I can feel myself going red. Am I?

"So," he says, "I've been trying to work out where we can go. You know, to—" He whistles and winks.

"What about the Blue House—when you stay overnight?"

"You don't want to go there."

I look at him. It's on the tip of my lips: I'd go anywhere.

The machine stops with a clang, and Stu wipes his hands, gets up, and starts transferring the wet sheets and tea towels and whatnot into the dryer. I'm buzzing from the idea that he's thinking about a place, and then I remember.

"We have a long weekend coming up. Most of the boarders go home. But my parents are in Singapore. I was going to stay with Jinx's aunt . . ."

"Mmm-hmm?"

"I could just say I'm staying at Jinx's aunt's—if we had somewhere to go . . . My face is flaming, combustible, and the sound of the tumble dryer is primal, matching my pulse. Oh! Hot, damp, thumping world!

"So, great," Stu claps his hands together like a broker at a business meeting, "I'll find somewhere."

He grabs me and kisses me. "I'm going to make you feel so good, Clem."

Back at the dorms, Old Joy has set up a crafternoon. We've been making bunting for the Winter Fair, personalizing little cloth triangles. The fair is a big fund-raiser for the school—it's all fuss and jostle and parental involvement.

I sit in a circle with Jinx, Iris, and Kate. Iris isn't speaking to me. Kate's in her own world. Jinx is making me laugh by decorating her bunting with vulva-esque motifs.

Old Joy strides around with her hands in her poncho pockets.

"Lovely, girls, lovely. I'm seeing patterns, and inspirational quotes."

A morose-looking girl puts her hand up.

"Miss, I can't think of anything to draw."

"Just draw what makes you happy."

I raise my hand.

Old Joy comes over. "Clem?"

"Can I use a photo as a reference? It's on my phone."

Jinx groans. Iris is glowering at me.

"Nice try," Old Joy says.

After 10 minutes, it's like a calm bomb has descended and we're absorbed in our sketching and coloring. Stu does this sort of stuff at his work—creative therapies. He told me he had one client, a teenage boy who had violent outbursts, couldn't stand being touched, and was a whole packet of trouble, but if he had paper and pens he'd draw amazing unearthly worlds. Stu said they were crazy beautiful.

Stu is crazy beautiful.

I'm trying to draw his face from memory. I should be able to do this, but my hand and mind aren't communicating. His brow's too big and his chin's too small. His head looks like an alien's egg-shaped dome and his lips are pushing up a sinister moustache. I cover the mess up with swirls and add his initials and mine, entwined. I'm obsessed, I know. If I don't stop thinking about him, I'm sure I'll explode from repressed desire.

"Hey." Jinx leans on me. "Are you getting excited about Canberra?"

"I guess."

"When are you going to come back to us?"

"What's she talking about?" Iris says peevishly. "Are you still not swimming?"

Kate paints tiny dots. "Does she have to swim?"

"Yes," Jinx says. "She's good."

Iris is staring at me. I refuse to look at her.

"I don't get you," Iris says in a small voice. "Swimming's your thing. You love swimming. What's going on?"

"It's about a boy," Jinx says.

"What boy?" Iris wants to know.

"Jesus!" I snap. "Stop sticking your nose in it. My life has nothing to do with yours. And don't even think about telling Mum and Dad."

"What boy?" Iris persists. "Is that where you went today?"

I get up and take my bunting with me. It looks like shit, so I chuck it in the trash on my way out. I go up to my room, find my old pilled bathing suit, and put it in my bag. I take the key to the new pool from Jinx's drawer, and head down there. It is true that the water feels like an old friend; I remember at once the pleasure of slipping under, the dreamy darkness when I close my eyes, submerged. I swim by myself, up and back, up and back until I can't feel anything but froth and churn and my heart feels too big for my rib cage, and my throat is tight and my legs feel like sandbags. When I finally get out, it's late. The night seems to press against me. I thought swimming would make me feel better, clearer. But, in the end, all I feel is exhausted.

WEEK 4

SELF-ESTEEM

Wellness

Monday, August 1
Dr. Peter Malik

Week 4: Nurturing Self-Esteem

Provocation

What lies behind us and what lies before us are tiny matters compared to what lies within us.

—Henry S. Haskins

Self-esteem is confidence in one's own worth or abilities. It's made up of the thoughts, feelings, and opinions we have of ourselves. Today we reflect privately on how we see ourselves, and discuss methods to improve our sense of self-worth.

Points for Discussion/Reflection

Each of us is an individual as well as a member of various groups—family, community, school, friendship. Our identity is developed through a combination of our personality, our beliefs and values, our cultural background, our opportunities and privilege, our experiences and actions, our defining moments.

- What are your five best qualities?
- What do you see as your greatest talent? If you can't decide, ask the people in your group.
- What factors affect your self-esteem? (Consider family, peers)
- Does your self-esteem ever fluctuate? When is your self-esteem at its highest? When is your self-esteem at its lowest? What factors might be lowering your self-esteem?
- Discuss some practical ways you could boost your self-esteem.

Task 1

Complete the Rosenberg Self-Esteem Scale. Developed by sociologist Dr. Morris Rosenberg, the Rosenberg Self-Esteem Scale measures self-esteem by asking you to reflect on general feelings about yourself. Indicate how strongly you agree or disagree with each statement.

Statement	Strongly Agree	Agree	Disagree	Strongly Disagree
On the whole, I am satisfied with myself.				
At times, I think I am no good at all.				
I feel that I have a number of good qualities.				
I am able to do things as well as most other people.				
I feel that I do not have much to be proud of.				
I feel useless at times.				
I feel that I'm a person of worth, at least on an equal plane with others.				
I wish I could have more respect for myself.				
All in all, I am inclined to feel that I am a failure.				
I take a positive attitude toward myself.				

Scoring

Items 2, 5, 6, 8, 9 are reverse-scored. "Strongly Disagree" 1 point, "Disagree" 2 points, "Agree" 3 points, and "Strongly Agree" 4 points. Add the scores for all 10 items. Higher scores indicate higher self-esteem.

PSST

RATE THE BOARDERS—ST. HILDA'S, SACRED HEART, CROWTHORNE

1. Angela Bannon—fucking hot. number one boarder id do
2. Jinx Benedict—shit face but gives excellent head
3. Carla Walsh—better from the back
4. Josephine Parker—good tits, average ass, okay legs
5. Grace Wang—get her drunk at parties thats all im saying
6. Helena Parks—total dog but gr8t body
7. Maddie Plom—puts out at every party
8. Sarah Lim—excellent handjobs if yr desperate
9. Bernadette Smith—shit handjobs but gr8t fuck
10. Kate Turner—weird mute, but if yr desperate at least she won't talk back. and it's the quiet ones that really go off

Bizjiz: feminazi jinx needs a good fuck.
sufferingsuffragette: It's absolutely outrageous that you think you can do this.
Bizjiz: yr just mad yr not on the list
Ericsonic: i would def do kate t.
renterg: maybe if she wore the lab coat on her head.
clydesc: id like to make her scream
closetgman: shes so weird man and olivers on that anyway
fridgeman: really? didn't know he was so desperate
homeboy: josephine parker did me in bathroom at party
nombomb: i want them all together all at once

Kate

Monday, August 1

I get up as quietly as I can, but Iris opens her eyes before I leave. I give her a hesitant smile, and she waves—a signal that she really has forgiven me.

At the pool I set up my computer in the deep end, tune my cello, close my eyes, and put myself back into the darkness of the club. I know it doesn't make sense, but I felt my future in that place.

"Your future?" Iris said Saturday at breakfast, carrying on the quiet fight we'd started the night before. "You want to be onstage, is that it? With everyone watching?"

I stopped talking then, stopped trying to explain that it wasn't about being on the stage or about impressing Oliver. It's about playing old notes and making new sounds. Using the computer. Doing something I love.

"You love science. You want to be a doctor," Iris said.

That would be a perfectly fine future, a bearable one. But the other possible future is brilliantly lit.

The girl onstage at the club—Juliette—played sounds that made every part of me want. She was confident enough to be playful. She's studied for years, I'm sure of it.

Late Sunday night, after a day of polite and angry quiet, Iris sat on my bed. "Okay," she said, her voice switched to practical mode. Motioning for my notebook, she turned to a blank page and wrote a list in her careful handwriting.

Where will you get a music teacher?

How will you afford a music teacher?

Will you tell your parents? Or will you lie to them, and say you still want to be a doctor?

Will they think extra experimental lessons are a waste of money that could go toward your expenses next year? Because you're already in the orchestra and they're paying for that.

I try to force all other thoughts out of my head and play, but thoughts are stubborn, so I give up and call Ben. I tell him I'm feeling stupid and defeated.

"It's Monday," he says. "People all across the country are feeling stupid and defeated."

"Usually I love Mondays."

"I do, too," he says. "All normal people across the country are feeling stupid and defeated."

"Still no luck making a friend?" I ask.

"I'll assume that's a rhetorical question. What's the core of your defeat?"

I tell him about the weekend, Oliver, the money problem, about needing a teacher I can't afford. "You need a cello study partner," he says. "You can't ask the Oliver guy?"

"She's too stubborn to ask the Oliver guy."

"Is that the Oliver guy?" Ben asks.

"It is the Oliver guy. Who are you?" Oliver asks.

"I'm Ben."

"Nice to meet you, Ben. What's your relationship to Kate?"

"None of your business, actually," I tell him.

"Best friend," Ben says. "And you? Why do you keep turning up?"

"Today, I brought Kate a CD that I thought might help."

"I don't need help," I say.

"You just said you did," both of them say.

"Well, I'm taking it back." I don't know why, but I find it impossible to accept help from Oliver. I can't quite look at him now. I feel like he's been wearing a mask since I met him, and now that he's taken it off I can see the guy in the T-shirt onstage, playing in a band.

His hand is still out, and Ben is still listening, so I take the CD and turn it over. The back cover is blank. "Who is it?"

"Someone you need to hear," Oliver says.

"Is it you?"

"Let me know what you think after you've listened to it," he says, and walks off.

"Is he gone?" Ben asks.

"You need to start living your life and stop living mine vicariously," I tell him, and hang up.

I'm on my way out of the pool, the CD in my blazer pocket, when Joseph turns off his leaf blower and walks over. "Tell your friend he can't come here anymore. I've ignored him so far, but I'm supposed to report it if I see a boy on the grounds."

"He's here for orchestra," I say.

"Not at 7:30, he's not. Lately he's even earlier. Lately, he's here from the second you start playing."

I drink my coffee, stare at the blank back of the CD, think of Oliver, and feel strange. He's been watching me from the second I started playing? Meaning, 6:00 a.m.? What's he doing on school grounds at 6:00 a.m.?

When I walk into orchestra, he's already tuning. I'm about to tell him what the groundskeeper said, and accuse him of stalking me, but he looks up and gives me a small smile, which is unexpected and actually nice. I find myself giving a small smile back.

"Thanks for the CD," I say.

Iris walks in and ends the conversation before it starts. "I need to talk to you," she says in a breathy whisper that smells of cornflakes. "It's about PSST."

"I'm tuning," I tell her, and point at Mrs. Davies, who's already here.

She won't give up, though. "Have you seen it this morning?"

"No, because it's misogynist crap. I've told you bcforc, it has nothing to do with me."

"You need to read it," she says, holding out her phone. I'm about to tell her it's none of her or my or anyone's business when Oliver says quietly and seriously, "Forewarned is forearmed."

Other people are walking in, setting up. They all glance at me as they sit down, which is new. I pull out my phone, ignoring Iris's. If I'm about to read shit about myself, which is clearly what's about to happen, then I'll read it on my own device, thanks very much.

As soon as I look, I wish I could un-look. The topic is "Rate the Boarders," and there's a list of 10 names with descriptions. I'm number 10.

Kate Turner—weird mute, but if yr desperate at least she won't talk back. and it's the quiet ones that really go off

I read through the offensive comments (so *unbelievably* offensive) and stop when I get to a comment that mentions Oliver's name.

olivers on that anyway

I look over at him. "What have you been saying?"

"Nothing, I swear."

Mrs. Davies taps her stand.

I play with fury.

"Kate!" Oliver calls as I leave practice. I walk faster so he has to jog to keep up. I wish I could just start running, but I don't want Oliver thinking I'm crying over this and, besides, it's impossible to run with a cello.

"KATE!" Oliver yells again, and sprints toward me. For a studious guy, he's amazingly athletic. He moves ahead of me, turns around, and runs backward.

"You'll fall."

"I'm aware that I'm taking a risk," he says.

"I do not want to talk to you or any male at this point."

I actually don't want to talk to anyone. I've gone from fury to rage to humiliation and back to rage. Who do those people think they are? Commenting on me, on Jinx, on all of those girls? Imagine them typing away, thinking they have the right. "Who the fuck do they think they are?" I ask Oliver.

He holds up his hands in surrender. "Whoever they are, they're idiots. And I need you to know that I have never, at any stage, made any suggestion to anyone that we are together or having sex."

"Is that why you were at the pool this morning? To tell me?"

"I came to help—"

"I don't need your help. I don't want you listening to me at the pool, invading my privacy. If Joseph sees you again, he will kick your ass onto the street."

"Who's Joseph?"

"Stop talking to me!"

Like I said, it's hard to run with a cello, but I get pretty close to it. Oliver gives up jogging in front of me. I keep walking and leave him behind. I feel ridiculous: a huge, stumbling turtle.

"Kate goes wild," some girl yells on my way past, but I don't see who. I keep moving until I get to the music room, where I place my cello into a music locker and fight the urge to stuff myself in with it.

I think through the full version of my morning and everything has a humiliating tint to it. Oliver listening as I try to write music at the pool, giving me the CD out of pity because I'm a mute geek and I'm trying to be something else, which he thinks is impossible. Because the only time I could possibly be loud is when I have sex?!

This is not true. One, I haven't had sex. Two, I don't think I'd be loud. But if I was loud, whose business would it be but mine and possibly the person I was being loud with?

No one's.

♦

In wellness, the talk before Dr. Malik arrives is about the PSST post and who's doing it and if people agree with the ratings. Lola's thinking aloud in a bored voice that it's a good thing. "I mean, at least someone's noticing the boarders."

Jinx puts her hand on my shoulder as she passes and says, "If I was having sex, I'd be loud as hell," and Angela says she wishes she was, "But what's there to yell about?"

Whether people are being nice to me or not, it just makes me angrier. They've messed with the wrong tech-head. Because now it's on my list to find the losers and expose them. *Find the fuckers,* I scribble in my journal, feeling guilty because I should have scribbled that the first time anything was posted.

"Prepare to be well," Clem says, as Dr. Malik walks in.

He hands out a survey that's designed to help us measure our self-esteem. I don't need a survey to measure mine. It's zero and plummeting.

I don't bother completing it.

I spend the class thinking about the Haskins quote. *What lies behind us and what lies before us are tiny matters compared to what lies within us.* What lies within me is rage at the moment. And humiliation. Everyone's looking for the cracks in people to expose them. What's the point?

I stare out the window, pondering that question until the bell rings.

On her way out, Ady walks past my desk. She drops her folded-up survey in front of me. I open it. Scrawled across the top is: *Don't let them inside your head.*

I fold it back up, so I can carry it with me all day.

Ady

Monday, August 1

What factors affect your self-esteem? Try getting attacked by PSST. Try being Kate Turner or the other girls on that list. Try pulling yourself out of the slime pit where some anonymous piece of shit is imagining you having sex and posting their pathetic opinions about it online. Try turning your back on that and polishing up your self-esteem and having a great day. Wellness class is a good idea, no doubt, but it floats above the surface of what's really happening.

So, the survey? Phenomenally irrelevant and useless, Malik. No. Just, no.

At times, I think I am no good at all. I certainly feel useless at times. I wish I could have more respect for myself. I feel that I have a number of good qualities . . . For each statement I tick all four responses: *Strongly Agree. Agree. Disagree. Strongly Disagree.*

Ten statements. Forty ticks. I feel about each one of the statements the way people's compasses acted when the Krakatoa volcano erupted. So much shit in the air that the compasses spun around in circles. When I say *shit*, I mean iron dust or something. But, whatever. Spinning. All options equally plausible. Okay, I realize I can do something useful with this survey, this piece of former forest: I write a note to Kate.

In class we are finishing off bunting for the Winter Fair while Malik talks about self-esteem. There's been a bit of talk about the PSST post, but my friends don't even seem to care about it that much. It's as though what happens online is ugly wallpaper that we can half-ignore. Lola actually thinks it's nice that someone's including the boarders for a change. I'm going to give them a big feminist motivational talk one of these days.

Malik tells us that doing something crafty with our hands means our brains will connect to everyone else's brains in a different way because we have a shared goal. We are being altruistic and purposeful. Imagine back through the centuries to when we had to come together to build shelter. And now he's like, when we help others (the school), we tend to feel good about ourselves. It's a pretty tenuous link between our slave labor on the bunting and the class topic of self-esteem, in my opinion. Anyway, he says it's also neuro-diverse, or neuro-responsive, or neuro-annoying. Words to that effect.

So we're cooperating on making bunting. I'm here in theory, but community arts isn't really my thing. I'm definitely more in the auteur camp. Or, if you prefer, I'm a control freak. My kinder teacher, Ms. Zink, told my parents I was *aggressively expressive* when it came to my art because I had a tantrum when she put her brush on my paper and "corrected" (i.e., ruined) a chicken I was painting. I felt that my parents were on my side. But Clare heard about it and, being a complete smart-ass six-year-old, she didn't hesitate to use it against me: *Mu-um, Adelaide is being aggressively expressive again.*

The school should look at its own self-esteem, anyway. Private schools never stop their competitive jostling, each one trying to outdo the others. Why do they expect us to find our quiet confidence when they clearly haven't found theirs? Malik said teenagers hate hypocrisy because we are emerging from the protective half-truths of childhood into the reality of adult life, and we don't want any more lies. Personally, I'd make an exception for Santa Claus and fairies, but I know what he means. He means our sharp eyes are fresh and hypercritical. It's true. He said it's one reason we're so harsh on our parents during these years.

So, swear to God, despite the stupid questionnaire, Malik is quite often 100 percent correct. It's like when my father used to be drunk, I didn't even really notice when I was little—what would I have been comparing him to? But anytime my friends have seen him like that in the last couple of years—even if it's in the middle of a fun-looking party—I'm embarrassed. I am hypercritical. I do judge him.

Clem nudges me, holding up a finished flag end to tie to my finished flag end.

"So, you're part of the loop relay at the pool opening?" I ask, making an effort since she is in my thumb-group.

"Yes." She looks uncomfortable. "It's not like I've got a choice."

"Didn't you hurt your wrist or something? Is it better now?"

"Yeah."

"Try to curb that wild enthusiasm."

"I'm excited. Who doesn't want to perform like a gibbering dolphin? I'm just out of practice."

"I don't know how you swimmers can stand those early mornings. I can't even pretend I'm human until around eight o'clock."

"And even then . . ." Tash chimes in, giving Clem a dismissive look and leading me away.

"We need to talk about Friday night," she says. "I mean, what the hell, Ady?"

Her net-ball training at lunchtime gives me a reprieve until after school.

Kate

Monday, August 1

I lie on my bed, headphones on, music loud. Songs to ease the pain—"Never Be Like You" (Flume), "Step Up the Morphine" (DMA's), "The Less I Know the Better" (Tame Impala), song after song of Chet Faker.

I keep looking at myself in a small mirror I borrowed from Iris. Every time I look I see myself a little less the way I saw myself yesterday and that makes me angry because, who are they to tell me who I am? Last time I checked, I didn't have a friend called fridgeman and I don't ever plan to.

While Iris is out of the room, I call Ben. "Search PSST," I tell him.

He puts me on speaker and I listen to the familiar roll of his chair, the sturdy wheels on hardwood, his predictable complaining about slow internet; it's the sound of a good, old friendship. I imagine myself into the room with him, sitting in the blue wicker chair in the corner, my feet up on the windowsill, staring at the lemon tree out the window, the green and yellow ripeness.

I hear the small inhalation of breath when he finds the site and reads the comments. Then the wheels of his chair move as he pushes himself away from the desk and stands. "I would like to hit something, but I have nothing to hit."

"Times the feeling by a million," I say.

I wait for him to say something that will make me feel better. If anyone can find the words, Ben can because he's known me forever. The words aren't out there, but I hope for them anyway.

There's so much quiet on the other end, and I'm about to let him off the hook, when he says my name. Just my name. Spoken in his sensible voice, his gentle way, it reminds me who I am.

After we hang up, there is a new comment.

BenTran: Kate Turner is the greatest person I know.

I focus on Ben's comment and not the loser who asks if Ben is "doin' me."

What lies behind us and what lies before us are tiny matters compared to what lies within us.

What are some practical ways to improve my self-esteem? I start making a list.

At the top of it: *Find the fuckers who run PSST and shut them down.*

Ady

Monday, August 1

I have an annoyingly confusing final period of math. I do dummy math and still it's hard. My pals do brainy math. Although, let's be frank, Lola can only keep up with help from a private tutor. I cannot wait to graduate from dummy to zero math next year. It's simply not the way my brain is wired. I'm chill-blasted during the five-minute walk between school and Muse, our near-school café. When I see Lola and Tash and Bec sitting there in a cloud of self-righteousness masquerading as concern, I'm tempted to brave the cold again.

Kate is sitting at a corner table where Max has just arrived and is unscarfing and settling down next to her. I give them a wave. Max is not wearing a school uniform—my dream—because she goes to MCA, Melbourne College of the Arts, a specialized high school where students get to exercise a bit of freedom instead of being slowly asphyxiated by a thousand and one rules.

I drop my coat, scarf, and gloves, and order a hot chocolate.

Tash is the lead inquisitor. "I hope you caught up with Rupert. He was so *sad* on Friday night."

"Yeah, he came over yesterday." I don't mention that I asked my mother to come upstairs and make a little mother speech about leaving my bedroom door open. "I think he's recovered."

"Where *were* you?"

"I told you—it was just spur of the moment. Anyway, I don't even know Sam that well."

"But that's a reason to go, to get to know your boyfriend's friends."

"It looked weird that you weren't there," says Lola.

"Like you two were fighting or something," says Bec with a worried frown.

"We weren't. I know it. And Rupert knows it. And you guys know it."

"And you were really with *her*?" Tash asks, glancing over at Kate and Max.

"Yes." I eat a half-melty pink marshmallow from my spoon. "Her. Kate. She's . . ." I think of all the nice and unusual things Kate seems to be, and how you certainly couldn't sum her up in just one word.

"Weird," Tash finishes for me.

"Look, it morphed from our Malik thing. We had coffee and then we went back to my place—"

Tash nearly chokes on her coffee. "You invited her to your place?"

"Sure."

They all give me the side-eye of disbelief. I know. I don't really believe it myself. If you'd told me a week ago I'd be hanging out with Kate, I would have laughed. "So, how was the party?"

Significant looks.

"I think I might like Sam," says Lola.

"You love him," Bec tells her.

"Great," I say. Great, the heat's off me. "So, let's all do something together over the weekend. I'll ask Rupe."

I look over to where Kate and Max are sitting. Max is offering Kate an earbud to listen to something.

"Hey." Tash waves her hand in front of my face. "Do you want to go over and sit with your friend?"

I need to smooth the feathers a little more.

"I am sitting with my friend," I say, putting on my best happy face, giving her a hug, and tuning in to whether Lola should ask Sam to the formal or wait for Sam to ask her.

Clem's Wellness Journal

Monday, August 1

I'm lying in bed, waiting for Jinx to come back. She's been in the shower for ages. Way too long—the water must be freezing by now. When we saw the PSST post, she tried to laugh it off at first. "Everyone knows it's bullshit." I mean, we all say it, but, I don't know, the bad feeling just seems to hang around. I wish I knew what to say to make her feel better. She says she's just creeped out. "How do they even know my name?"

The girls whose names were listed looked a little fragile today. When I went to Iris's earlier, I wanted to say something to Kate, but Iris was being all protective.

"School boys suck," I said. "Fucking Basildon."

"You don't know it's them," Iris said.

And of course I don't. But it's someone. Or some few. Makes a case for older men, I say. Stu would never be so disrespectful. Stu likes girls.

A thought: Should I be wondering why MY name wasn't on the list? Not that I want to be on it but, at the same time, am I so forgettable? Probably. I tried to do that stupid self-esteem scale. I scored 28 out of a possible 40. Jinx says that's all bullshit, too.

Okay. She's definitely been too long. I'm going to go and find her.

Kate

Wednesday, August 3

I stop thinking about myself and focus on practical things. Other people are being wrecked by PSST, and I can help them. Step 1: Look for clues. Idiots always leave clues.

There's a photo of me on the page, a shot from my old school in the country. I'm in science class, wearing protective goggles and a white lab coat, frowning slightly in front of a Bunsen burner and holding a test tube. I'm in study mode, looking studious, which is why my old school asked if they could use the photograph. I'm the poster-girl for the well-behaved. So no clues there; anyone could have pulled my photo off my old school's website.

I scroll back through old posts. It's not just about people from our school or Basildon. There are comments about girls from other private schools. There are comments about guys, too, but only the ones who don't fit the mold. I make a list of all the private schools that are linked to the posts, and all the ones in the area, but it's way too many to make the problem solvable.

It could be anyone, is the depressing fact. I think it's a guy, but all that does is narrow what it is an impossibly large field. Ben has a theory that anonymity sets the id free. Looking at the posts and the comments, it's pretty clear he's on to something.

I can't hack it, and even if I could find out how, the source code for a site like this is basically untouchable. The simplest option would be to get the admin password. But getting that would mean I'd have to know the administrator, which I don't, and, besides, it wouldn't do me any good without their computer. If I had the computer, I could write a plug-in, and mess with the site that way.

I don't have time to keep going now because I have orchestra practice this afternoon. As the Winter Fair gets closer, we've been having extra practices, in addition to the one on Friday. This is annoying because I'm trying to avoid Oliver. I know he didn't say anything about me. I know he wouldn't. But every time I see him I think about how stupid I must sound at the pool. It's like the PSST post has colored everything about me. I'm fighting against it, but I'm not having a whole lot of success.

At practice, Iris is edgy because we have our tutoring session with Gregory on Wednesday afternoons and she doesn't want us to be late. One, he doesn't add on time at the end, and two, if he thinks we're not turning up, he leaves. Iris told him we'd be late, but Gregory suffers from selective memory when there's something else he has to do.

"Everyone has somewhere else to be," Oliver tells her, suggesting that she stop complaining because it only makes things worse. If I were talking to him, I'd agree.

"Are you still ignoring me?" he asks before we start.

"No."

"Have you listened to the CD?"

"Too busy being mute while having screaming sex."

"That has nothing to do with me," Oliver says.

You bet it doesn't, I'm about to say, but this isn't Oliver's fault.

"I know," I tell him, and put all my focus on the music and Mrs. Davies.

After orchestra, Iris has to get a book, so she rushes out and says she'll meet me in the library. I think Oliver's gone, too, but he's standing at the door of the auditorium.

I walk off. He walks off, too. I'm being an idiot, so I slow down and let him catch up to me.

"You need to play the CD."

"I really haven't had time," I say, and he writes his cell number on a piece of paper. The numbers are neat and square—like Oliver, I think—and then I remember him on the stage and now the numbers look neat and square and slightly edgy. "You can't win alone," he tells me.

"Thank you very much," I say, but I take the number.

He's got that look of fierce concentration that makes him strangely attractive, but I don't have long to contemplate it because Iris texts: *What's taking so long? Ready to start.*

I sit in tutoring, trying to concentrate on Gregory's voice, looking at the physics on the page, but hearing Oliver's voice and thinking about the CD. "Kate," Gregory says, and taps his pencil on the table. "The scholarship exam is hard. You might not know as much as you think."

I force myself back to the page and work through the problem he's pointing at. I've missed a piece of it, and my answer's wrong. I know it as soon as I'm done and I go back to correct it. If he hadn't made me look at it again, I'd have made a dumb mistake and lost points.

"He's right," I say to Iris on the way back to the dorms. The light is gone. I'd love this light if I were on the farm because I'd be inside with a fire. I'm hit with homesickness and I remind myself that I'll be home for the long weekend in three weeks.

"We'll study together," Iris says. "Get you caught up."

I'm grateful for her kindness.

Later, when Iris is asleep, I take the CD out of the drawer. I stare at it for a while, and think back to Oliver's fierce look. You can't win alone seems to suggest that I might win, if I'm not too stubborn to ask for help.

Mum told me once in a deep and meaningful discussion, that she worried about me sometimes. *Everything comes easily to you. You've never had to struggle.* "That's a good thing," I said. And she agreed, to a point. I don't remember what she said after that. All I remember is falling asleep and waking to a pink sky.

I haven't listened to the CD because I know who's on it: Juliette, the girl from Orion. Oliver's message will be clear: *Unless you play like her, you don't have a chance. Be like her*, he's saying. But I can't do that. I don't have the experience.

I put the music on, bracing myself for jealousy. Instead, I feel wonder. I listen to the most amazing music—wonky and rolling. A strange road, built out of notes.

It's Oliver. I've played next to him for long enough to know that. A playing style is as distinctive as a voice. Oliver is stubborn and authentic.

The other player sounds familiar but it's not Juliette.

I take out his number. *Who's the other player?* I text.

Finally, he texts back. *The other player is you.*

Sender: susanbeazley@sthildas.edu.au

To: clementinebanks@acaciahouse.com.au

Date: Wednesday, August 3

Dear Clem,

A note to let you know how happy I am that you've "dipped your toe" and resumed morning training. Next season is going to be massive! Just a reminder: There will be photographers at the Marlins' loop event next Sunday, and I'd love to see the relay team in their spiffy new uniforms.

Keep up the good work!

Kind regards,

COACH BEAZLEY (BEAZ ☺)

Ady's Wellness Journal

Thursday, August 4

Okay, confidence in one's own worth?

What am I worth?

My self-esteem is a seesaw.

My outside is confident, but my inside . . . ?

What lies within me is uncertainty. There are things I hadn't properly pieced together until recently.

All those fragments were "okay," because they're versions of my father, of the way he's always been. Stupid me. Wrong. Dumb.

I've half-known, but not understood it properly. But little-girl beliefs have to go the way of baby teeth.

All my parents' friends act like this. It's camouflaged him. My mother says people are "very silly" or "very naughty," when they're actually hammered.

I asked Clare why we never speak honestly about my father. No one says the words "drug addict" or "alcoholic," so when I say them, I doubt myself. I feel like a liar. A troublemaker. Clare said, Take a look around—it doesn't match the décor.

If everything looks all right, then it is all right. All right?

I don't want to be protected from the truth. I need to pop the delusion bubble and grow some fangs.

Here is a fun fact: You don't have to be dirty and furtive-looking with a scabby face to be a drug addict. You can wear designer clothes, throw great parties, and even have a "happy" family.

But your children will either run away, or grow up with no self-esteem because they've spent so much time not knowing what is true, and pretending that things are okay, and not sure exactly what the fuck is expected of them.

It would make a big difference to me if everyone would just use their words.

Strongly fucking agree.

Clem's Wellness Journal

Friday, August 5

What do you see as your greatest talent?

If swimming was my greatest talent, it's not anymore. I've trained all this week—in the old bathing suit; the new one is a disaster—and everyone's acting nice, but we all know I'm way behind.

I couldn't face it today. I pretended to sleep while Jinx crashed around getting ready. When I thought she'd gone and I opened my eyes, she was standing by my bed.

"Clem," she said. "There's this scorpion and he wants to cross the river so he asks a frog for help and the frog goes, 'But if I help you, you'll sting me.' The scorpion says, 'Promise I won't, cross my heart.' Frog goes, 'Oh, okay.' They set out and they're not even halfway across when the frog feels the sting in his back. And as they start to sink, the frog goes, 'Why?' And the scorpion says, 'It's in my nature.'"

She looked at me, waiting for me to get it.

"Okay," I said. "Am I supposed to be the frog or the scorpion?"

"You're both."

"Huh?"

"Shit." Jinx thought for a sec. "I think I said it wrong. Never mind. What I'm trying to say is, It's gonna get better. Swimming's in your nature."

Now I'm just sitting here, writing this, and feeling . . . I don't know—like I've been faking it for so long that I can't remember what real is. I'm dreading the fair. And I can't think as far as Canberra. At the crafternoon, when Iris said, "Swimming's your thing," I wanted to scream, IT IS NOT! I know it doesn't make sense. But just because you're good at something, does that mean you have to do it? I mean, I have other talents:

I have a talent for upsetting Iris.

I have a talent for sleeping in.

I have a talent for eating.

I have a talent for kissing Stu.

I'm not sure you would call these transferable skills.

WEEK 5

CHOICES

Wellness

Monday, August 8
Dr. Peter Malik

Week 5: The Road Not Taken

Provocation

Two roads diverged in a wood, and I—

I took the one less traveled by,

And that has made all the difference.

—Robert Frost, "The Road Not Taken"

Points for Discussion/Reflection

Are you a follower or a leader? Which is it better to be? Which is it harder to be?

- Do you believe in fate? Are our lives written for us, or are we able to write them?
- Discuss a time when you have taken a chance. What was the outcome?
- Make a list of things you would like to do, but don't have the courage to try.
- To what extent do you try to take the path "less traveled by"?

Task 1

Create a piece of prose, poetry, or artwork in response to the language and/or themes of the poem.

Task 2

Make a journal note to organize a second social outing with this same group in a month.

Kate

Monday, August 8

The other player is you. I am the other player. Oliver and I sound good together. We (maybe) sound good enough to win the scholarships. At least we sound good enough to try.

I spent the weekend pretending to study, but researching Iceland and the Harpa Academy and calling Oliver to see if he could send me a sound file of himself so I could play around with some mixing.

He didn't return my calls, so I walk into orchestra this morning wondering if maybe the CD was just a sympathy thing after all. Maybe he wanted me to feel better about how I played after being so humiliated on PSST.

"You called?" he asks, as I sit next to him.

"Did I?"

"Fifty-two times, in fact."

Fuck it, I'm clearly past the point of lying. "I'm obsessed with the audition."

"So am I," he says immediately. "I was at my aunt's wedding in Avoca. I spent the whole night on a dark hill trying to get reception."

I like how Oliver's not into pretending. He is what he is: completely and absolutely obsessed with music. He takes out a slip of paper that he says is a rehearsal timetable, but I don't get to read it because Mrs. Davies starts the practice.

It feels like Oliver and I are playing together this morning. Alone, among the other cellists. He plays the double stops and I can feel him nodding next to me as I play them, too.

"We could win," he says, businesslike, while we pack up. I open the schedule and read the amount of times he wants to practice: Monday, Wednesday, Thursday, and Friday; Saturday and Sunday when possible.

"I rent a studio on Wednesday," he explains. "On the other nights we can practice at my place. I have a sort of studio in my backyard."

"I can't do all these times," I say. "They won't let me out every night, for starters. I also have to get top grades on the St. Hilda's scholarship exam, so Wednesday is definitely out."

"Then we won't be ready," he says. "And there's no point. So make a choice."

I have made a choice. "All I'm saying is you need to ease up on the schedule a little."

"Wednesday is a deal breaker."

"It's a deal breaker for me, too, so maybe we could compromise."

"Compromise doesn't get us to Iceland," he says.

I know it doesn't get us there, but all I can offer is compromise.

I fold the schedule. "I need to ask my parents." If I don't ask them, then I'll have to lie to get passes for all the times he wants to meet.

"I can wait until Sunday for the answer," he says, and I know it's a definite deadline.

Dr. Malik reads us Robert Frost's poem "The Road Not Taken" in wellness this morning. Mum's read the poem to me before, and we studied it in English last year, but today it means more.

I feel the yellow wood, the grassy road that wants wear. I feel the pull toward things I want. I feel the pull toward Oliver and Iceland, toward that strange new road I heard on the CD. I wonder how we get to where we want to go, if where we want to go keeps changing?

Dr. Malik tells us our exercise this week is to think about the roads we choose. The other task is to create a work of art in response to the poem, and I know, as soon as he said it that I have been doing exactly this since I heard Frances Carter. I have been sitting in that pool, composing new roads. The old ones are perfectly fine. But they're not the ones I want.

I want to take the other road.

But I need permission to take it.

Mum sounds tired when she answers. Or maybe I'm reading things into her voice.

I've had several conversations with her in my head, trying to work out how to tell her that I want to ditch my scholarship tutoring sessions to play experimental cello with a boy she's never met to apply for a scholarship to spend the summer in Iceland at an academy that I've never told her about. And, by the way, could I borrow the money for the recording studio so I can offer to pay Oliver half?

Now that I'm on the phone with her, I can't read the speech I've written out. I stall, and ask her how she and Dad are doing.

"Same, same," she says, and she sounds more than tired. She sounds defeated.

"Tell me," I say. "Maybe I can help?"

"All we need is for you to keep studying and get the scholarship. You don't need to worry about us."

"What if I don't get it? What if I can't?" I ask. "After all the money you've spent on me?"

"You will," she says. "And then all the money will be worth it."

Ady

Monday, August 8

Malik's task this week asks us to look mindfully at our decisions. *Mindfully*. Ha-ha. How else are we going to be looking? Elbowfully? Ribcagefully? Sort of has to be the mind, Malik.

God. The roads I should be not taking.

Top of the list, I guess, is Rupert.

Beauuuutiful Rupe. Bec and Tash and Lola and I were so excited when he asked me out. I'm going to say it: We are the *perfect couple*. On paper, anyway. Short honeymoon.

The kissing weeks were fun. The gazing into his lovely face and knowing it was mine. The turning heads. The awwwwwws. The envying looks. The rightness of it all. I thought I might be falling. I waited, impatient, confident: Fall, Ady, *fall*.

To be honest, I was curious, the first few hand jobs I gave Rupert. The mechanics of it all. The penis is whack—strange and interesting. But the first time he put his hand up between my thighs I grabbed his wrist. Not to guide, but to stop. Instinct.

Why? And the look on his face? Pure relief. He wasn't going to have to navigate the girl-scape. Not such a reach for him to believe that getting him off was our shared goal. It's not that it does nothing for me. It's a pretty intense few minutes. If Rupert did put his fingers in the right place, he wouldn't find me unaffected by all that hot needing and coming.

What stopped me? Was *I* the only person who was ever going to flick my switch? Maybe I'm autosexual—is that even a thing? Hey, I actually haven't heard of it. I might have created a whole new sexuality. Google . . . Jeez, is there nothing on this planet that someone hasn't already invented? If only I were living a century ago, I'd be appreciated as a totally original thinker.

It's been a regular once-a-week thing for a while now. Party, his room, my room. Lots of spilly handfuls. Fun facts that surprised me: Semen emerges at a very warm temperature and at high velocity; it can really travel; cleanups in unexpected places are sometimes necessary. But I'm detached, on the outside of what's happening. Tissues at the ready.

Then, out of nowhere, he suggested that it was time for a blow job. That was it, right there—a road that I would not be taking. Nuh-uh. No way was I going to drink the stuff. How would he like it if I had really bad hay fever and I blew my nose and offered him the tissue—to eat? Who decided that ingesting guys' metabolic waste would be a thing?

So, "metabolic waste"—not the language of love, am I right? Surely love would nibble and sip and lap and suck with relish. Wouldn't it? Love would not speak of "metabolic" or "waste."

I know breaking up is the right thing to do. But even though I'm quite prepared to break up with Rupert, I am extremely reluctant to break up with my dream formal night, which includes Rupert. So, can I stretch things out for another month? Or should I set him free now? I can't just use him as a glamorous formal night accessory, can I? Would that be a dirty little secret road that I could choose? Well, sure. Could I live with that decision? Not so sure.

Does it have to do with how uncertain things are at home? Don't want to let anyone see how quivery I am inside, so I'm constructing a barrier to make myself impervious and impenetrable? Perhaps I've already formed an exoskeleton because of all the secrets I contain, all the versions over the years of pretending to the outside world that everything's okay at home when I'm not sure it is.

There'll be a line when he's out there and single again. Everyone loves Rupe. What's not to love? What's wrong with me?

My heart has stayed so slow and cool and empty for him, and it's my heart I want filled.

I knit and stitch love into the clothes I dream and make.

I made Kate's wild messy bun and poked those flowers into it with love.

I'm weak-kneed in love with beauty every single day.

I was jealous of Clem's rush to meet that boy. To see her usually scrubbed-clean sporty-girl face made up all wrong and shining eager. That's some sort of love, for sure.

Clem

Tuesday, August 9

Mum-and-Dad Skype is just Mum this week. But excruciating—she wants me to model the new bathing suit. "Seriously? How old do you think I am?"

Iris fails to hide her smirk. I feel like kicking her; if I was wearing something tougher than my Peruvian slippers maybe I would. She starts blathering about the Winter Fair.

"I wish we could see it," Mum says.

"It's dumb," I tell her. "All we're doing is swimming in a loop."

"Muuuuum," I recognize Iris's wheedling voice, and push my chair back a bit to give her the screen. She's after money so she can get her hair styled before the formal. I let out a groan of disgust. Iris glares at me.

I look across at Kate's pinboard above her desk. She has some interesting items on it: a picture of a man at a piano on an ice floe; a list of band names, hastily scrawled. There's also a photo of her and a boy—it must be from her old school in the country, because they're standing in front of a tractor. He's cute. I wonder if he's her boyfriend. I swing back around to Iris, and Mum on the screen. Unbelievably, Iris is talking about Theo. "He said I had 'good form,' and then he said, 'A bit of advice—if you don't mind: I've noticed you stay on the sides a bit too much.' And then he said, 'In chess and in life.'"

"Goodness," Mum says politely.

I mime sticking my finger down my throat and Iris's eyes turn to slits.

When I get back to my room, Jinx is writing in her wellness journal. She sucks on the end of her pen and says, "Hey, Clem, are you a follower or a leader? Do you take the path less traveled?"

I lie down on my bed. "I'm not a follower or a leader."

Jinx makes a wrong buzzer sound.

"And I don't feel like I'm on any path."

Jinx points her pen at me. "You're on the path to Canberra! To victory!"

"Maybe," I say. Then I turn to face the wall.

"Do you believe in fate?" Jinx asks, not getting the hint.

I think about Stu, the accident, the flowers.

"Maybe," I say again. I don't feel like doing the wellness work this week. It hurts when you have to be so conscious.

Ady's Wellness Journal

Tuesday, August 9

One night. Seeing my father vomit after my parents have had a dinner party because he's so drunk. My mother propping him up in the downstairs bathroom, saying, "Jesus, Hugo, you just have to stop opening bottles. How hard is that?" And him saying, "Not hard if you're a killjoy." And her saying, "Well, your killjoy is trying to make sure you don't pass out and choke on your own vomit, okay?" And then the sound of more vomiting. It's bad when your friends get wasted and vomit, but when your father does it, it's beyond bad. It's disgusting.

Another night. Late. Peeking through my door, opened just a crack, seeing him stagger home, hit the wall, giggle, fall down, go to sleep on the floor. Checking in the middle of the night, seeing that a blanket has been put over him. Checking again first thing in the morning. He's in the kitchen making coffee and pancakes. Did it happen or was it a dream?

Another night. My father not making it home for Charlie's birthday dinner. My mother telling us he was stuck editing. Me knowing it was a lie because he had no work. Him, away for two nights and coming home looking like death.

So many sad nights.

Ady

Wednesday, August 10

With just a little more than a month until the formal, Bec and Tash and I find ourselves saddled with a dorm representative on the organizing committee: Iris Banks. We can't leave the precious boarders out. She's completely redundant; we've got it all covered.

Basildon and St. Hilda's have always had a combined Sophomore Formal. It saves people from actually having to get dates. Although many of us will have dates.

The Basildon reps are Theo Ledwidge, Bryce Katz, and Jonno Nesbit.

We're sitting around a table in a quiet study room in our library at the end of the day, schoolbags strewn around the floor. It's our third organizing committee meeting; Iris's first.

"Hoxton can play at the formal," says Bryce.

"Wow, good get," says Tash.

Great get—Hoxton is mostly former Basildons; they've had a successful album release and done lots of touring in the last couple of years after they won a contest that led to a recording contract when they were seniors.

"I'm surprised they said yes—aren't they way too famous for a Sophomore Formal?" I ask.

Jonno is turning crimson, poor guy. "Hamish is my brother."

I can see it: Lead singer Ham Nesbit is a hotter, cooler, hairier, larger, older version of shy Jonno.

"His mum told them they had to do it," says Bryce.

"Well, send thanks to your mum from us," I say.

"They don't mind," says Jonno, crimson deepening further. Fascinating.

"So that's our work done—what are you girls bringing to the table?" asks Theo.

I like this dude a little less each time we meet. I know he's some kind of chess whiz, and he's kind of good-looking, but his manner is Mr. Patronizing. Iris has not stopped staring at him since the boys arrived. He hardly seems to notice her.

"Tash has a food report," I say.

"So, yeah, we've got tables and chairs rented, and we've booked River Café Catering. The menu is roaming appetizers with drinks, two types of paella and salads, and we'll be having a gelati and patisserie table. Every course has vegan, dairy-free, gluten-free, and fructose-intolerant options."

"Sounds good," says Jonno.

"It's no-frills, but yes-delicious," says Bec.

"We're putting together a 'Moments' PowerPoint—Basildon

and St. Hilda's fun times, year to date. You can send me pics that we might not already have," says Tash. "Combined activities only."

"And I'm editing some footage to play behind the band," I say. "Unless they want to bring their own stuff?"

"No, they'll do an hour and a half, and then we'll Spotify."

"Let's make sure we've got an agreed list," says Tash. "Lola's party list is excellent."

"According to . . . ?" asks Theo.

"Every partygoing teenager in Melbourne, basically," says Tash, clearly implying that he's not in that group.

"Agreed," says Bryce, tapping a note to himself.

I make a mental note to ask Kate for music suggestions, too.

"Who's having the pre-party?" asks Theo.

Bec and Tash and I sit tight-lipped. There is no way he's getting asked to ours, which is at Tash's.

"So," I say. Theo gives me a cold look. Tough. "Let's have two laptops that night. I need lots of muscle for the film, and we'll use a different one for lighting, I guess . . ."

Iris pipes up. "One from each school?"

"Sure," I say. "We'll do a tech check that afternoon."

"Kate Turner and I are St. Hilda's tech support," says Iris.

"And I'm Basildon's," says Theo.

"Dance floor's getting laid the day of," says Bec.

"Main decorative element is lots of potted trees with white fairy lights," I say. We can get them at a super-cheap rate from Lainie's parents, who own a party rental company—Henry the Hirer.

“Okay, that’s it for now, then,” says Theo. “Unless you want some help with editing the footage, Ady?”

“No, thanks—I’ve got it covered.” I haven’t actually, and I need to get started, but I don’t want to spend hours in front of a computer rubbing shoulders with Theo Ledwidge. Seriously.

Kate's Wellness Journal

Friday, August 12

Dear Journal,

Ways to please my parents and still get what I want:

1. *~~Ask Iris to shift our tutoring session with Gregory to Sunday morning.~~ (Didn't even bother to ask. She plays chess every other Sunday.)*
2. *~~Ask Iris to shift to any other day but Wednesday.~~ (Just asked her. She said I could ask Gregory to have a separate session with me, but I can't afford it, so scrap that idea.)*
3. *Ask Iris for the notes and skip the tutoring session with Gregory entirely (a possibility).*
4. *Lie to my parents and do what I want, but study every spare second I have so they never know I lied and I can still pass the exam.*
5. *Beg Oliver to give me a break.*

Kate

Sunday, August 14

I've spent most of this week trying to work out how to get what I want without breaking any rules. How do I keep everyone happy? The old Kate keeps chiming in, informing me that music is a dream. How will I feel if I fail the exam and have to go back to Shallow Bay next year?

I will feel like shit. Thank you, old Kate.

I wake up on the morning of the Winter Fair, convinced that I just have to explain the problem fully to Oliver. If I do that, he'll be reasonable. He'll tell me that, together, we can work something out. For now, choosing one road closes off the other, Robert Frost. So why can't I stay at the crossroads for a while and hedge my bets? This seems like the obvious, sensible solution.

I recite all this to myself as I head across to the auditorium. I told Iris I felt like being alone this morning and left early. I haven't been speaking much to her this week. She's been accusing me of being in a bad mood, and, even though I denied it, I have been.

At her, at the old Kate, at Oliver, at my parents, at everything that is making what should be a good thing difficult.

Oliver is out in front of the auditorium when I arrive. Here early, like me. I explain to him all the reasons I need him to bend a little on the times we practice. I go through all the lists I've been making, all the reasons I can't ditch the exam, how I want to do it all and how I can't see why I shouldn't be able to.

He listens without interrupting. I can't tell from his face if he's going to say yes, but I don't think he's going to immediately say no. People from the orchestra start arriving as I finish my speech.

I wait for Oliver to answer, keeping my nerves in check by counting the number of tents set up on the oval. I get to 30.

"When can you practice?" he asks eventually.

"Friday nights I can get a pass, no problem. Mondays are hard because it's after the weekend and they don't like us going out, but I could maybe do Tuesday. Not Wednesday. Saturday morning is okay, but Sunday I have to study."

"So, Friday night, maybe Tuesday and Saturday morning."

"Two nights and a morning," I say.

He looks at his cello, then nods at some people going inside. "It just seems like you're not serious. And I know it seems like I'm being harsh, but we won't be ready if you can't commit. Do you know how competitive this thing is? The other people auditioning have been working for years."

He waits for me to change my mind. I wait for him to do the same thing.

When we can't wait any longer I pick up my cello. *Please compromise*, I think. *Please, please, please.*

But he doesn't.

And I can't.

"Then I guess you have to ask Juliette to partner with you," I say.

And he agrees.

Clem

Sunday, August 14

I wish this dressing room was a TARDIS. If it was, I would go forward to tomorrow so this day could be over.

Jinx thumps on the door, "Clem! Come on!"

There's nothing I can do. I have to go be a Marlin, loop the loop, in public. My bathing suit is bifurcating me. I cover myself up with my tracksuit and my bomber jacket, and reluctantly open the door. Jinx does a little dance. I feel numb all over.

When we get to the pool, the crowd is already filing in and filling the seats. There must be a thousand people and all the glass and concrete is hurting my head; it's a prism. I want to die.

Beaz's face never shows surprise. She nods at me when I come out of the stall, red-faced in my pinchy suit. I see a few looks from the rest of the girls. No one says anything, though.

"Clem, you're in the third stream. After Jinx."

I nod, but I'm feeling sick. Outside, announcements are happening. There's applause, and then silence, then we file out. It's horrible standing out there in front of all those eyes. I remember to breathe, try to grasp some sense of calm. But there are photographers, and smirks, row upon row of ancient, death-masked alums. Special guest singer Deity Haydn-Bell dances in, swinging her hair extensions. She starts to warble; the acoustics are sonic-spectacular and my sick feeling intensifies. At the end of her song, Deity cuts the ribbon and it flutters into the pool. Principal Gaffney gushes, the press take photos. The first Marlin dives and then the next and the next and soon it will be my turn.

On the block there's a roaring in my head. I pinch my arm, but my skin feels like rubber. The water's so very blue. The trail of bubbles from Jinx is fast disappearing. A voice hisses, "Clem, GO!" But I can't seem to move. I've broken the loop and it's obvious. I look up. Faces blur. Everything blurs. I feel a shove on my back. I suck air and smack water. I swim, but not in the direction anyone's expecting. I cross two lanes to get to the ladder and climb up and out. And then I run. I am cold, but I am on fire. I bolt the length of the pool, past the crowd, who are all staring at me and not the elegant athletic display that I've just wrecked. I run outside to the quadrangle, smack into the nonchoreographed heart of the seventh graders' silent disco. Fifty kids, wearing headphones and spandex, shaking like maniacs, inadvertently blocking me. I stop and sink onto the asphalt. Mini disco divas circle me, dancing and staring with serious faces.

Firm hands pull me to my feet. Kate and Ady half-guide, half-shove me out of the disco mob toward the old building. The reception area is empty. We pad down the hall with its ancient plaques and photographs, into the Oak Parlor, the wellness room, but there isn't a beanbag in sight. It's set up with refreshments—

cakes, pastries, fruit, and cheese. Ady closes the door and it's like the outside world has evaporated. For a few seconds, all we do is look at each other. The muffled quiet of the room makes it feel like a compression chamber.

Then Kate plucks a lemon tart off the table and polishes it off in one mouthful. Ady finds a plate and starts cruising the table, making selections. She presents it to me.

"You've had a shock. You need sugar."

The tart is sublime, and so is the brownie. The almond croissant is perfectly flaky. I don't feel numb anymore. I don't even feel cold. The sugar rush is making me giggle. I pull off my swim cap and slingshot it across the carpet. We start laughing—we laugh for ages. It's not that funny, and yet . . . it's something. Something unexpected.

When we're stuffed full, Ady sits at one end of the window seat and I sit at the other. Kate takes the piano stool, tinkles the keys.

Ady looks around. "It feels wrong without the beanbags."

"Do you think Malik was at the pool?" I can't bear to think of him seeing me like that.

"What happened, Clem?" Ady asks.

"I don't know. I just . . . I couldn't stand it. Everyone watching." I stare down at my bathing suit. "This stupid suit."

Ady looks around. She picks up the piano cover and drapes it across my shoulders like a cape. I hold it out to read the school motto: *Orta recens quam pura nites.*

"Newly risen, how brightly you shine." Kate translates.

"So, so bright," I say. "I fucked up."

"Do you care?"

I think about it. "No." I feel strangely light at this admission.

"I really don't. I'm sick of this place. I'm sick of all of it. I'd happily go back to my last school. Any school."

Kate says, "There are good things about St. Hilda's."

"Like what?"

"More opportunity. At my last school, most of the students had dropped out by sophomore year, so they could help on the farm or do some apprenticeship. No one goes anywhere."

"Wake up and smell the privilege!" It's one of Jinx's sayings.

"My mum went here," Ady says. "Her mum, too. They both married Basildon boys."

I look at Ady, think about her photo-perfect Basildon boyfriend.

"Are you going to keep the tradition?"

Ady doesn't answer. She pops some brownie in her mouth.

And then I hear myself say, "What's it like?"

The question hangs in the air.

Ady's face shifts. "What makes you think I know?"

I shrug.

"Don't believe everything you read," Ady says softly.

I feel chastened, but also disappointed. I'm desperate for tips, advice, strategy. I used to get all my information from Iris, but I'm not going there with this. The other night I googled "first time sex" and saw some things I can't un-see.

"Fucking PSST," Ady says.

"I hate that site." Kate thumps the ominous lower keys, playing monster music.

"Hey," I say. "You think we can count this as our second social outing, for Malik?"

Ady groans loudly and I laugh like a seal. Kate's monster

music morphs into ragtime. I guess we go a bit delirious. In all our scoffing and scrambling, we don't notice the door opening until it's too late. Principal Gaffney and Deity Haydn-Bell enter laughing, but their laughter turns to shocked silence. Gaffa serves us her steeliest stare.

"Girls!" Her voice sounds demonic. "WHAT is going on?"

Kate, Ady, and I freeze. We have violated the green room and decimated the dainties. I'm wearing a piano cover and dripping water on the carpet. I glance at Ady. Her lips are pressed tight together and her shoulders tremble with impending laughter. It's because Kate's still eating the brie. We are deeply fucked.

Ady

Sunday, August 14

If we'd analyzed what we did in advance, each one of us would have known we were heading for a Saturday detention. But it was one of those glorious moments when three people make an unspoken pact: Let's just do it.

So now I'm waiting for the official talk from my parents.

I didn't actually see Clem's failure to launch; I walked into the buzz and confusion that followed it when I left the equipment room, where I'd been to meet Rupert.

I slipped into the equipment room—a room filled with squad kickboards, and lane floaty things, and water polo stuff, and containers of chlorine—while all eyes were on the brand-new turquoise investment.

I knew Rupert would be expecting that we'd mess around a bit, and I had firmly decided to delay the breakup until after the formal. (Don't judge me.) When he came in, looking gorgeous, I knew I'd made the right decision.

He kissed me and, before my brain could intervene, breakup words started coming out of my mouth. It was like a wellness class override coming into effect.

"I'm sorry, Rupe, I think we've got to break up." I put my hand gently on his cheek. Not one pimple. He's like a god. You could cast him as the younger brother of Sam Heughan and people would totally believe it.

He looked at me with a wary smile. "Are you joking?"

"I'm really sorry."

"Why?"

I was as surprised as he was to hear it come out of my mouth: "I'm not in love." It's not like we'd ever even mentioned *love*.

"Me, neither. But that's not a problem, is it?"

"Well, yeah—I mean, maybe."

"Is there someone else?"

Such an annoying response.

He obviously misinterpreted the pause. "Who is it?"

"There's no one else. And I'm kind of hurt that you'd think that."

"Well, I'm kind of hurt that I'm getting dumped for no reason."

"No offense, but 'not in love' is not 'no reason.'"

He was silent. He looked sulky, broody, like a model for an edgy fashion label.

"I am sorry. I mean it. Wait a few minutes before you come out, okay?"

"Okay."

I planted one last kiss on his manly cheek. He flinched. Unnecessary dramatics, Rupe.

Anyway, that's how come I left the pool hot on the bare heels of Clem, and how I found myself soon after eating a delicious and entirely unexpected morning tea.

My parents are not impressed.

I'm knitting my new project, a stripy cardigan that will have rainbow wings or petals erupting from the shoulders, budding, opening up further down toward the elbow. I am knitting because I'm impatient to make something the minute I think of it, and because I know it will annoy my parents that I'm not concentrating fully on their message to me about what a disappointment I am.

"Do not smirk, Adelaide," my mother says. It wasn't a smirk; it was a little ding of recognition about why I was finding myself interested in Kate and Clem. I don't know what either of them will do next. I could write the script for Bec or Lola or Tash. But these two—nuh-uh, never at all what I expect.

"I'm not."

"What you did was childish and so disrespectful. You ruined a carefully planned afternoon tea. You're lucky it's just a Saturday detention."

"Yeah, I feel so fricken lucky."

My mother goes into her annoyed lip compression mode. "You could have been suspended."

"Like you were," I say, looking at my father. How can they be so self-righteous? It's a family joke that he was suspended from Basildon, for smoking, when he was 16.

"We're talking about you, not your father."

"No, we never talk about him, do we?"

"Could we lose the attitude, please?" my mother says.

"I know that we're in trouble. I can hear you fighting. I don't know why you even care about this. It'd be better if I got expelled. Then you wouldn't have to pay my school fees."

My parents exchange a long look.

"Ady, we do want to talk to you . . ." my father starts.

"But not now." The way she looks at him! She's clearly the source of my death-stare powers. Exactly what are they not telling me?

My father's look concedes my mother's right to call the shots. He leaves the arena with a parting platitude: "School's a game, Ady; you've just got to play along."

"You two think you're so cool, but you're such losers." I count some stitches.

My mother yanks the knitting out of my hands and slams it down on the table.

"Could you stop deflecting attention from yourself and try for one minute to take this seriously?"

"I know. If only I was perfect, like Clare."

I can tell my mother is using all her self-control not to bite back. "I'm not going to keep talking to you while you're being such a smart-ass. But do think about it. What you did was—"

"'Childish and disrespectful.' I get it."

"You have so many opportunities, Ady—don't be the person who takes that for granted."

She walks out of the room, leaving me alone with my dropped stitches.

Happy families.

I wonder how much trouble Kate and Clem are in.

To say that Clem took the road less traveled today would be the understatement of the century. That Kate and I followed her is another unexpected result of the world according to Malik.

Kate

Sunday, August 14

"I can't believe you ate the brie," Mum says.

I can't believe the brie is what she's fixated on.

"She said you ate the brie *after* she specifically told you to put it down. She said you ate the strawberry, too. You don't even like strawberries."

"Why, Katie?" Dad asks.

"I was hungry," I say.

I can't explain to them how good it felt to be with Ady and Clem in the Oak Parlor, to be letting things spill, to hear them spilling. It felt so good to hear Clem talk about the water and how she was willing to give it away, to listen to Ady's certainty, to eat the brie and not care.

On my way out of the room, I didn't feel ashamed or worried. I felt reckless. I felt good. I felt desperate to call Oliver and tell him that I'm not giving up the audition.

"Something's wrong," Mum says, taking the phone back from Dad. "I can hear it in your voice. Something's going on."

I almost tell them.

But they're about to go to bed early so they're up in time for backbreaking work.

"Were you led by someone?" Dad asks.

"She's not a follower," Mum says.

I think back over the day and aim for the truth. "I was inspired."

"Well," Mum says, "I hope detention on the weekend is equally inspiring. I hope you're also inspired by the fact that you're not getting any more passes out of school until after your detention."

"I really need the passes," I say.

"Why? You've got all the cheese you need right there in that school. We're paying a heap of money for you to be there, Katie. We're paying it because you said it's what you want."

"It is," I say.

"Then act like it." She hands the phone back to Dad.

"It was just a slight malfunction of character," I tell him.

He says he knows it was. "It happens to us all." But he doesn't say I can have my pass privileges back.

I hang up and Iris is looking at me with her I-told-you-so eyes. We've been fighting since I walked into the room and she launched at me because everyone had heard what we did, and she couldn't believe I'd be so stupid as to get involved with Clem.

"I didn't get involved with her—I was helping," I said.

"And look where it got you. That goes on your record. Your permanent record. It affects your chance of a scholarship."

"Principal Gaffney said it wouldn't."

"You really think she gives you a free ride after that? You need to stay away from Clem, work hard, and not get into any more trouble."

Iris looks genuinely upset for me. Which is why I don't tell her what I'm about to do next. I take my toiletry bag. I say I'll be back in a minute.

I walk down the hallway calmly, but make a turn before I get to the bathroom, toward the basement. I take a second, not even that, to consider what I'm about to do. The road not taken, I think, and head into the darkness, past old costumes and suitcases and broken desks and chairs, feeling my way to the portal. It only takes one strong push.

And I'm free.

"Hello?" Oliver answers his phone.

"Hello," I say, stomping my feet partly because it's cold, and partly because I'm nervous, and mostly because I'm incredibly scared that I'll get caught.

"Kate?"

"Oliver?"

"Now that we've established our identities," he says, "why are you calling?"

"I escaped," I tell him, still slightly out of breath. "Through the portal."

"The what?"

"The portal in the basement." I give him far too much information about how to get in and out of it. I'm just babbling now, so I get to the point. "Don't ask Juliette. I want to start.

Tonight. Only, I don't have my cello." I look down at my feet. "I don't even have shoes. I'm in socks."

There's a pause. I wait anxiously, hoping it's not too late. "You don't go through a portal in socks," he says. "Don't you know anything? Stay put. I'm coming."

He doesn't take long. He doesn't live far from the school, as it turns out. "Just around the corner," he says, looking at me and then at my feet. He says we can't walk anywhere if I don't have shoes, so we sit at the tram stop.

"I'll have to lie," I tell him, "which I don't mind. Only now that I think about it, escaping with a cello will be difficult."

"You can use my dad's. He won't mind."

The sky, the lights, the night are all telling me I made the right decision. I get the strangest thought sitting here. As though inside is a landscape and I am at the very best part of me now. I've run right to the end, to the cliffs of myself.

"I have to tell you something," Oliver says. "I spoke to Max tonight, told her about what happened at orchestra, about how I wouldn't budge so I lost the chance of working with you. She said I had to tell you, and I think I need to tell you, too."

I turn a little more toward him and wait.

"It has to do with what you call me," he says. "The anally retentive fuckwit."

"I'd forgotten I called you that."

"Alas, it's not so easy for me to forget."

"Sorry."

"No, it's okay. I am sometimes, about music, and when I'm nervous. And both things are happening when I'm around you. You make me nervous."

"Because I'm so good?" I joke.

"Partly," he says seriously, but doesn't elaborate on the point. "I brought some music I thought you'd like." He hands me an earbud so I can listen. He puts the other in his ear. I've never heard the artist before.

"It's like Zoë Keating, but not."

"Julia Kent," he says. "This is 'Gardermoen.'"

"The album?"

"Song. The album is *Delay*."

A tram pulls up, but we don't get on. I wonder what we look like, to the people in there, staring out. Two people, joined at the ears by music.

"How will you get home?" he asks.

"I haven't thought that far."

The stars sharpen up.

The world becomes more.

Ady's Wellness Journal

Sunday, August 14

Clare just told me that "The Road Not Taken" is one of the most misinterpreted poems around. So it's possible I've been thinking about it all wrong. Whatever. She also told me that our father is heading for rehab one of these days in the not-too-distant future if our mother's plans hatch, so my parents will be dis-united again before long. De-united? Un-united? Disintegrated? Checking my "emotional temperature" . . . I feel completely miserable about that. I wonder how much my father's addiction is because he is a father, with all the bills and staying in one place, etc. that involves. In my listening-in over the years, I've put together a picture. My mother and father met in law school. He dropped out and went to film school. He made ads, but always wanted to make a feature film, too. She had Clare and me and only did bits and pieces of volunteer work. He became super successful directing ads and never quite got to the film. He directed some music videos. One night when they had friends over and someone asked him whatever happened about his plans to direct a film, he said, "Oh well, the music clips are like short films," and my mother said, "They're really more like long ads, when you think about it." It sounded mean. When we were little, he used to go over to LA for various meetings and Clare told me we'd probably be moving to Hollywood, but nothing ever came of it, and then they had Charlie. So maybe it's our fault. Maybe he's so frustrated that he never got to do what he really wanted and he became an addict. The end.

Now it's late and I've worried myself into unsleepy-land.

WEEK 6

THE IDEA OF PERFECTION

Wellness

Monday, August 15
Dr. Peter Malik

Week 6: The Idea of Perfection

Provocation

Song: Lou Reed, "Perfect Day"

Points for Discussion/Reflection

- What's your idea of a perfect day?
- Is there such a thing as perfection? Is perfection even possible?
- What influences your idea of perfection? (Peers? Art? Media? Family?)
- Perfection is a myth promoted by the media.
- What are your flaws? How do you live with them?
- Perfection is boring. Flaws are what make people interesting. Beauty is subjective.

Task

In your journal, reflect on what your perfect day would be. Write an itinerary. Who would you be with? What would you be doing?

PSST

FAT CLAM'S WALK OF SHAME

Patrons of the St. Hilda's Winter Fair were terrorized by an unidentifiable fleshy mass. It came out of the water and remains at large. Heh heh.

diddywah: Some like 'em lardy.
K-bomb: That's the most DISGUSTING thing I've ever seen. My EYES!!!
Ericsonic: Krispy Kreme.
Wylderworld: How about you Bizjiz? Up for jabba-action?
Bizjiz: Ha! My dick'd get lost in there.
StHildasSuffragette: Bizjiz—your dick's so teeny-weeny you wouldn't be able to find it in the first place. K-bomb—you're the disgusting one. The fuck is wrong with you guys?
Ericsonic: Anyone harpooned that??? rate and review fresh meat for Rate the Boarders

load 96 more comments

Kate

Monday, August 15

Iris follows me to the bathroom this morning, still going on about how stupid I was to sneak out last night, something only topped in stupidity by Clem, Ady, and me eating the food in the Oak Parlor.

"Did you think you wouldn't get caught?" she asks again, putting her toiletry bag on the shelf in front of the mirror and taking out her toothbrush. She's asked me the same question at least 50 times, so I no longer feel like it requires an answer.

"You've changed," she says.

She says this like it's a bad thing, but people need to change. What if I stayed the same person all my life? I brush my teeth for a good long while, giving myself time to think about that, while Iris launches into a speech about how this is the kind of thing that happens when people hang out with Clem.

"Did you see the photos?" she asks, sawing floss between her teeth.

She takes out her phone and shows me as I spit. It's another post on PSST, and as soon as I look, I wish I hadn't. It's Clem, a shot of her at the fair, running beside the pool.

"What do they get out of posting that?"

"She's fat now," Iris says matter-of-factly. "It's the truth, and I can say it because I'm her twin. No one else better say it, though."

"She looks better in a bathing suit than I do." I look away. I've seen enough to know there are no clues there as to who posted it, and I don't want to size up Clem as fat or thin. She looks hunted, and I hate thinking about her like that.

I head out of the bathroom and walk to Clem's room. She doesn't answer my knock, so I go to breakfast, but she's not in the dining room. I text Ady while I'm eating my toast. She texts me back immediately: *Already on it. A.*

Iris takes a seat next to me with her usual breakfast—orange juice and cornflakes. Will she be eating that for the rest of her life? "There's more," she says, but this time she doesn't seem happy about it. Her twin protection instinct is finally kicking in.

I don't want to look at what the "more" is. I don't want Clem to think for a second that I was part of it, but Iris pushes the phone in front of me and I see a flash of too much skin. You can only see a small curve of her breast, a thin moon of flesh. If she were going out, wearing a dress, it wouldn't matter. It's seeing it in combination with her lost face that makes me feel like we're looking at something private.

"Should I do something?" Iris asks.

"Ady's got it under control," I say, getting up and walking out quickly so I can't be followed.

I knock on Clem's door again, but she still doesn't open it. I see Jinx in the hallway and she tells me Clem's "sick" in air quotes.

I decide to skip orchestra so I can talk to Ady. Making music is the last thing on my mind today. Clem is the first. The second is how to mess with PSST when the opportunity arises.

"She does this," Iris says before I go. "She gets people into trouble."

"She didn't *get* me into trouble. She isn't leading me astray."

Or if she is, I like it.

I don't know Ady well, but I'm starting to know some things about her. One, if she says she's on it, then Clem will be okay. Two, she won't want me turning up at her front door without some notice, so I head to a café not far from her place and the school. *At the Organic Grocers*, I text: *Meet me?*

I'm drinking my second coffee before she texts back: *On way. Stay there.*

She takes off her coat and hangs it on the rack at the front when she arrives, then looks around to find me. When I first saw Ady at school, her hair with the kind of shine I envy, surrounded by similar-looking girls, I immediately slotted her into the kind of popular crowd I'd never connect with.

"Coffee before speaking," she says, putting up her hand.

We sit in a warm square of sun that's coming in the café window until she's had her second coffee, and then she starts talking. "I'm working on something to lessen the pain." She slaps honey on her toast and licks the drips from her thumb. I don't push her on what it is. If Ady says she's got it under control, then she has.

I fill her in on what happened with Oliver and she smiles.

"It's strictly work," I say.

"It can't be both?"

"It can be, but it's not. Anyway, he's probably got a girlfriend."

"Probably doesn't mean definitely," she says. "The formal is coming up. If I were you, I'd find out if he is single and then multitask." She stands. "I'll take care of Clem. You go forth. Make music."

I use the portal again tonight, so I can meet Oliver. He lives two streets away from the school, toward the river, and I walk there. It's dark, but there are people out. I'm not afraid. The nerves are all anticipation.

His house isn't what I expect. It's small, a single-story Victorian, with a terrace and an overgrown garden. I see a brief glimpse of a narrow hallway and low ceilings when he opens the door. A vase of lilies on an old sideboard. A worn carpet runner. A dog trying to nose its way out the front door.

"Good fella," Oliver says, pushing him gently inside, then leading me along the side of the house. There's only room for single file. I follow behind him, careful not to trip on cracked concrete.

In the backyard, tucked behind a shirt-filled clothesline, there's a brick shed. He opens the door. "This is my studio and my bedroom," he says, and I walk into a room not much bigger than mine at school.

The walls are covered with egg cartons and then soundproofing foam; even though it's a myth that it completely blocks sound, it muffles it a little. The brick keeps it watertight. There's a heater and a tiny makeshift kitchen—kettle, microwave, tea, coffee, and a mini-fridge. There's an electric piano, an assortment of wind instruments, and Oliver's cello next to what I guess must be his dad's. Oliver's computer equipment is set up on a desk in the corner. His bed has a gray cover and blue sheets, neatly made. There's a black-and-white cat sleeping on his pillow; her name is Bach, he tells me.

"I miss cats," I say, scratching her ears.

He doesn't answer, and I figure this is Oliver being nervous, so I try to get some conversation started. "When you said a studio, I assumed you meant, you know, not a shed."

"Let's play," he says, ignoring the comment.

And that's when everything really goes downhill.

The two people sitting next to each other at the bus stop, listening to music, disappear.

Oliver tells me he wants to start by playing the song that's on the CD and seeing if we can add to it. I've brought the piece of music I was playing on that day, and he's got the music he's playing on the CD, and we try over and over to reproduce the sound of us, but we're terrible. First I start too early, then he starts too early, then we both start too late and when we play it back and mix, it doesn't work.

We try for hours and get nowhere. "Maybe we just need to take a break. I have to go back now anyway," I tell him, and he accuses me of not taking things seriously enough.

"I'm taking it seriously enough to sneak out and risk expulsion," I say, packing away his dad's cello.

"I'll walk you back," he says.

"Don't bother."

But I can't shake him. He stays behind me all the way.

He texts me later that night and says that if I'm not serious I shouldn't bother turning up on Wednesday. *I don't want to waste my studio time.*

Fuck you, I text back.

I wish I hadn't, but I'm glad I did, and then I can't sleep for thinking about how to talk to Oliver. Surely we can talk if we play together like we do on the CD? But we didn't play like that tonight. Maybe we're a one-off? I lie awake, listening to what he and I could be, that wonky road we're on, rolling around me in the dark.

The music makes me feel better after a while, and that gives me an idea about Clem, who's still not answering her door. Around 3:00 a.m. I give up trying to sleep and decide to do something useful with my insomnia. I make her a playlist.

1. "Angel Down"—Lady Gaga
2. "The Skies Will Break"—Corinne Bailey Rae
3. "Dream Girl"—Jack River
4. "Feeling Good"—Nina Simone
5. "Respect"—Aretha Franklin
6. "There's Always Someone Cooler Than You"—Ben Folds
7. "Perfect Day"—Lou Reed

Kate's Wellness Journal

Monday, August 15

Dear Journal,

I've put some music under Clem's door to make her feel better, and now I'm in the sophomore bathroom—typing this because I still can't sleep. I'm playing the Lou Reed song that we read about in wellness class—"Perfect Day"—and I'm thinking about how none of us is perfect, and how sometimes you can really fuck things up trying to be (e.g., Oliver and me tonight). What you need are people around who think you're okay: people who don't care about the size of your body, or whether you wax, or if you play right the first time. You have to forget that you're not perfect, because no one is.

So what would be my perfect day? Not a perfect day. Just a day when I was with people who wanted to be with me.

I send Oliver a text with "Perfect Day" attached. I tell him I want to sample the song for the audition.

One of my favorites, *he texts back.*

I think maybe we were trying too hard to be good, *I text.*

I think I was being an anally retentive fuckwit, *he texts.*

I think I was being one, too.

No, you weren't, *he texts.* You were being your usual self.

Is that good?

You mean, is your usual self good? Yes. My usual self is good, too, by the way. I'm not my usual self this year.

Because?

Because my mum decided not to come back this time from her tour. She left Dad, but it feels like she left me. Max thinks that I've become ever more obsessed with perfection since then. Like I'm trying to get her attention with the Iceland audition.

Are you?

I don't know. Is this too much information?

No. I'm just taking a while to reply because I'm trying to find the right words.

They don't exist. But I'll take some wrong ones.

I would miss you, if I went on a tour. I would miss you and I would come back.

Thank you, Kate, *he texts.* In future, let's not aim for perfection in life.

Is that what I do? *I ask.* Is that how I seem?

You work harder than anyone I know.

I need to work hard to save my parents. *(I didn't know I was going to text that last bit. That just came out.)*

Aren't they old enough to save themselves?

Probably.

Do you want to go to Orion with me this Friday night?

Yes!

I'm making a record of this conversation here—a record of the first time I really spoke to Oliver.

Ady

Monday, August 15

I see all the photos of Clem on PSST. Images don't die; they don't even fade anymore. The best you can hope is that different shocking images supersede the images that are making you want to die or fade away.

Malik starts the class in classic Malik style: "Doesn't the notion of perfection depend, for its very existence, upon the idea of imperfection?"

Someone, I'm pretty sure it was Lainie, does an audible fart.

Malik politely ignores it, but it takes a couple of minutes for everyone to settle down. Lainie's other trick is to burp the word pardon. It's a dilemma for teachers.

"Dr. Malik, all our wellness sheets have quotes from men," I say.

He looks shocked, even though he must have put them together. "We'll have to rectify that."

And then he goes straight into showing us some slides to demonstrate how much Photoshopping goes into images that are published in fashion magazines, so I'm glad Clem isn't here. It would be a bit close to the bone.

"It's up to you to reject these dated ideas, girls."

"Not so dated," says Jinx.

"They are if we make them so," Malik counters.

"How long did it take you to put your outfit together and put on your makeup and do your hair, compared to the women teachers?"

Malik does his serious smile. "Point well made."

"Anyway, Dr. Malik, it's not just magazines that criticize us," says Lola. "It's online commentary." She's giving a troublemaking smile to Tash, whose look dares Lola to continue.

Malik registers the exchange. "Is there any particular online content that you're thinking of?" he asks.

I imagine Lola showing the Clem pics to Malik for a laugh, and know that Clem would be horrified.

"All of it," I say. "Pornography, for example—it gives everyone a false idea of what genitals are supposed to look like." A few titters and snorts burble out. There—I've successfully derailed Lola, who mouths *spoilsport* to me.

Malik is now treading carefully through the minefield of our genitals, making general comments about the lack of respect shown to women across a range of media platforms, and getting the hell out of porn land and back to the safe shores of us contemplating what a perfect imperfect day might look like.

Reframing imperfection as individuality, being less self-critical, being our best selves, practicing self-love. It's not that simple. *If only* we just worried that we're not pretty enough, or thin enough, or that we've got pimples. For us, the message that you fail to attain someone's idea of perfection is a wash that colors EVERYTHING. It is the air we breathe. Sure, we're getting better at calling it out, but that doesn't make it go away.

It's not just stupid fashion magazines—it's every dude checking you out and ranking you with a look on the street, every PSST post, every ass-grab. It's everyday sexism. It's the fricken patriarchy.

It's also something internalized and regurgitated by women. Again, insights courtesy of Clare, but when she told me I totally got it.

"Did you see your new Malik bud on PSST last night?" Tash asks in our mid-class stretch-and-breathe break.

"Maybe her perfect day could include a fucking bikini wax," Lola says, apparently disgusted that such a thing as pubic hair still exists. "Nobody should have to look at hairy tufts sprouting from a bathing suit."

"Nobody said you have to look." Even as I say it, I know it's ridiculous. We all look at PSST.

"She is carrying a lot of extra weight," says Bec.

"It's not like that's a crime," I say.

The three of them look at me in disbelief: Of course it's a crime.

The difference between their reaction and Kate's. And mine. That's some huge distance.

There's no doubt that Clem looks out of condition for such a star athlete, and whoever posted has done some really mean close-ups, but it's her face that gets me. She looks so lost—no, worse: scared. The panic in her eyes, I recognize that.

I'd just never let it show.

And the comments. *Fat slut* times 100 variations. I feel a surge of pure hatred for the evil idiots—from Basildon, I assume—who keep this site fueled.

I head over to the dorms after last period. The door is answered by a junior boarder who takes me up to Clem's room.

"Go away," Clem says, muffled, as I knock and walk in.

She emerges from her duvet, cried-out eyes, propping herself up on one elbow. "What do you want?"

"I came to see how you're doing."

We're both half-nervous to be in Clem's bedroom like this, based only on some Malik maneuvering that involved thumb lengths and ended up with us accidentally getting into trouble together. I push some clothes off a chair and sit cross-legged in it. Clem sneezes, blows her nose, and chucks the tissue in the general direction of a tissue-filled garbage can.

I open my folder and drop the worksheet from today's wellness class on her. "Malik's latest. It's a meditation on the idea of perfection. Spoiler: There's no such thing. Tell him all about what a humanly imperfect 'perfect' day would look like to you."

"It would involve no one posting horror pics of my fat bits." Clem flicks the sheet onto the floor without looking at it. "Who is it doing this PSST stuff? Is it your friends?" She sits up properly, shuffling and punching her pillows into place.

"Doubt it. We're some of the favorite targets. Could be anyone, from any grade, who took the photos. The quad was packed."

"What are people saying?" She pulls her pajama top up by the collar to hide the bottom half of her face. She wants to know, and doesn't want to know.

"A more polite version of what the comments said."

"I'm fat. I should kill myself, apparently."

"Ooh. Which reminds me . . ." I'd almost forgotten why I'd bothered to schlep into dorm land.

In my parents' study there are boxes and boxes full of postcards, bought in handfuls from every museum and gallery they've ever gone to anywhere in the world. I figured they wouldn't miss a few.

I rummage in my backpack for the cards, get up, and let the ones I've chosen rain down on her. Clem picks them up, looking at each one in turn. A series of beautiful women, all shapes and sizes, painted by Raphael, Renoir, Modigliani, Matisse, Bonnard, Manet . . .

"Jaysus, she's got an owl between her legs," says Clem, picking up a postcard of a marble figure by Michelangelo. She turns it over and reads: "*Allegorical figure of Night, tomb of Giuliano de' Medici*. Weird breasts." She looks at me. "What is this? Another Malik idea? Visit a fatty?"

"I'm sick of all the little anonymous judges waiting around to pile on the criticism about nothing. I'll bet none of them has a trophy. Besides, what is fat? Maybe you're not super-fit-you at the moment, but so what? And who gets to say what the right size is?"

"Easy for you—you are the right size."

"Well, that's a boring idea. And who cares? I like all sizes. I like the dance companies that let people be big or little or round or square or whatever, not the boring, identical, starved same-samies who look like robots with skin. And that's who I want to wear my clothes. Everybody. Every. Body."

"*Your* clothes?"

Oops. "The stuff I make. If I ever get to do it as a job someday."

Clem picks up the cards and puts them together in a pile. "Thanks for coming. This was a nice thing to do."

She still looks a bit suspicious. But only a little bit. She opens the drawer of her bedside table and gets out two mini Kit Kats, chucking one to me.

"Are you coming back to class tomorrow?"

"I guess. I mean, if I don't then it's all like, *Oh it's such a big deal, she's so torn up about it.* And I kind of am, but I don't want anyone thinking that."

"Good call." I unwind myself and check my phone. Ten messages from Lola and five from Tash. Three from my mother. Zero from Rupert.

As I walk home, the rain holds off, despite broody mauve clouds. I don't want to call Tash back. She's been asking lately when my parents are going to have their next party. Since eighth grade, we've all floated around at those parties sneaking drinks and good food, and watching the grown-ups misbehaving. Maybe she smells blood.

I've also been refusing all shopping invitations to hunt for formal dresses, seeing as I've been told not to spend any money on clothes and to find something at home or make something for the formal. Even when Tash is peak-happy she just wants to bitch about every single person we hate and every single person we like, and gleefully unpack and pick over all the latest PSST crap. My bestie loves nothing more than finding someone's weak spot and poking at it until something breaks.

When I get home, there's a car in our driveway. I freeze, watching unseen from the other side of the garden as my father gets in the back seat and the car backs out. My mother puts a hand up in farewell. She turns and heads back toward the house. I've never seen her look so exhausted. Things are getting less perfect by the minute.

Clem

Monday, August 15

It's 9:00 p.m. I've been deep into duvet-land. It's the only place for me. In addition to being Fat Clam, I have a shitty head cold and the world can go fuck itself. I have to meet with Gaffney and Beaz tomorrow. I don't know what to tell them. I've got "issues." I'm self-sabotaging. I didn't want to swim the stupid loop, so I didn't. I am no longer a team player. Why? Why is the sky blue? Why do birds sing? The thing is that by the end of Sunday—cold aside—I was almost feeling okay about things. Not swimming, cutting out, it felt like a statement. Then Jinx came in and told me about the photos. She said I shouldn't look at them—but how could I not? FAT CLAM'S WALK OF SHAME. The photos were bad, but the comments were brutal—people calling me Orca, saying I was so fat I should kill myself, so ugly I should be raped (WTF?).

Iris turned up after dinner with a mug of soup and a roll. She just sat on my bed and stared at the carpet

"Stop looking like that."

"Like what?"

"Like you feel sorry for me."

"But I do feel sorry for you."

"Well, I don't want you to."

"What happened with Gaffney?"

"Nothing yet."

"What about swimming?"

"I don't want to talk about it."

"But I want to help you."

"Why?"

"What do you mean, why?"

"Why do you want to help me? Newsflash, Iris: We don't get along."

"I know, but—"

"I think you're happy," I said.

"Why would I be happy?"

"Because you like to see me taken down."

"I left a comment defending you."

I dunked my roll in the soup and ate it without tasting it. It was a nice thing for Iris to do, a small gesture, a warming thing, but I didn't feel grateful. I felt mean. She was looking at the photos around my mirror: the family snap from happier times; the one of me and Bronte Campbell, who won gold at Brazil; the one she defaced, Thing One and Thing Two.

"I'm sorry I did that," she said.

"I don't care. Nothing happened because of it. It's not like you can put Wite-Out on my face and I'm going to disappear or anything."

Jinx's bed was empty and Iris kept looking across at it. Then she said, "Are you going to stay with Jinx over the long weekend? I'm staying at Kate's."

"You don't have to organize me, Iris."

For a second she looked like she might cry. "What did I ever do to you?" I couldn't answer. I don't know what the answer is. Iris is like a pebble in my shoe, and I can't ever quite lose her. I walk a few steps and there she is, grinding again, making me feel stuff when I don't want to feel anything at all.

Today, when Ady visited, at first I was suspicious. I pictured her reporting back to Tash, telling tales of Fat Clam, marooned in her dorm room. But no—she'd brought me the wellness sheet—on the idea of perfection—and a gift: some art postcards, beautiful women, fatties all. I shuffled the cards in my hands and I could feel my eyes getting hot. I didn't want to cry in front of Ady—Ady of all people—but the tears leaked out. And Ady put her arm around me, like we were friends.

Jinx walked in. Ady left.

"What's that all about?" Jinx asked.

"Wellness homework."

Jinx nodded, but I don't think she bought it.

"Do you want to talk?"

I shook my head. Jinx smiled sadly and put her headphones on. She lay back on her bed.

I looked around our room, tried to see it through Ady's eyes. It was so jock: trophies, ribbons, posters of the greats, energy bar wrappers, and sweaty socks scattered all around. My eyes went to my mirror, the photos in the frame. I took Bronte Campbell down and put Ady's fat ladies up.

Clem's Wellness Journal

Monday, August 15

Is there such a thing as perfection? Is perfection even possible?

I'm not perfect and I will never be perfect.

When I was first getting really hard-core about swimming, I lived on protein shakes and read online forums for tips. If my time was off, I'd force myself to do extra practice. I was never good enough. But if it wasn't swimming, it would have been something else. We all do it. Every girl here. We're all trying so hard to be what we're not. Skinnier, prettier, smarter, better.

"Oh my god you look so skinny. Oh my god I feel so fat."

I'm not perfect and I will never be perfect.

My legs will never be long enough. My cheekbones will never be high enough. Stu says he's into me, but if he saw me naked in broad daylight, he'd probably puke in his hands. I imagine him seeing the PSST photos and I want to puke in my hands. Thank god he's outside school, outside all of the shit.

Ady

Tuesday, August 16

So, Clare was right about rehab. Of course. The morning after my father gets picked up, things are quiet and cold. My heart rolls a slow, sick somersault, remembering him slumped in the car and my mother's look of complete exhaustion. Still, no one's talking about it. We didn't have dinner together last night because our mother was at a meeting at school.

Charlie has already eaten and run. Bowl and plate in the kitchen sink. I'm wondering how Absent Dad will impact on Mr. Routine. He's mostly coped with conflict by not being here much. Helpful habit.

The buried hum of hot-water pipes signals mother shower, so I can eat breakfast without a side order of uncomfortable heart-to-heart, if I hurry. I want to talk to her and find out what's happened, but at the same time I can't stand the idea of talking to her and don't want to know what's happened.

Domestic trauma never dulls my appetite. Two eggs, fried.

Two slices of toast, buttered. A slurp of sriracha sauce. A handful of spinach leaves. Slap them together and yum. Thank you, genes, for the metabolism that lets me eat everything I want and never get sucked into the misery of limiting food, rationing food, cutting out whole delicious food groups, fearing food. Food is my friend.

Clare debrief before inevitable mother deep encounter might be an idea. She will be sipping her—at least—fourth cup of tea from her glass infuser teapot, positioned at exactly ten o'clock relative to her laptop. She will already have finished her disgusting own-recipe, Tuesday breakfast: extra-ancient grains, brain-food Bircher muesli with brain-cell-building nuts, served with a glass of fresh orange juice for vitamin C to keep away any disempowering illness. Clare says no to losing even one optimal study day. She carries a disposable surgical mask on public transport and does not hesitate to use it if there's any snot or coughing in her vicinity. Good practice, too, for getting used to the breathing restriction when she is eventually an actual surgeon in a surgical mask, if all goes according to plan A, which of course it will.

The distant muted thumping is her maniac 40-second flat-out spin on the exercise bike in her room. She does that a few times a day. It keeps her fit without eating into any significant study time. I'm really going to miss her next year. Not at all.

Living as she does in the super-fit study zone, alert, one ear cocked like a dog, Clare always knows more than I do. She instructs me with a downward glance to lower my sorry-to-interrupt-your-study chocolate frog onto the side table arranged at a 45-degree angle to her desk.

"You might have to be the one to find your next school, you realize that?" she says.

"My what?"

"St. Hilda's has refused to continue the fee repayment scheme our idiot parents entered into."

"The what?"

"They've been paying our fees in small, affordable installments for the last year, but they've missed the last couple of payments."

"They have?"

"School has waived my final year's fees, as a 'scholarship,' because I'm obviously going to ace the year, so it looks good for them."

"Our parents?"

"The *school*. Wise up, Ady. You're a different case." She softens for a nanosecond. "If they had scholarships for great art, you'd be fine."

It becomes clear. "Wow."

"She had a meeting with the school accountant and Gaffney last night."

"Do you think they'll get divorced? Who will we live with?"

"I'll be in Sydney. You and Charlie will be with Mum. Dad's got too many substance abuse problems to get custody—if they do go down the divorce road."

Fuck my life. "You don't seem fazed."

"Can't afford the time."

"How has this happened? What about all his awards?" A whole crowded shelf of them. He's like the king of advertising.

"It's not that he lacks talent." Clare shrugs. "Forty-four is pretty old for advertising. Newer, younger, better directors have come up behind him. It's the way of the world."

She jots that down, *the way of the world*. She must be going to use it in some killer essay. Can't wait for that one.

She sees me looking at her note. "Congreve," she says impatiently.

I have no idea what that is or means. "How do you know about our life, and I don't?"

"I asked Mum. You should try it some time."

"What's she going to do?"

Clare has a very expressive way of raising her eyebrows. "Well, she's rewatching *The Good Wife*."

"But she hasn't worked as a lawyer since . . ." When, actually?

"Yup." Clare has already spun back around to face her desk. "So: Find a new school. Sorry I can't help you out there. But I'm happy to check out your short list." She puts her earbud back in.

I only ever warrant one earbud out. I wonder what it would take for her to remove them both.

Clem

Tuesday, August 16

I dress carefully, hair combed, tights straight. I don't have to fake a contrite expression. Last night Jinx was trying to brainstorm excuses for me: "Say you had temporary insanity, you slipped in the change room and hit your head." But we both know it's hopeless. When I open my door, there's a package for me in the hallway. It's a CD with a note from Kate. She's written: Music helps. A CD? How old school is Kate? No time to listen to it now. I shove it in my bag and make my way to Gaffney's office for my big dressing down. The office lady lets me in. It's Gaffney and Beaz and they've brought Malik in as well.

Gaffa says, "Clementine. Sit, please."

I sit. The old pleather chair farts and I dare to smile, but only Malik smiles back. The fact that Beaz doesn't almost breaks my heart. Gaffa goes straight in. "Clementine, we need to talk about your attitude. Ms. Beazley tells me you've missed quite a bit of practice this term. And after Sunday's debacle I'm afraid you leave us no alternative but to act."

"Maggie Cho is replacing you on the relay team," Beaz says. "And you can't come to Canberra." She's looking at me like I'm supposed to say something, so I say, "Yes," and look down. Beaz is in her civvies and it just looks wrong—like an alien trying to join the human race. She's even wearing lipstick.

"You had a setback. No one expected you to jump straight back in. But, Clem, enough. I'm supposed to be your coach, not your babysitter. Something's going on with you. I think it would help if you told us what it is."

Malik has a turn. "Clem?"

I feel sick. The oatmeal I ate for breakfast sits high in my throat.

"We'll need to inform your parents," Gaffa adds.

Malik clears his throat. "Maura, if I may—perhaps Clem should have the opportunity to talk to her parents about this first." He looks at me. "Take a couple of days, if you need to."

"Yes," Gaffa says. "That will be satisfactory."

I can't face class. Jinx and Lainie will be at me, wanting to know what's gone down, so I go to the old pool. It's full of trash from the fair—with all that crap and the leaves you can hardly see the bottom. I lean on my tree and think about how disappointed Mum and Dad are going to be, and how they'll know I've been lying to them. At least we'll have a screen between us. I can turn the camera off; that way I won't be able to see their faces slide. I feel a bit lost—which is unexpected—I thought I didn't care about swimming anymore, but now that Canberra's not happening, I know it's really over. No more Swim Clem, at least, not like I was. Now the future is just like a white blur of skywriting that time has made unreadable.

Just as I'm wishing I had someone to commiserate with, my phone vibrates in my pocket. A photo from Stu. His face with a thought bubble drawn on. *Thinkin' of you.* I pause—he's sent me this photo before. Is it a bad sign that he's already recycling his photos? But he looks so cute, it's enough to carry me through the rest of the day.

Ady

Thursday, August 18

I haven't spoken to my mother alone since my father got picked up. Even though I feel sick every time I think of that scene in the driveway, I need more information.

She's packing some of his clothes into a suitcase.

"How long's he gone for?"

"It's a six-month program."

"He didn't even say goodbye."

"I'm sorry we haven't talked properly. I was trying to sort things out with your school, and trying to get your dad into this clinic."

"Yeah, so don't worry, Clare already told me I have to leave." I'm angry, even though I've done my share of avoiding her. My adrenaline doesn't seem to know whether it's flight or fight time.

"Sorry, Ady, the last few days have been a nightmare of forms and consent, and—you don't want to know . . ."

"No, it's fine. I get it. You protect Charlie and you talk to

Clare, but you don't give a shit about me. I can go to hell and get yanked out of my school and lose all my friends."

"You know that's not true, Ady. I am sorry about St. Hilda's, but, to be perfectly fair, you've done nothing but complain about it for the last couple of years."

"Everyone complains about school. It's still where all my friends are."

"I'm sorry it's happening like this."

"I feel so embarrassed." That sounds childish as it tumbles out of my mouth, and I wish I hadn't said it.

"Addiction is a sickness—it's no more embarrassing than . . . having cancer."

She wouldn't have done so much venting lately if she really believed that. She thought he should just get his shit together. She said it often enough. At least cancer is something people understand.

"Everyone's going to think we're such losers."

She smiles, which is infuriating. "Real friends won't think that. Your dad's going to get better. I'm going to get a job. And we're going to live within our means, for a change." Now she's sounding evangelistic. Come back, sole remaining parent.

"Why is he even like this? Why couldn't you help him?"

"Sometimes people need things to get . . . really bad . . . before they can even admit they have a problem."

"Will we be able to see him?"

"Not much for the first month or so, and then, yes, of course."

"I don't even want to see him."

"Well, that's up to you."

"Are you getting divorced?"

A pause. "Not at this stage."

"Is this what happened in seventh grade, when he had to go away to 'work in Sydney'?"

"Yes."

"Will he have his own room?"

She does the reassuring smile. "Yes."

She opens her arms and offers a hug. Crossing my arms, I turn to leave the room. I won't be able to hold my tears in if she starts hugging.

"We still need to go through your wardrobe. We'll get some Figgy's apple cake for energy and do it this weekend?'

"I've got detention, remember?" Obviously not.

She sighs as she zips the suitcase closed. "Okay. We'll do it another time. The hug's here when you're ready."

A suitcase should be on its way to somewhere good, greeting you at a funny angle on an airport carousel, not heading for rehab.

PSST

ADY ROSENTHAL LIKES IT UP THE ASS,
COURTESY OF RUCKMAN RUPERT
GO, BASILDON!
DON'T FORGET TO SHARE THAT SWEET ASS AROUND, RUPE

rateme: good take down for a StH stuckup bitch
h0RnyT0bi@s: Id tap that one just to teach her a lesson
noBs: chix like the ruffstuff true
Hilarian: Loving the advanced spelling skills of you PSST pea-brains. It meshes well with your understanding of the world and the size of your dicks, no doubt.
rateme: you want to be raped
Hilarian: No, rateme, I don't. And I'm sure you don't want to be raped either. But I hope you enjoyed typing all the bad words, you fool. Biggest thrill you'll ever get, I imagine.
rateme: yur prob 2 ugly to rape anyway, just die
noBs: u wouldnt waste a load on ugly sluts
sufferingsuffragette: It is a comfort to me knowing that you strange little fossils will never attract partners and reproduce

Clem

Thursday, August 18

At dinner everyone is buzzing. Iris sidles up.

"Did you hear?"

"What now?"

"Rupert gave a report on Ady—sexual proclivities and so forth. It's all over PSST. That means your photos have been bumped down."

"Great," I say, thinking that PSST, like life, rolls on inexorably. I'm about to do the same, but the mean glint in Iris's eyes stops me. She barely knows Ady. She's never even had a conversation with her. The way she says "sexual proclivities"—so prudish; so the opposite of what I'm sure the post actually says. I bet it calls Ady a slut. Because, according to PSST, all girls are. Sluts and bitches and skanks and hos.

"Why do you even care?" I ask Iris.

Her face shifts to sour. She doesn't have an answer.

"I don't want to hear about that shit," I say, "and you shouldn't be spreading it."

"I'm not spreading it. God, you make it sound like I'm personally responsible. Get a clue, Clem."

"I'll get a clue when you get a life."

Late in the night I listen to the CD with Kate's mix and scroll through my Stu gallery. Just when I'm thinking about turning in, my phone pings. A photo of Stu's ankle.

He texts: *Your turn.*

I take a photo of my knee. It looks like a lumpy face. I can't send Stu my knee.

I'm waiting.

I want to tell him I miss him. I want to tell him what my week has been like. The PSST photos, the canceled Canberra trip.

I text*: I want to see you.*

He texts: *I want to see you too.*

Followed by: *All of you.*

I look across at Jinx, dead to the world, her mouth quivering in snores. I take my PJs off and lie back and try out a few poses, shuffling my camisole off one shoulder, sinful skin-full, promise of curves. I take a full frontal, neck down, because cyber safety, then I sketchify it. Send.

Wow. You're so beautiful. Zaftig Clem.

I have to google zaftig. It means deliciously plump, ripe, juicy, sexy. Beats being called Orca. So weird how one pretty word can almost cancel out all the ugly ones.

Ady

Friday, August 19

When I wake up at 6:30 a.m., I read it again.

Could my life actually get any worse at this stage?

I am still numb.

I read it again again again again again . . . Heaps more comments have been added, are being added, as I read.

People are so happy to join in.

I like it up the ass?

It's not true.

What's true is I'm a virgin.

Not that being a virgin is a virtue. But it is a fact.

So the facts of my life get kicked away and I'm not a virgin anymore because someone posts lies?

I lose my virginity without getting to have actual sex?

Seriously?

I texted Rupert as soon as I read it last night.

He hasn't talked to anyone about what we did or didn't do together.

I believe him.

He doesn't know who writes this shit.

Says it's not fair that it's always the girl who gets the slurs.

I agree.

And I'm left alone to deal with it.

So—I have to say something at school.

What, though?

Eight forty-three. The usual homeroom buzz. I stand at the front of the room, staring down at the teacher's chair upholstery fabric—turquoise tweed—trying to calm the thudding pulse in my ears. Silence drops like a blanket over the class. Unheard of. I've got maybe one minute before Yelland arrives. Winging it, totally. Breathe.

"It's all true. Like it up the ass? That, my friends, is the understatement of the century. Rupert and I actually broke up, for anyone who's so out of the loop they haven't heard, but when we were together, we were basically never out of each other's bottoms."

I look around and see a variety of reactions: blanks, shock, and some amusement. Tash's eyes are round with disbelief.

Making a joke of it is the biggest "fuck you" I can come up with. I hope word gets back to them that I sent the whole thing up—that I couldn't care less. Which, of course, isn't true. I feel undressed, humiliated, disrespected, but I'm not about to show that in public. "And, hey—how come we're not reading that Rupert likes it up the ass, or Bryce is a slut, or that Nick's a frigid virgin? Why isn't it about me sharing some 'sweet Rupert ass' around? Because, misogyny, that's why."

"Preach," says Jinx, as Ms. Yelland walks in.

My perfect day? Easy: Rewind this week. One, my father is still here and magically doesn't have his addictions; and two, someone has destroyed PSST and caused great pain and public humiliation to its creators.

I'm going to art first period, but my usual favorite place at school is no longer an escape—I won't even be here for much longer.

Things are the opposite of perfect for the foreseeable.

5:00 p.m., text from Tash: *Call me, lady.*

5:03 p.m., text from Tash: *Like now*

8:35 p.m., text from Tash: *Why the hell did you say that today?*

8:38 p.m., text from Tash: *Adyyyyyyyyy wtf???*

10:00 p.m., text from Tash: *I mean it—call me!!! and we can figure out how to minimize damage*

11:53 p.m., text to Tash: *Sorry couldn't find phone tonight—many panics—in wrong bag ☹ We'll talk soon, promise, feeling a bit tired and a bit sad and a bit angry still, nighty noodles xxxxxxxx*

I haven't told Tash about Dad being in rehab.

I didn't talk to her about the PSST post.

She's still acting as though we're best friends, and we are. But are we really?

Ady's Wellness Journal

Saturday, August 20

Clare came into my room last night, late. Big news. My room. Zero earbuds in. She sat on my bed and said, So I heard what you did at school today. (Clare doesn't actually read PSST, for real. She thinks it's beneath her, and that thinking about it and getting angry about it is a waste of energy and brain space. It is. But that doesn't stop anyone else from reading it.)

And so I'm like, And?

She laughed, ruffled my hair up with both her hands, exactly how she knows I hate, and said, My brainwashing has not been in vain.

She left the room still smiling. Okay, patronizing, but also affectionate. I'll take it. I think she didn't disapprove, which = good response from the lofty one.

But Clare being nice just seemed to add fuel to my crying night. How does niceness unpick the stitches that keep you together?

Weird moment when I woke up—a conversation between my mother and father in my head. It was about a year ago. He was home from a long, long lunch with a record producer, very drunk. She was reminding him that they had people coming for dinner in an hour, including a creative director who was a possible source of work. She said, Get out of my sight and straighten the fuck up. I think she was telling him to take cocaine so he wouldn't seem so drunk.

Kate

Friday, August 19

I shove the portal door open and escape, heart beating quickly, nervous breaths exploding as I hit the air. I skirt around the parts of lawn that are exposed by emergency lighting. There's always a moment when I stop and take it in: the flood of grass rolling toward the gate, the line of darkness that runs along the edges, the strangeness of being the only person out here, awake, in a world that feels like it's sleeping.

Oliver is waiting at the gate, looking unsettled. It's how he's looked all week. In orchestra practice he's been concentrating so hard on playing he's been making mistakes, which is, as Mrs. Davies commented, very un-Oliver.

Our session on Wednesday at the studio felt like a waste. Every time we tried to play, we sounded wrong together. "You need to relax," I said, to which he gave the fair response that it's hard to relax after someone's told you to relax. "I don't know what it is," he said, as we walked down Lygon Street, basking in the smell of pizzas and garlic, our stomachs rumbling. "I can't seem to play."

"Maybe the audition's freaking you out?"

"I've performed all my life," he said.

"You look nervous," I say tonight.

"These are legitimate nerves. I don't want you getting caught."

"Does your dad know you're out with me?"

"Yes," he says, and we start walking to the tram stop. "He doesn't know I'm helping you escape. He thinks you're a Max. She has permission to go out at night as long as she has her phone and her parents know where she is at all times."

"I'm envious," I say, and he wonders aloud if I am.

"You think I like escaping through the portal?"

He puts his hand out for the tram instead of answering.

I don't dislike it. I don't want to get caught, but I like the rush. "I like taking control."

He nods.

Oliver is quiet.

I like Oliver's quiet.

It's not really quiet. It's a pause.

There are only two seats on the tram, facing each other. Things I've learned about him this week: He is as obsessed with the Iceland scholarship as I am. He isn't anally retentive, but precise when it comes to music. He concentrates. He wants to be as good as humanly possible. When he plays, he sees color beneath his closed lids. His mother gave him his first lessons, and eventually he got a teacher (David) who is the most serious man I have ever met. He was at Oliver's house when I arrived on Tuesday night. They'd just finished Oliver's lesson and David, at Oliver's request, showed me how to really play the double stops.

Oliver watched from the sidelines, grinning, as David informed me of the finer points of stops, gently adjusting my technique with his soft voice, eyes intent on my hands, taking in tone, movement.

"Good," he said after 30 minutes of playing, and I knew why Oliver strove so hard to hear that word from him. Oliver isn't anally retentive. Neither is David. They're serious about their craft.

I study Oliver's reflection tonight—his eyes look straight through himself to the world outside the window. He's off somewhere in his head—in a piece of music, thinking about his mum, maybe—I want to know where he is.

Without warning, his eyes shift, and stare at the eyes of my reflection. I stare back.

We are crossing lines. I don't know what they are exactly, though. Or where they lead.

The line for Orion is long, but we walk straight past it. "We're not going there," Oliver tells me, and before I can protest, he pulls out two tickets. I read the front of them. Frances Carter, Concert Hall. "I can't afford this ticket," I tell him.

"You don't have to."

"*You* can't afford this ticket," I say.

"I don't have to," he says.

Turns out it's Oliver's birthday and he asked his mother for tickets to Frances Carter. "For me?" I ask, and then immediately feel like an idiot. These tickets were bought months in advance. I guess his mum couldn't make it home.

I think about that in the dark, as Frances Carter plays. I think about a lot of things. That I am learning even still. That I thought there was nothing more to the world than St. Hilda's and then when I got here I thought there was nothing more to the world than Orion. The world keeps opening up more, note after note, unfurling. Sitting here tonight, the cello aching in my chest, surrounding me, I am filled with the thought that there's nothing more thrilling than all those things in your future, waiting to be known.

We can't go straight home after the concert. We're too full of cello.

"Coffee?" Oliver asks, and he leads the way to a small shop, hidden in an alley, with dimly lit small rooms that run off each other, an open fire, red checkered tablecloths that could be cheesy, but aren't.

"You think we'll get better in time for the audition?" I ask, while we wait for our order—coffee and Portuguese tarts.

"Can we maybe not talk about that tonight?" Oliver asks. "Let's talk about other things."

"Such as?"

"Such as anything. Such as your week, as it does not pertain to music."

"You have an odd way of speaking."

"I play better than I speak. Usually." He leans back to let the waiter put our tarts and coffee on the table.

"You look disappointed," he says.

"They're small."

"Try them."

"Okay," I tell him after I've taken a bite. "No longer disappointed."

"Your week?" he asks.

"It'll lower the tone of the conversation," I say, and when he indicates he doesn't mind, I tell him I've been thinking about PSST and who might be running it and how I might bring down the site.

"How's Ady?" he asks.

"Are Basildon guys talking about it?"

"Pretty much nothing else. First the post, and then Ady in class."

I don't want to talk about Ady, not even with Oliver. It feels disloyal. But I want to know if he has any thoughts on whether it's Basildon boys.

"Maybe," he says, picking up the last bits of pastry with the tip of his finger and eating them. "But it could be anyone. You can't stop it, so ignore it."

"Ignoring is not an option and I am stopping it."

"By?"

This is obviously the problem. "It's someone who knows Rupert and Ady, right?"

"A lot of people know Rupert and Ady. They're like the King and Queen of private schools in the area."

It's true. But I ask Oliver to keep his eyes and ears open at Basildon and to pass on anything he knows.

"What would you do?" he asks. "If you found out."

I tell him exactly what I would do, and his eyes glaze over halfway through. "Okay, I understood *nothing* of that. You would what with a what? How did you get to be this smart?"

He has a small piece of pastry on his chin. It looks lovely. I'm disappointed when he brushes it away. "Why did you lie to me about the Orion sticker on your cello case?" I ask, and he acts as though he's giving it quite a bit of thought.

"I don't know," he says in the end. "I wanted to tell you all about it, and then, in that moment, I decided not to. Max has a theory."

"Which is?"

"Ridiculous, so I'll keep it to myself."

I resist the urge to text Max right this second to ask her.

Kate's Wellness Journal

Friday, August 19

Dear Journal,

What would be my perfect day? Not a day. A night. This night. Looped over and over and over again.

Clem

Saturday, August 20

Detention goes like this:

Me, Kate, and Ady, laughing, swearing, delirious, armed with hot water and suds, and super-sized garbage bags. Our task is to clean up the old pool, but our rubber gloves are so big they're useless for anything other than surrealist mime. Ady's brought snacks. Kate's brought portable speakers. She plugs her iPod in. Out here we can be as loud as we want to be. The music spills out, wild beats and street swagger with an infectious disco sample. It makes me want to dance, so I do, and soon, we all are. If Iris could see us, her lip would curl. Her mouth would sling itself open, like, *Huh? You and her and her?*

Detention shouldn't be fun, but this is easily one of the best mornings I've had all year. I feel free. Like I don't have to explain myself to anyone, like I don't have to try. I can just be Clem. We work fast and demolish the snacks. And we talk.

How we talk!

We talk about wellness and boarder microaggressions; we talk about bests and worsts—movies and books and rumors and personal disasters; and we talk about PSST, who might be behind it.

"Anyone with a computer could be," Kate says. She starts up with the tech talk but after a bit Ady and I are rubbing our foreheads.

I say, "No wonder Iris loves you."

"She doesn't love me anymore," Kate says. "I've ditched our study sessions in favor of Oliver. She thinks I'm distracted."

"You're 16," Ady points out. "You're supposed to be distracted."

"True enough."

It takes forever to clean the pool, but it's a nice kind of eternity. When our talking subsides I feel hit with a feeling that's something like "homesick." Homesick for life before St. Hilda's, life before high school, the kingdom of childhood. Maybe I'm mourning swimming.

"Earth to Clem!"

Ady throws her sopping sponge at me. I scream and throw mine back at her. Kate moves onto the grass to do some hard-looking yoga positions.

"My back is killing me," she says.

"I thought you'd be strong from lugging your cello everywhere," I say.

"I am strong. But there's a limit."

"Someone's phone's ringing," Ady says.

It's mine. It's Stu. I know it. My phone is in my jacket pocket—but where is my jacket? I find it too late. Missed call. When I try calling back his line is busy. A voice-mail message pops up, and then I hear him. He says there's a house-wrecking party, his band is playing, do I want to meet him there, and he tells me the address. I can bring people. The more the merrier . . .

I put my phone back in my pocket and do a little happy dance.

"Wow," Ady says. "Is he that good?"

"He's amazing."

"But you haven't . . . ?" Kate's voice trails off.

"I'm dying to, but there's nowhere to go." I tell them about our plan to rendezvous on the long weekend.

Ady's frowning.

"What?" I say. "He's not sketchy."

"How old is he?"

"Nineteen."

She's still frowning.

"What time is it?" I ask.

Ady checks her watch. "Ten to four."

I look at the pool. "You think this is finished? I'll bet they make us come back."

"I don't even care," Ady says. "What the fuck. It was fun."

I grin. "What the fuck. It really was." Then: "Hey, what are you doing tonight?"

Kate says, "Well, I've got a pass. Officially, I'm staying at Ady's."

And it is decided: Kate, Ady, and I are going to the house-wrecking party.

"We'll do it for wellness," Ady says. "Our second date. You guys . . ." she raises her eyebrows ". . . things are getting serious."

Clem

Saturday, August 20, later

Ady kicks a heel against the tram floor. "Whose house is this anyway?"

"Danny. He plays music with Stu. He's super hairy."

Kate perks up. "What kind of music?"

"Stu calls it 'noise.'"

I don't tell them how old Danny is. I don't want to put them off.

It takes a while to find the house. It's on a massive block, with a wild, overgrown garden.

"I'm going to wait for Oliver," Kate says.

I zoom ahead of Ady, down the long driveway. In front of the house is a bonfire stack. People are lugging the furniture out and breaking it up, adding it to the pile. I stare at it, transfixed, until Ady catches up.

"Hey, girls, are you lost?" A guy wearing jeans so slashed you can't even call them jeans comes out from behind a tree. His eyes are wrecked. He's carrying a puppy. I worry about that puppy. He doesn't wait for an answer, just wanders off into the house.

The front door has already been dispatched to the bonfire pile. The first thing we see as we go in is a man with a screwdriver taking down another door.

"Burn, baby, burn," he says with a wink.

"Okay . . ." Ady looks after him warily.

I head for the band and just assume that Ady's following, but when I see Stu, everything else falls away.

He looks grungy, like he's slept in his clothes. For some reason he has bare feet and a hairclip in his hair. He's playing guitar, but the sound can't be what he's aiming for, because it's like ear torture. The other people in the room are all older, black-clad, not dancing. The smell of dope fills the air. Dope and beer and apathy. I stand in Stu's eye line, waiting for him to see me, but he's lost in his noise.

Finally, he looks up. He stares at me blankly for a moment—a terrible moment—and then he smiles and triumphantly sends more unearthly sounds into the ether.

Seconds are swallowed by minutes. The trouble with Stu's music is that it has no end point. Every time I think we're close, Danny steps in and plays something on his saxophone and they're off again. I'm getting sore feet from standing around. I can't not notice that the girl from the pub is here, watching Stu. And I can't not notice that there are other girls, too. When he finally, finally finishes, it's like there's a pool of us, offering things: a drink, a word, a hug, ourselves—but he slings his arm around me—me!—and kisses the curve between my neck and shoulder. He stoops so that his eyes meet mine.

"Let's go someplace quiet."

His eyes flash. I can read my future in them.

We try the upstairs rooms first, but one is barricaded and the other is occupied by the puppy guy, shirtless now and looking even more wrecked than before. Stu steers me to a small room with an open window. He climbs out the window. I stick my head out. He's on the roof of the garage—it's flat, and someone's had the foresight to drag a couch out there.

Stu dusts the couch off. "After you."

From where we're sitting, we can see the lights of the city and the dark ribbon of the river. Our breath makes clouds in the cold night air.

Stu's lips are soft. His hands are fast and fervent. My cardigan is off, my dress pushed up, my tights and undies down. I'm trying to arrange myself so he can't see my fat bits. He takes his jeans off. He lies on me, warming me up, and the couch creaks under us.

"Uh . . ." I stop. I'm feeling . . . overwhelmed. Overpowered and blocked and chaotic, like the world is tilting, like I'm falling or maybe flying. Things are happening too fast. What about the weekend? What about finding a place? Is this our place? I want to stop but I can't say it—it's like there is no room for words—there is only kissing and touching and—

"Okay?" Stu's breath is hot. He's tussling with a condom. And I want to laugh, but that's just nerves. He's gone all strategic—eyes unfocused, hands downtown. Then he's pushing—for a moment I think it's not going to happen, but then it's in. And it hurts. Stu stops. Starts. Stops. Repositions. I don't know if I'm supposed to move or what. He doesn't speak or look at me, and over his shoulder the sky is black and the stars seem not like fixed points, but like a wild swirling.

While it's happening I'm trying to capture it. I'm trying to think of the words I'll use to talk about it. In movies, sex goes on for ages but here on the couch on the roof I'd put it at four minutes, tops. Afterwards Stu passes me his shirt to wipe myself with. He lights a cigarette and asks me if I'm sore. "It gets better," he says. And all I can do is laugh and cover my face.

We return to the party. Once we get downstairs we separate—this feels okay, like the mature thing to do. I find Ady outside by the fire, with a cool-looking girl who must be Max.

Ady checks me out. "Uh-oh."

"How do you know?"

"Special skill."

The party's gone over the edge. There is a drunk girl dancing to no music. A guy in a MOTHERFUCKER T-shirt tries to dance with her and she flings him off with crazed drunk-strength and he falls into the fire. He runs out screaming, his long hair ablaze. He rolls on the ground in the fallen leaves. We watch, frozen in place. Ady grabs my arm and there's no time to find Stu to say goodbye.

On the tram back, it all seems like a fevered dream: first-time sex, a man on fire. But the proof comes with a tantalizing ping.

That was fun, Stu texts. *Are we still on for next weekend?*

When I get back to school, the grounds seem eerily quiet. I edge around the back and shove the portal door open. I'm shuffling through the dark basement when I hear footsteps above. I tuck myself into a cavity, the shower stall. The light goes on. I hold my breath. It's Old Joy and I'm done for. This is it. But after a minute the light goes off again. She retreats.

I wait in the damp until I'm sure it's safe, then I creep up the stairs back to my room.

People say you don't feel any different. Lainie said she didn't feel any different—but that's not true for me. My pulse throbs. I am tender everywhere.

I am not who I was yesterday or last week or last year.

Kate

Saturday, August 20

I walk behind Ady toward the party, with the brilliant day I've had moving through my head—Ady lounging in the sun and Clem dancing around the pool in slow, swimlike moves to the strange beat of Zoë Keating's "Escape Artist."

"Play some music that's me," Clem had said, and I immediately thought of the song with the throaty cello lines, the unexpected beat. When I put it on, she arced her hands around her to the sound of those sliding notes, slicing them through air, telling us dangerous secrets about her and Stu.

I'm hoping he loves her. I'm worried that he won't.

Ady's worried, too.

But I'm tired of worrying. I want to do.

It was strange spending time with Ady and Clem at the pool, at my pool. It felt right, though. It felt good to clear out the rubbish that people had thrown into my space, clear out the leaves. I didn't even mind that. Time for some new sound.

As Clem spoke about Stu, I thought about Oliver. Not platonic thoughts, either. I let myself give in to the thought that I want to kiss him. I don't think he wants to kiss me. He's so serious, about music and winning. We are crossing a line, but it's a line that has to do with music, I think. I don't know.

Today was the first time I've let myself actually have the daydream. Rules felt suspended today. What would it be like to kiss him? Would he kiss as seriously as he plays? With the same attention to technique? The thought found the sweet spot in my body and I shut it down before I melted in the cleaning suit that Ady called a giant condom.

"I thought about Oliver quite a bit today," I call to Ady, who's ahead of me. Clem's far ahead of her, so far I can't see.

"I never would have guessed," she calls back. "Are you drunk?"

"I have not touched a drop. I'm drunk on having friends. I called Max and invited her tonight. I gave her your number so she can find you in there if she can't find me."

"Did you invite her hoping she'd invite Oliver?"

"Not entirely." I want her here. But I want Oliver, too.

"Just call him, Kate. He'll come. Don't say anything but your name."

"If I were you, that might happen."

She stops walking, turns, and looks at me. The smell of garden—dark and green—is all around. "Do it now." There's a flower hanging above her, a white burst on a tall bush. It makes her look otherworldly, like she's wearing a crown or her aura is showing.

I take out my phone, and key in his number, and when he answers, I look at Ady and say my name.

Wait, Ady mouths, and I do as she says. I wait for what feels like a long time.

Eventually he asks, "Where are you?"

I give him the address and hang up. "That was amazing. I mean, that was a-mazing. I said my name, and he said he'd be here. Are you a witch? That worked like a spell."

She grabs both my shoulders. "You're gorgeous, you're smart, you're talented. Any guy would be lucky to have you, but you're a geeky guy's dream."

"I'm going to wait for Oliver," I say, excited by these revelations.

She keeps moving forward toward the party. Her steps certain, calm. "Ady," I call, and she turns.

"Come to the farm with me for the long weekend. Sit by the river. Eat spectacular food."

"Apple pie?" she asks, only slightly making fun.

"If you order it," I say. "But I suggest the plum cake."

"Plum cake it is," she says.

I text Max to look for Ady when she arrives: *She's alone. You need to find her.* Then I wait.

I'm wearing a dress of Ady's, the silk one I'd seen on her before. I asked, and she said yes without a second thought. "Don't wear tights," she said. "It feels great on your skin." When I said I might be cold, she offered to lend me the coat she was wearing that day we had coffee.

It takes Oliver a while to get here. I search for his face in the groups that walk past. I think about how strange it is that I like him now, and wonder when it was that I started to, and then think about how I probably started before I knew I'd started, and how strange it is that changes can start in us long before we know they're starting. It's a long thought, a string of beats that I follow from one to the other, so I've forgotten to watch for Oliver and then, without me noticing how he arrived, he's standing in front of me.

"Proof of my theory," I say.

"And what theory is that?" He laughs nervously.

I fight the urge to tell him to relax.

"Do you come to these kinds of parties a lot?" he asks, staring behind me in the direction of the noise, at the people walking past, people already drunk and smelling of what even I pinpoint as dope.

"It's a friend of Clem's," I say, as screaming laughter starts up behind us.

"Interesting friend."

We're back to being awkward again because I've made the strange phone call and I'm dressed up and I've asked him to a party that I'm not exactly invited to, so I decide that we need loud music and crowds to drown out the fact that we're not talking.

Before we get to the door, there's a huge crash on the lawn, and then the sound of splintering. "Oh my god!" Oliver yells. "Oh my god! Kate, I think someone just pushed a baby grand out the window."

He's running, and when I don't follow he comes back, grabs my hand and pulls me in the direction of the drunk, stumbling crowd that's gathering. People above are laughing, staring out the window, and people below are starting to contemplate how "close we were to fucking dying." Oliver has pushed his way through them and cleared a circle so he can kneel next to the piano as if it's a living thing.

"It's not a baby grand," he says to me. "It's an old Yamaha." He presses a key and it lets out a sad plink. "They pushed a piano out the window. A piano." He looks up at me. "I would like to leave here, Kate. And I would like you to come with me."

We decide to walk for a while, and to hail a taxi from the street.

It's now that I see Oliver. I don't think I really saw him before, at least not properly. He looks as if he's much more comfortable with a cello in his arms. He doesn't quite know what to do with his hands, so he shoves them in his pockets. Brown hair. Tall. Tall enough to play the double bass, actually.

"Why don't you play the double bass?" I ask.

"I heard the cello," he says.

I think maybe Oliver is looking at me for the first time. At least looking openly, his whole stare on me, on the dress, and my eyes and my skin.

"Borrowed," I say.

He touches his shirt. "Borrowed also. Dad and I have been lazy with the washing."

Seeing a piano fall from a window and smash at our feet seems to have had a relaxing effect on Oliver. He scoops up three pebbles and juggles for a while. I'm impressed and I tell him so. He shows me the trick, and for 10 minutes or so, we stand on the side of the road, juggling and dropping pebbles.

"So, how did a girl like you end up at a party like that?" he asks, once we've started walking again.

"A girl like me?"

"Serious."

"I'm not entirely serious."

"I like serious."

"I'm a little bit serious," I admit. "Clem told me about the party. We were in detention today."

"On a Saturday? You get more and more interesting."

"Are you flirting with me?"

"No. Maybe. I don't know what I'm doing. This is new terrain. I've been trying to flirt with you for a while."

"That's worrying." And exciting.

"Why were you in detention?" he asks.

"I ate a piece of cheese."

He laughs.

"No, really. I ate a piece of cheese. A big piece of cheese. And a strawberry. In the Oak Parlor at the Winter Fair with Ady and Clem."

"How long can you stay out tonight?" he asks.

"As long as I want. I've served my detention. My punishment is over. I have a genuine pass that says I'm staying at Ady's."

"Don't they know most cheese eaters are recidivists?"

"Apparently not."

A taxi approaches. We hail it and run to where it's waiting.

Lights, trees, the broken night rhythm moves past the window and Oliver takes my hand. It's comfortable and exciting at the same time. I'm not drunk, but I feel as though I'm floating. I stare out the window and think about happiness.

We get out of the cab and a light goes on in a room of Oliver's house. An older version of Oliver opens the window. "Good party?"

"They threw a piano out the window," Oliver says.

"Good god."

"Indeed," Oliver replies. "Dad, this is Kate. Kate, this is William, my dad."

"So this is the beautiful cellist," William says, and gives me a wave.

I wave back. *I am the beautiful cellist?*

"You are," Oliver says, which I assume is mind-reading until later when he tells me I spoke out loud.

We walk down the side of Oliver's house to the shed, but it feels different this time. I feel trees brush my arm and smell jasmine. There's a wall of mint that I didn't see before, and Oliver breaks off a leaf as though it's his habit, and hands it to me.

I think of kissing.

We set up, an unspoken understanding that, since I'm here, we'll practice.

Practicing is our way of talking, I realize, and tonight something has shifted and the conversation isn't awkward, or even slightly awkward. Maybe it's because the secret is out, and we're not playing around it anymore. I like Oliver and he likes me, and we're both obsessed with music and we both want to win.

We play without worrying about the mistakes. If I make one he waves his hand for me to go on, and when he makes one I do the same. Once I stop him because the mistake sounds good, and he agrees and we decide to keep it.

We sample Lou Reed.

We listen to the song over and over to choose the part we want.

We loop and mix and play it back.

"It's good," Oliver says, but I disagree, so we loop it again until we're both happy.

I lose a sense of time while we're playing. After a while, I take over the computer and looping while Oliver makes tea because computers are what I do best. He puts a cup in front of me on the table.

He takes a sip.

I take a sip.

"Listen," I say, and play back what we've recorded. He takes over the computer, changes some things. Then I take over and change some more.

My concentration starts to drift. "Long day at detention."

"What's the punishment for eating cheese and strawberries?"

"Cleaning out the pool wearing giant condoms."

"At a later stage we might get into that, when I know you better."

He's lying on his bed now, hands behind his head. He pushes himself up and puts on a record. It's Bowie. I like it. There's nowhere else to lie but his bed, and it's comfortable, and it's next to Oliver, so that's where I rest myself.

"Will your dad mind if I stay here?"

He says no.

The track changes.

"One of your eyelashes has escaped," he says, taking it off my shoulder, hands shaking as he flicks it into air. "I find myself thinking about you," he says.

"I find myself thinking about you, too," I say.

"You make me nervous."

"I would like, very much, to kiss you," I say, imitating Oliver's formal tone.

Oliver is, as always, really good at what he sets his mind to. Later, I will remember this as my first real kiss, with someone I respect, like, need. I will remember Bowie playing in the background as Oliver's hands find their way. I will remember falling asleep, records spinning.

Ady

Saturday, August 20

Through the cypress hedge to an overgrown, weed-thick front garden with 1960s-style planting—pittosporums, oleanders, lilly pilly, japonica—I pick my way through the trash, strewn along the broken concrete path to the front door. People are piling up pieces of furniture in a clear patch of lawn near the hedge. Kate is staying outside, waiting for Oliver. I turn back as she calls my name. She invites me to her place in the country for the long weekend. She is as impulsively kind as Tash is impulsively harsh.

Clem has floated on ahead, drawn by Stu's pheromones, no doubt. Her hair looks so pretty all pinned up like a spiky little tiara. This party is already boiling over and it's only 8:00 p.m.—it's a potential riot or cop callout for sure. Stu's band is so loud I don't even penetrate the front room where they're playing. Wouldn't mind a couple more allies here. I told Kate I was glad she'd asked Max. Glad doesn't quite cover it: I feel helium-fueled over-the-moon excited and nervous.

I text Tash: *At that party, yawnies. See you tomorrow?* I told her that tonight was strictly Malik homework, a second date with the thumb-group. Keeping Tash happy suddenly calls for determined insincerity. She replies: *Poor bb with the dorks. Brunch at Figgy's 11ish, loves* ☺♥ . That will put another hole in my gram birthday cash with nothing on the horizon to replace it.

The place reeks of weed, and ticks my number-one bad sign of a party: too many dudes. I smile and think of Flight of the Conchords, "Too Many Dicks (On the Dance Floor)." Flight of the Conchords is one of those parent-kid crossovers in my family. Stomach lurch as I remember: It was my father who brought them home, and now we are fatherless, for a stretch.

A guy is smiling at me. I avoid eye contact, vague-smiling as I walk past him. "Bitch," he says. God, the tiresome small dealings with random dudes. I couldn't count the number of times I've been a frigid bitch or a stuck-up slut just for not talking to or smiling back at guys who are complete and utter strangers to me—since eighth grade, since the first hint of breast. I send up a prayer to the party fairy for a night of no ass grabs; I get so tired of having my guard up the whole time. Based on the amount of beer swilling around here, I'm not going to be hanging around for too long. A moment of missing my soccer-physique Rupert companion, walking further in, comfort-touching the edge of my phone in my jacket pocket. That thought makes me angry, too: feeling safer with a big guy next to me.

Clare told me about an article that floated the idea of a curfew for guys, so women could feel safe roaming the world at night. Uproar against the idea, of course; how ridiculous, hysterical—why should all guys be penalized for the actions of a few? *But why not?* All women are penalized because of the actions of a few (guys). We're all forced to modify our behavior, or risk our safety, all the time. So why shouldn't all guys have a turn at the world not being guy-friendly for a change? I imagine the girl-friendly world—streets at night full of girls and women. God, it would be so lovely. Walking anywhere we want, wearing anything we want, staying out late, shouting, singing, drinking. Never worrying about attracting unwanted attention from dickheads. All the taxis and Ubers driven by women, so you don't have to sit there holding your phone, ready to speed-dial for help if they take a wrong turn on the way home. Women in the trains and trams, laneways, highways, parks, beaches, pubs, parties, clubs—all safe, all night. Things would be . . . unrecognizable. Imagine slipping out for a full-moon midnight walk just because you could. We'd start to swagger. We'd own the streets, own the night.

There would have to be a device ready to pick up any men who broke curfew—maybe a drone with a clawlike attachment. Men's neck implants would start beeping if they were out after dark, so the drones could locate them right away. And women would finally feel—*be*—safe in the dark hours. After centuries, millennia, of not.

I wander deeper into the house, wondering if I'll get to the heart of this party. Parties have such unpredictable anatomy, so you don't always find it. Looking for the heart is why you end up staying too long at some parties. It can be dancing when the perfect track comes on and getting that mainline hit of collective euphoria, or eating a souvlaki on the way home when you're stoned and starving, or talking your head off to friends you've spent all day with, or kissing someone new.

It feels mildly creepy here, not quite safe. I feel a small pang of longing for the party Lola, Tash, Rupe, and the others are at—dancing to Queen Bey with the girls, parent-funded booze, nice food of some sort. Here, I don't even want to sit down—that orange sofa looks like it would have a liquid level somewhere not far beneath the surface.

The wrecking vibe is warming up. Front sitting room walls have already been graffed: dicks and balls (*why*?), lots of tags. Two girls, each wielding cans in both hands, are creating some pro-looking tentacular sprouting around a window frame, the solvent smell mingling sickly with the weed and beer. The lighting is crime-chiaroscuro from a couple of portable film lights pointing up in two corners of the room.

I head upstairs to keep exploring. This house is a tatty Florence Broadhurst–esque dreamscape—a delicious clash of time-travel furnishing. I wish I could have seen it in daylight.

I open and close one door—humping; a second door—shooting up, *eep*; a third door—ah, just right—empty room. O, wallpaper, lit by the streetlights—a hot pink, black and white wicker-weave pattern. Be still, my hammering heart. It's the real thing: Florence, and the perfect backdrop for my dress made from decommissioned Gram curtains—Marimekko: big black-and-yellow geometric daisies. I shine my phone flashlight around. This must have been a library or a home office; it's lined with shelves now empty except for junk. There are piles of magazines, a broken *The Sims 2* box, a small space heater with its plug cut off, and a shelf of phone books with the 2001 White Pages L–Z on top. I think about taking it home—it's super-thin paper, good for papier-mâché . . . What am I—crafty craft kindergarten girl? No! Resist!

I find the clearest stretch of wallpaper, lean back against it, and paste on an enigmatic smile suitable to the pattern clash. Arm out, flash click, check, edit, filter, post. I have eight likes as soon as I refresh. Thirty when I refresh again. And a message from Max: *Are you where I am?* I message back: *idk—I'm having a wallpaper love-in upstairs—come join* ☺

Max comes through the door with a blast of party sound and a smile. We sit at opposite ends of the window seat, knees up, toes not quite touching.

"Tell me these are not your friends," she says.

"These are not my friends. It's an unfortunate friends of friends of friend situation. Hey, I'm looking for a new school. How do you like MCA?"

"I like it lots. It's perfect for driven arts tragics. There's no wellness program, but there is ample wellness."

"St. Hilda's thinks it's an antidote to online meanies."

"Kate said they posted about you. That sucks."

"I chose not to take it seriously. At least not in public. There's no good way to deal with that stuff."

"When did everyone decide it was even a thing to be anonymous and evil?"

"It only takes a couple of people—and it's like everyone is waiting, ready to follow the mean lead. It's easy to set up a new site if one gets shut down. It's like Whack-A-Mole. You don't have stuff like that at your school?"

Max shakes her head. "People would think it was too—nasty.

Uncool. We get a lot of private school rejects. Not looking for any trouble. Recovering from trouble." She gives my foot a gentle nudge. "So, Kate's been telling me about her perfect day assignment—it was writing music and performing it. What's yours?"

"I don't know—playing with fabrics, dreaming up clothes that don't look like other stuff. What about you?"

Stu's band is starting up again and we mirror-grimace.

"Oh, I've got a thousand perfect days. They all involve books and movies and music," Max says, trying to compete with the band's volume.

"I can hardly hear you."

"We don't have to talk."

She swings her feet to the floor, tilts her face toward me, and checks with a look that she can keep going. My smile says yes, and, right here in the pull and glow of our kiss, I find the heart of the party.

Later, just before some idiot threw empty spray-paint cans into the fire, just before they exploded and caused a fireball that ignited the old cypress hedge in a burning whoosh, just before we made our escape, laughing, and feeling lucky that we hadn't been standing on the other side of the fire, just before all that, I saw Stu standing under the lilly pilly tree, kissing a black-haired girl, his hand down the front of her jeans.

Lying in bed, too hyped to sleep, I see it clearly, looping like a scene from a film. I'm worried about how to tell Clem and don't come up with a single good way to do it. She looked so happy coming home on the tram. I don't want to shatter her happiness.

Text from Tash: *We're all going to escalatorrrr, COME TOOOOOOO, YOU LAZY WENCH xxx*

I put my sound-of-rain app on and go to sleep thinking about kissing Max, and when I can kiss her again.

Kate

Sunday, August 21

Oliver's dad cooks us breakfast in the morning. He hums at the stove, making scrambled eggs and toast. The kitchen reminds me of the one back at the farm. It's used. Garlic and lemons on the bench. Herbs on the sill. The dog (called Inca) licks my hand and begs for bacon that I'm allowed to give him, but only after we've finished eating.

Oliver walks me home. I'm thinking about waking up next to him and the feel of sleepy kisses. I'm thinking about going to Iceland and all the new things that I'll learn. "We're close," I say. "We'll practice every day next week until the long weekend?" I ask, and he confirms that we will.

"And then on the fourth we will blow them all away," I tell him.

"The third," Oliver says. "The audition is on Saturday the third at 10:00 a.m."

"You mean the fourth."

"Are you messing with me?" he asks, smiling and putting a piece of hair behind my ear.

"Yes." No. *Shit.*

"Show me your calendar," he says.

"*Oliver.*"

"I know I'm being crazy, but I just want to make sure you have the right date and time."

"I have the right date and time. Nothing will keep me from being there."

"Nothing," he says, with absolute faith in me. "And we'll win."

This is problematic but not unsolvable. Surely I can take the scholarship exam at another time?

When I get back to the dorms, the first thing I do is knock on Old Joy's door.

"Come in," she says, and waves for me to take a seat. "What's up?"

I fill her in on my problem. "It's an audition for Iceland," I say. "So I have to be there. But I have to take the scholarship exam, too."

She actually looks sympathetic. "Kate, girls all over the state take the exam. They can't move the date for one person."

"But I could take it early?"

Even as I say it, I know that's impossible.

"Why do I have to choose?" I ask. "Why can't I be a musician and a doctor?"

"You can," she says, not understanding, but understanding enough.

"But now I *have* to choose and my life will go in either one direction or the other."

"Bit dramatic," she says.

But that's how it feels. "I want to be everything," I say. "Everything I want."

"And you can be," she says. "But at this particular moment in life, you have to choose. One way or the other. You can always go to Iceland next year."

She starts shuffling papers and looks toward the door, so I leave but I can't find the energy to walk any further than the seats outside her office. I need to make a decision before I go back to my room, before I see Iris. Because, as annoying as she is, she talks sense and she's certain about things. Her certainty will infect me. I flick through my phone, look at the calendar again. How could I have been so stupid?

But I was that stupid.

So now I have to decide.

And I have to decide soon, so Oliver can get someone else.

But he can't get someone else. It's too late for him to get someone else.

He got me.

And I'm about to fuck him over.

I'm *possibly* about to fuck him over.

Or I'm about to fuck over my parents.

And fuck me over, the old Kate says. Because if I don't take the exam, I go back to the country next year.

If I don't audition for Iceland next year, I won't ever go to the Harpa International Music Academy. And I won't audition next year. I might tell myself that I will, so I feel better now, but I won't. I'll get the St. Hilda's scholarship, I'll study math and science, and I'll take that path. If I go to the audition and succeed, then that's a whole other life. Maybe one is just as good as the other. Maybe it isn't.

Old Joy walks out of her office and sees me still sitting here.

"Why don't *you* decide what you want, Kate?" she says. "You're a smart person."

I feel pretty dumb today.

I walk into our room and find Iris sitting on my bed, staring at the door.

"Where were you last night?"

"With Oliver. I had a pass."

"Not to stay at Oliver's."

"To stay at Ady's. Clem had a party. We went straight there from detention."

"So you're her friend now," she says.

I know Clem's awful to Iris sometimes, but she's not awful to me. "I think it's a sister thing," I say to her. "But I can be friends with both of you."

"You'll find out the hard way what she's like," Iris says. "Don't say I didn't warn you."

I sit next to her. I'm tired, and now I have to figure out what to do about Oliver. Iris will find out anyway, so I don't bother hiding from her what's happened.

"You can't audition," she says without hesitation, like I knew she would. "You can't throw away your future for a guy."

"It's not about Oliver. It's about Iceland, and all the places that leads." It's about who I want to be.

"No scholarship, no St. Hilda's."

I hate that the choices about my future can be reduced to

that clipped sentence. Futures need long sentences, with lots of parentheses (maybe you might change your mind), go this way (but don't worry, you can come back), try this for a while (see where it takes you).

"Why are you so judgmental?"

"You asked for my opinion," she says angrily, which is a fair point.

"Can I still come to the farm?" she asks, after we've been sitting in silence for a while.

I try not to think about how Ady and Iris will clash. "Of course," I tell her.

I walk to the Organic Grocers later in the afternoon. Ady's agreed to meet me. She's sympathetic when I tell her about my problem, but she doesn't have an answer. I don't need her to have one. I just need to tell someone who'll understand how much life sucks sometimes.

"This I can do," she says, and then leans back. "If I knew something about someone you'd kissed—scratch that, someone you'd had sex with—something like he'd kissed someone else, would you want to know?"

"Oliver kissed someone else?"

"You and Oliver had sex?"

"Who are you talking about?"

"Stu," she says. "I saw him and a girl. I don't know whether to tell Clem."

"You should tell," I say immediately. "Especially if they've had sex." I pick some seeds off the crust of my toast. "How do you know they've had sex?"

"Some things you know."

"Oliver and I didn't have sex. We kissed. A lot."

"I know," she says.

"How do you know?"

"There's a hue about you," she says, waving in the general direction of my face.

She puts on her coat. "I have to tell Clem."

I ask if she wants me to come with her.

"I think one on one is better for this," she says. "But thanks."

Ady

Sunday, August 21

When Tash arrives at 10:50, my mother is in the front garden pruning the quince tree. Charlie is helping, stacking offcuts.

"That looks like a job for Robert, Jen."

My mother looks at Tash, then looks at me, and I could swear she's deliberately trying to scare Tash off. "No more Robert. No more Marion. This is the era of austerity at 22 River Place, Hawthorn, Tash. At least until I get a job."

The bemused look Charlie gives me reminds me so much of our father that I get a lump in my throat.

Tash's eyes are gossip saucers. She looks at me with pity and loathing, the only response she knows to a "coming down in the world" story. The pity component is a down payment on friendship retention in the event that we pick ourselves up again.

My mother lops off a branch that I'm pretty sure Robert would have left on. Farewell sweet-smelling, fuzzed quinces that will never germinate, grow to maturity, and sit in the large blue-and-white bowl making the sitting room smell mysteriously pretty.

No more Marion? Are the bathrooms going to clean themselves? My heart sinks. Noooo. I'm too young to clean bathrooms. Or too old to start. Or neither. I just don't want to do it.

Red Hot Chili Peppers is filtering into the garden. My mother is singing along, grimly, to "Scar Tissue." This is her "I had a life before I had children, you know" music. It's also her "40-something lawyers are cool, too" music. Maybe it's "I managed to use cocaine and let it go, but it got its claws into my husband good and proper" music, as well. Who knows what's going on in there?

Tash is texting most of the way as we walk the six minutes to Figgy's, but I'm just happy not to be getting 20 questions about why I said what I said in class, or about the economy drive at home, so I don't even ask who she's talking to.

At the back table in Figgy's, sitting with my bestie—who looked like she despised me just 10 minutes ago—I'm knitting a *birdie* cardigan sleeve as though it's just any other day, when Lola and Bec arrive together.

Tash jumps up and walks over to the door to meet them. Why? Advance party to let them know we can't afford a gardener or a housekeeper anymore?

I've just worked out how to make little slits in the sleeves—mid-row casting off seven stitches and then continuing on—so I can sew in fabric petals to form wings running from the shoulders to the elbow. It's not the sort of thing you'd wear very often. Oooh, plan: I'll wear it a couple of times, label it, and put it out in the world to be shared. Share-wear-ware. It feels like it fits in with Malik-world, but I'm not sure exactly how.

They all say at the same time what a great night I missed at Escalator. A round of giggles and smirks loops and repeats as they settle and sit.

"Well, spill," I say. "Something juicy obviously happened."

Tash says, "Let's order first; my hangover needs food."

We have the usual. Me: breakfast burrito; Tash: the hotcakes that she'll half-finish; Lola: avocado, haloumi, and heirloom tomatoes on sourdough, with a side of spinach; Bec: fruit salad that she'll devour, following which, still hungry, she'll finish Tash's hotcakes. The others each order freshly squeezed orange juice, eight bucks a pop. I'll have to ask if we can pay for what we order rather than split the bill. Coffee plus burrito plus two-buck tip will clean me out.

"What are you wearing, hon?" asks Tash, as though she's only just noticed my clothes. My mother has enough odd designer clothes that Tash has to check before she knows if she should praise or condemn, just in case I've borrowed something expensive. It's not so bad. Almost the entire world relies on other people's opinions to tell them what to think.

I'm wearing a new ensemble made from the Gram upholstery fabric treasure trove. It has completely different fabric front and back. An exaggerated onesie shape, like a paper doll, three-quarter sleeves, and leg length.

I put *birdie* down, stand up, arms out to the side facing them, and then turn the other way before I sit back down, smiling. "It's called, *now you see me: escape-wear for parties*."

Tash looks at Bec, eyebrows up.

Bec responds. "Since when do you give your clothes *titles*?"

"I don't know." I don't want to say: *Since I started thinking they're my art*. I start knitting again, and shrug. *Since why the fuck not?* "Since *birdie*, I guess. But there are lots more in my head with titles." It gives me a spurt of happiness, even with the family shit happening, even with PSST horrors, to think of all the things yet to be made.

"You know, you look—" Lola starts. They look at each other, as if three-way glances zipping back and forth above ricotta hotcakes and blueberries will come up with the right party line—or as though they've had the conversation already, without me. "Okay, Ady, we've been noticing lately . . . you've gone from being a bit arty, and kind of cool, to looking—"

"Peculiar," finishes Tash. "As though we're not even the same *species* anymore." She laughs lightly, not unkindly. I know this laugh. This laugh lets you get away with saying the nasty stuff because you're sort of kidding. I use this laugh myself, regularly.

Looking down at my cardigan sleeve in progress as though it might be diseased, Tash raises an index finger to the passing waiter, and checks with us. "More coffee?"

I think of the austerity drive. "Not for me, I've only got a twenty."

Tash looks impatient. "I'll get it for you."

Bec makes sympathy eye contact with me. "No, I don't want another coffee, either."

"Just two more skinny lattes," Tash says, as though Bec and I are being difficult.

"Thanks," I add to the girl taking our order. My family might be kaput, and my clothes might be too much for some people, and half the world might think I'm a fan of anal intercourse, but at least I say thank you to the person waiting on my table.

"So, too bad you couldn't come last night," says Lola.

"I got social outing number two crossed off the Malik list, so that was good," I say, smiling, remembering the party, remembering Max, and wondering how Max and my friends would get along. Not quite seeing it.

Friends. Interesting. I see Clem asking me if I'm okay at detention, and Kate inviting me home with her for the long weekend before I see these guys, my actual friends.

"Poor you. Wasting a whole night with the boring boarders." Tash eats a micro-mouthful of hotcake, like you hear actors have to do when they are performing scenes that involve eating and talking.

"It wasn't so bad."

"You're too kind."

"They're okay." I think about detention and the party, and I don't want to sell them short anymore. "They're better than okay, they're nice. I like them."

Tash starts and the others follow—incredulous laughter. It's contagious. I give in.

"I know, all right. But I do! I didn't know them before."

"You'll be telling us you like Iris soon." Another peal of laughter.

"Don't be silly. I have to draw the line somewhere." Feeling a tiny bit guilty. Why did I have to laugh and seem to agree like that? And shocking bore though Iris is, even Clem manages to avoid her and not say nasty things about her.

"Good to hear you haven't completely lost it," says Tash.

The three of them exchange looks again.

"What is it with you guys? Do you have something to say? Say it."

Bec starts. "Well—we thought you went a bit too far with the PSST response."

Tash's lip curls. "No guy wants his ex saying things like that, even if it's meant to be a joke."

I look at them. I'm the incredulous one now. "No girl wants a scummy social media site telling the world she likes it up the ass, either. I decided it was better to go for humor than to get defensive and deny it."

"You were pretty unfair to Rupert, that's all."

"Well, tough. It's his stupid school all that PSST stuff comes from."

"We don't know that," says Tash, as though I've offended her.

"What, are you Basildon's best friend suddenly?"

The looping looks do another lap of the table. Things are smelling ratty. I have one of those leaps of gut instinct that leads me to a nasty place: That's the juice—Tash and Rupert.

"You didn't!" I've known Tash for long enough to see when she's squirming. "How could you?"

"Who told you?"

"Nobody."

"Well, you made it pretty clear you don't want him. And he's not likely to be alone for long."

"What happened to the one-year rule? It's barely been two weeks."

"I don't even know why that's a thing," Tash says.

The others are quiet. They know she's in the wrong, but they also know she's the strong one at the moment. That strength oscillates between me and Tash, and the others always know where it lies.

But I'm not putting up with this. "Oh, okay, sure—recap:

"In case your *friend* changes her mind and wants the boy back.

"To avoid hearing or engaging in inappropriate pillow talk about your *friend*.

"To punish your *friend's* ex for whatever part he played in dropping your friend, or, acting like a douche and deserving to be dropped by your *friend*, by denying him alternative nice girlfriend.

"To avoid the possibility of any unfortunate *friend*-to-friend comparison by the ex.

"To avoid any uncomfortable *friend* witnessing of friend hooking up at parties with the ex within close proximity of her having recently been the one hooking up with him."

I look around the table. "So, that's how I remember it—it's pretty friend-friendly. Did I miss anything?"

Bec shakes her head. She looks close to tears.

We wrote the rules down at the beginning of last year. And kissed the notebook with lipstick lips. (I know. But it was freshman year.) The rules are—were—sacred. It's not as if I want Rupert back, but this disrespects me, and it disrespects our friendship.

"I refuse to let this affect our friendship," says Tash.

"Too late for that, *girlfriend*." I roll the word in acid, carefully pack up my *birdie* sleeve and knitting needles, leave the twenty on the table, and go.

Walking into the hard winter sunshine, past the elementary school where Tash and I started in Prep together, before we both moved to St. Hilda's in seventh grade, my pace is fueled by anger over Tash's shitty behavior. I'm also worrying about the whole family nightmare and imagining my dad sitting in some horrible room with a single bed, but then, like a huge happy wave knocking everything sideways, I'm thinking of Max. I kissed Max last night, and she kissed me. Not a posed, fake, music clip kiss like we used to do at parties in freshman year—cringe. No. Long, slow, real kisses full of sex and romance. And what comes next? I look again at the text from her that I woke up to. No words, just a screen full of ladybug emojis. I told her that I love ladybugs, and I do.

WEEK 7

RETREAT, REFLECT

Wellness

Monday, August 22
Dr. Peter Malik

Week 7: Retreat, Reflect

Provocation

In order to understand the world, one has to turn away from it on occasion.
—Albert Camus

The three grand essentials of happiness are: Something to do, someone to love, and something to hope for.
—Alexander Chalmers

Points for Discussion/Reflection

- Happiness is an industry and an illusion. Discuss.
- What are your "Grand Essentials of Happiness"?
- We cannot know happiness as it is happening, only after.
- Happiness cannot be planned or predicted.

Task

On this long weekend, I hope you will find the time to unplug, switch off, tune out, and take a quiet moment in nature to meditate, to reflect. If you like you can journal your reflections. Ask yourself, What does happiness mean to me? Create a happiness plan.

Kate

Monday, August 22

Oliver's rented studio space for Monday. I should have told him there was no point in paying for an extra session, but I couldn't bring myself to say the words. I want another session. I want hundreds of other sessions. I want to ditch life as I planned it and spend every second composing with Oliver.

I walk along Lygon Street, thinking about the ideas that Dr. Malik talked about in wellness today. Happiness *isn't* simple. There's always something practical getting in the way of our dreams. If I ditch the exam then I have to go back to the country. And if I go back to the country, I will have lost both futures.

I walk slowly toward the library, dragging out the seconds until I see Oliver and have to tell him. Garlic, tomato, coffee, books—this part of the city feels like freedom to me. I wonder how many of the people around me got to choose their lives, and how many had to make compromises along the way, ending up in a place that was okay but not the one they were desperate for.

I see Oliver's cello case from a distance, resting against the wall of the library. He's tapping on his Mac with his left hand the way he does, his right hand steadying it, and every now and then scratching at his chin. He looks up and scans the street, but he's scanning in the wrong direction, so he doesn't see me approaching. He's got one earbud in: one ear in music, one ear to the world. His eyes find me when I'm close enough. He sees me. I see him. We see each other seeing each other.

"Are you ready for the fusion of information architecture and classical music?" he asks.

"I dressed for it," I say.

"So did I," he says, and looks down at his feet. He's shined his old boots. "An occasion such as this calls for clean footwear."

"I never know when you're joking."

"Assume that, when it comes to music, I'm serious. Assume all else is a joke."

We walk through the glass doors into the library, up the stairs, and into the studio. *Last time, last time, last time,* I think, to the beat of all our steps. There's no window to the world in the studio, only one to another room. It's airless and tiny, which didn't bother me before.

"You look grim," Oliver says.

I give him a small smile to convince him that I'm fine, and take up my bow.

I close my eyes and I get this image of the two of us building a city together, a metropolis. Behind my lids, in the darkness, I see the streets forming, the paths bricked by us, these skyscrapers growing. The more we loop and layer, the bigger the city, the more beautiful.

At the end of our session, I open my eyes. "We're ready," Oliver says, and it's the saddest sentence. Because it's true. All the practicing, arguing, composing, kissing, living have added up to this piece of music.

And it's been a waste.

We walk out of the studio, back down the stairs, and onto the street. Later, I might remember all the things we talked about on our way to the tram stop: looping software, Zoë Keating, Emilie Autumn, electronica, the dusky sky, the cloud above us shaped like a mouse, the myth that egg cartons can soundproof a room, the hassle of taking cellos on public transport, the Iceland auditions.

But I have a feeling all I will ever remember from this day, this year, is the look that will be on Oliver's face when I tell him I can't audition.

"Oliver . . ." I say, about to lay the problem out for him so he can help me decide.

"All your thoughts move across your face while you're thinking. You know that?" Oliver says.

"What am I thinking?"

"You mumble. I can't quite understand it. When you play the cello your face is dead serious and twitching."

"Oliver," I say again, and then he leans in and kisses me.

"Can I come to the formal with you?" he says. "I mean, will you go with me?"

"Yes," I tell him, and decide to give us this moment, this night.

I'll tell him when I get back from my weekend at home. I think maybe I'm hoping for some kind of miracle.

Ady's Wellness Journal

Tuesday, August 23

Yesterday in class Malik was all about how it's helpful to see happiness as a by-product of what we do, rather than a goal. What about unhappiness? Is that just a negative space? It doesn't feel that way. It feels like a commodity that's always overstocked. Unhappiness? Sure! We've got a heap out the back. Wait right here. If I tell Clem about Stu, that's a large express delivery of unhappiness. I let myself imagine that Clem and Stu have an understanding—they can both see other people. Then I think of the glow around Clem. Of course there's no "understanding." Not in her mind, anyway. Do I need a plan? Yes. Do I have a plan? No. Easy plan: Don't tell her; she'll find out soon enough. Right plan: Tell her. Kate thinks the same. Isn't it obvious? You treat friends the way you want to be treated. I'd want the truth. She is going to be unhappy about Stu. She's going to be unhappy with me. Some days are all cloud and no lining. Suck it up, I guess. Hmmm. I've started to think of her as a friend, and a friend is someone who deserves my honesty.*

**btw, the way I want to be treated by my mother but I never fricken am*

Clem

Wednesday, August 24

A text from Stu: *Hey Zaftig Clem, we've got a room! Belongs to a friend-of-a-friend. Abbotsford.*

A note from Iris: *What's up with you? Are we Skyping tonight? Why won't you answer my messages? When are you going to tell Mum and Dad about swim squad/Canberra? Are you staying with Jinx for the long weekend????????*

Being in love is like being in a fog.

I think of Stu when I wake up and then pretty much all day. I go to sleep hoping I'll dream about him, too. Jinx is sick of seeing me staring at my phone. "You're boring, Clem. You're like a zombie. Who is he, anyway? What school does he go to? It's not Anton D'Angelo is it?"

"No. Ew." I tell Jinx a little, but not everything. If she knew how old Stu was, there's no way she'd cover for me. I've never been to a Feminist Collective meeting, but I'm sure they spend the whole time making up new categories for skeevy guy behavior.

The rare moments that I come out of my love fog, what I see is enough to send me straight back. Winter just won't go—everyone's got colds and is sniffling and covering their mouths with their sweaters so they can't catch germs. And PSST just keeps on giving. My fat photos are history, but on Sunday there was a double whammy. First, a photo of Lainie sitting on some Basildon boy's lap, with the quote from him saying St. Hilda's girls would benefit from a master class on hand jobs. Lainie came to wellness class, her face gray as a slug. She'd had a crush on that guy for ages. She thought he really liked her. Malik talked about the importance of self-care, and Lainie said, "What I really want to know is, How come boys are such pigs?"

Malik: "I, uh, some context, Lainie?"

But she just closed up again.

What would he do if he knew? Would he do anything? We're supposed to report this kind of thing, but no one does, and anyway, what would the teachers do? What *could* they do? Turn off the internet! HA.

Yesterday, there was a new twist on Rupertgate—Tash and Rupert have hooked up. Ady's walking around, acting like it doesn't bother her—but I know better now.

After history, Kate and I confer.

"I read the St. Hilda's bullying policy," I say. "We could

report it. Girls are twice as likely to be both perps and victims of cyberbullying."

Kate frowns. "It can't be a girl—what girl would say stuff like that?"

"It's because we're brought up to be all nice and smiley and agreeable. It's not acceptable for girls to act on their aggressions, so we have to get creative. At least boys get to duke it out."

Kate's quiet. The way she's looking at me—something else is going on.

"What?" I say.

"Did Ady talk to you yet?"

"About what?"

"She's in the assembly hall. You should go see her."

"You're being very mysterious. Hey, Stu texted me—we've got a room. I think it's in his friend's house."

"You know, if you want to come to the farm on the weekend, you're welcome to."

I look at her—didn't she hear me?

"Clem—" The bell rings and Kate looks relieved.

I make my way to the assembly hall. Ady, Tash, and Lola are walking around with measuring tapes and clipboards. There's a plate of doughnuts on the table in front of them, untouched. I linger by them and wait for Ady to come over. Tash and Lola act like I'm not even there.

"Hey," Ady says.

"Kate said I should come and see you."

Ady looks cagey. Whatever she wants to tell me, she won't do it here.

"Meet me in the quiet area."

"I go here, I go there," I complain, smiling, swiping a doughnut on the way out.

The quiet area is a small square of garden, paved with commemorative bricks. I sit on the bench and read the names of families who donated money and feel the warmth of the winter sun. Ady comes through the door, looking grim. My good feeling starts to slide.

"What's up?"

"I wanted to talk to you."

"So talk." I tear off some doughnut and pop it in my mouth.

"Okay." She exhales. "This is hard. Saturday night, at the party, just before we left, I saw something."

"What?"

"Stu with a girl. They were kissing. He had his hand in her pants."

The doughnut tastes like mud. I stop. Swallow.

"I don't think so."

"I saw."

Ady's gray eyes look right into mine. I wait for her to smile and say, *Joke*! but she just continues looking worried, and I'm holding half a doughnut I can no longer eat.

The quiet space suddenly feels loud. Ady is sitting too close.

"But—he wouldn't. *He was with me*."

Ady bites her lip and looks down at her nails.

I try to come up with reasons for what she says she's seen.

"It was dark. It was some other guy. I don't believe you." Suddenly I'm shaking. Full of lava. "You bitch!" I shout. "Why are you saying this?"

I throw my doughnut at her. Ady ducks, but some Nutella has

stuck to her hair. She combs it out with her fingers. "I'm sorry," she says, standing. "If it was me, I'd want to know."

"Well, that's the difference between you and me, isn't it? Go back to your real friends and leave me the fuck alone."

I text Stu.

I need to see you. I'm having a bad day.

I'm at the Blue House all night.

Can I come there?

Tricky.

I wait, holding my breath.

It's quiet time after seven. Don't ring the doorbell. I'll meet you out back.

He texts the address. I feel like running back to Ady and waving it in her face. There has to be some way to turn this day around. There has to be. I go to the rest of my classes but I can't concentrate. I don't believe Ady, but why would she make it up? She must be mistaken.

Iris is looking for me. We're supposed to Skype Mum and Dad, but I manage to dodge her. I stay in my room until everyone's gone to dinner. Then I fling on a T-shirt and my old green velvet jacket. I put on lipstick and stare at my reflection for a good few seconds. A wild, awful feeling beats inside of me.

The Blue House is right next to the train line. I have to walk down an alley to get to the back. It's a dark, dark night. No stars. I wish I had my scarf and gloves. The back of the house is just a cement area with dead ferns and a washing line with some men's underwear on it. There's an overflowing ashtray and a couple of crates to sit on. I sit and text Stu, *I'm outside.*

Ten minutes pass. Ten long, cold minutes. I can hear shouting from inside the house and it makes me nervous. I shouldn't be here. This is where he works. It's where his clients live. I'm trying to tell myself that it's just like my dorm, but I know it's not. Stu tells stories—like the one about the guy who lost it because someone ate his pie. He shat on a plate and put it in the fridge. "The things that I have seen, Clem, the things that I have seen."

The back door opens. Stu presses a finger to his lips. He takes my hand and leads me up the narrow stairs. I can see three people in the TV room watching *The Bachelor*. They don't see us. Stu's room is tiny. It smells like old socks and energy drinks. He has a single bed, a clock radio, his guitar, and a handful of books—that's all.

As soon as he closes the door, Stu is all over me. I don't stop him. We don't even make it to the bed. He unbuttons my jeans with one hand, while working his jeans off with the other. And then it's the condom, the silence, the weight of him. Stu keeps his eyes closed. It doesn't hurt as much this time; it just feels like he's in a hurry. I wish I could lose myself. I want to get it—*IT*—the feeling people write about in songs and books, of being so connected, so close you want to die.

This time is even shorter than the last. As soon as it's over, Stu starts putting his clothes back on.

"What?" I say. "No afterglow?"

"No time for it," Stu says.

I find my clothes, start getting dressed. I can't help thinking about what Ady said. If I'm looking at Stu suspiciously, he doesn't notice. I'm trying to think of a way to ask him about the girl at the party, but then shouts rise up from downstairs. Shouts and thuds, like a fight is breaking out.

"Shit. Wait here." And he's gone.

I stand up. My mouth is dry. I'm pulsing all over. I see Stu's scarf on the back of his bed, and I put it on and breathe in the scent of him. Stu's phone is on his bedside table. I don't know why I pick it up—it's just an impulse—but the second I do a message arrives.

I stare at the name on the screen.

Anna.

I click on the message and then wish I hadn't. It's a photo, like the ones I've been sending, only not remotely arty.

The shouts from downstairs get louder.

I go to Stu's photos. My pictures are in there, and the ones he's sent me, but there are also photos of other girls. So many. A gallery of pink. I track back the messages he's sent Anna and they're a variation of all the ones he's sent me.

I put his phone down. My head fills with noise. And, god, I'm such an *idiot*. I haul on my jeans and grab my jacket. I run, out the door, down the stairs, past the TV room, where Stu's sitting on the floor, hugging a guy who's rocking and moaning.

Once I'm on the street, I walk for ages. I don't even know where I'm walking to. I walk past a bar where a group of guys call things out. And past a restaurant where a loved-up-looking couple are eating off each other's plates. I walk past posters for a "gentlemen's club"; someone's scratched the model's nipples off. And I walk past a church with a shop attached: a thousand plastic Jesuses showing me their wounds. Stu calls once, twice, but I don't pick up.

I get back to school to find that no one has missed me. The world hasn't ended, but it feels like it has. I have a long shower and then I cry myself to sleep. I don't even care that Jinx can hear.

Clem

Thursday, August 25

I'm lying in bed, staring at the ceiling, trying to track the pattern in the ceiling rose. I'm thinking about the coming weekend—the room, how much I wanted it. I'm not going, but some small idiot part of me kind of wants to. It's the same part that makes me sniff Stu's scarf—like, I hate him but I still want to smell him. He's sent me three texts: Where did I go? Did last night really happen or was it just a wild sex dream? *Call me, Zaftig.*

I know if I talk to him I'll cry, or whine; I'll show my age, I'll be pathetic. I hate feeling so desperate. Why can't I be enough for him? He's enough for me. It makes me think maybe none of it was real. Maybe I made it all up. I think about the quote on the wellness sheet: Happiness is an industry and an illusion. "Better we talk about joy," Malik had said. "Because the con with happiness is we think it's everlasting."

Four months ago I didn't even know Stu existed. And maybe

I wasn't completely happy then, but it wasn't because of missing him. Now I can't imagine being happy again. Today I went to class. I masked my sadness and kept to myself at breaks. I must have had a fuck-off vibe; no one came near me, not even Jinx. In the afternoon there was a message from Mum and Dad. Iris didn't Skype them and they wanted to know why.

I wish I'd never come to St. Hilda's, never had the accident, never fallen for Stu's smile.

There's a knock at my door. Iris.

"Go away," I say.

She ignores me and closes the door behind her.

Her glasses hang on the granny chain around her neck. Her sleeves are stuffed with tissues and her face looks like she's been rubbing it with stinging nettles.

"Are you still sick?"

"No." She scowls and sneezes; snot flies out too fast for her to catch it. We both stare at where it lands on the carpet. Then Iris bends to wipe it up.

"It's just a cold," she says, her voice thick. "What's your excuse?"

"My excuse for what?"

She waves her hand to indicate my general funk. Her eyes go to the mirror, Thing One and Thing Two. She's having a good look at Ady's fat ladies.

"Do you want to Skype Mum and Dad?"

"No."

She's silent, looking at me all judgy.

"Can I help you, Iris?"

"You never talk to me. You don't respect my opinions."

"What do you want?"

"I want to know how you are."

"I'm fine."

"You don't look fine." She sits on Jinx's bed. She looks like she's got something to say, like she's been thinking about it for ages, and then she says it. "I used to hear Mum talk about you to her friends and get so jealous. You know, you suck up a lot of energy."

"Me? You're the one they're proud of. You've got the bright future. You don't even need people."

"I need people," Iris says. She starts coughing. I wrap Stu's scarf around my mouth as a protective measure.

"How long have you had that cough for?"

"About a week."

"It's sounds bad."

"Whatever."

"Hey, Iris?"

"What?"

"I had sex."

"You did not."

I nod. "Twice."

Her eyes go wide. "Does he go to Basildon? Are you taking him to the formal?"

"It was the guy I ran into—who brought flowers."

"Him? But he's so old!"

I'm enjoying shocking her. Talking to Iris I can pretend that Stu and I are still a thing, still what we never really were—boyfriend and girlfriend. "I don't know if he'll come to the formal. It's a bit . . . babyish. You and Theo will have fun."

"What do I do if Theo wants to—you know."

I start laughing.

Iris goes red. She looks like she wants to hit me.

"I can't see it," I say.

"Why do you have to be such a bitch?"

"I don't know. Because I feel like it, I guess."

What is it like to be Iris? So closed off, so self-sufficient. I remember her Google search—*How do you know if a boy likes you?*—and I want to laugh, because it's such an innocent question. But even now, even after having sex, it's still *the* question. I feel myself soften toward her.

She starts coughing again. It sounds like someone tearing off huge strips of wallpaper. She blows her nose copiously. Then she lets out a wail of frustration. "I hate being sick! I've got Kate's this weekend."

"You know, Kate invited me, too."

"She did? Why? I mean, I know you had that thing for wellness, but . . . Kate's totally not your kind of person, Clem. She's refined. You're like . . . primitive."

"What, like a monkey?"

"I didn't say that." But she's smiling. And I'm smiling. It's sort of funny.

Iris spits phlegm into a tissue. She stares at it. "It's yellow. Does that indicate infection? Or is that when it's green? Or gray? Or bloody?"

"Go see the nurse. Get some antibiotics."

Iris stands up, but she lingers at the door. I'm flashing on a hundred childhood photos of us—where one or the other of us is always pushing to the front. Where if one of us looks happy, the other looks destroyed. The way we roll.

"What are you going to do if you're not going to be a champion swimmer?"

"I don't know. I'll just be nothing. I'll just be me."

Iris shivers, like the thought of that is a fate worse than death. Then she sneezes three times and leaves.

I go back to staring at the ceiling rose, thinking about Stu, feeling stupid. Maybe I *could* go to Kate's. Maybe getting away would be good for me. But Iris would hate it if I went. And Ady might not be so happy about it, considering the doughnut.

Ady was right. Iris was right. Jinx was right. I should have been more careful.

The sun sets outside my window and the heaters click on. Just before dinner, Jinx comes in and tells me that Iris fainted in the nurse's office and has been ordered to bed. "She's going to have a great long weekend in sick bay." Jinx shakes her head. And then, when I fail to move, she adds, "Aren't you going to go and see her?"

I make a care package for Iris. Chocolates and some DVDs, and, only because I'm pretty sure I'm not going to need it, *How to Hook Up*, the booklet from Fuss. I think about writing some words of encouragement regarding Theo, but can't think of anything to say. Because I still can't see it. But what would I know?

Clem's Wellness Journal

Friday, August 26

My rules for the weekend:

1. *I'm not allowed to say Stu's name.*

2. *No phone.*

We're on the train, going to the country, dressed in casual clothes. We're sitting in four facing seats, but there are only three of us. When I told Iris I was going to go to Kate's, she just nodded dully—she was very medicated—and when I gave her the care package she looked like she might cry, so I got out of there fast. I know it's mean, but I'm glad she's not here. It works better, just the three of us. Iris would have brought all our sisterly baggage. She would have been weird around Ady and possessive of Kate. She would have spilled our childhood everywhere. Here's the thing I can't really explain: I love Iris, but I don't like her very much.

This train is so much nicer than city trains—it has velour seats and clean toilets and a water dispenser. There's even a little café, selling cheese puffs and sausage rolls and almost-real coffee. The other passengers look like country people. They are jeans and Ugg boots and flannel shirts; tired-looking mothers with rough skin and raggedy kids; men with whisky noses talking loudly about soccer or farm equipment.

We've been traveling for about an hour and the window shows rolling green hills and blue skies and cloud mountains.

Kate has her eyes closed, her headphones on. Ady's reading. I don't want to hear my ringtone. Or people coughing. I don't want to hear my head. I am ecstatic to have ditched St. Hilda's, PSST, fluey Iris, but most of all Stu. The further away I get, the clearer the picture becomes. I never asked him about other girls because, in some deep down part of me, I knew.

When I told Ady about the photos on Stu's phone, she didn't say "I told you so." She just hugged me and told me about this thing the Japanese do: If they break a pot or a cup, they don't try to make it perfect; instead they fill the cracks with gold-dusted lacquer. She said, "They believe that when something's suffered damage and has a history, it becomes more beautiful. Like, it is more beautiful for being broken. Maybe all our heartbreaks will be like that and when we're old we'll look crazed with experience. In both senses of the word."

Kate

Friday, August 26

God I've missed the river, I think, as we round the last bend to home. There were whole years where it had dried up, and Ben and I stood on the side, longing for it to come back. *It's nearly full again now,* Mum wrote in her last email and I imagined swinging over the water, anchored by the rope that's tied to the ancient eucalyptus. I imagined myself floating, faceup, ice-cold body, sun-warmed face.

I've missed everything about the farm. I've missed the house—huge, rambling, comfortable—sitting in the middle of the fruit trees. I've missed the wisteria, working its way over the iron frame that Dad built so it can't pull down the house. I've missed the honeysuckle and the ancient rose. I've missed the kitchen, with the old Aga, the old floorboards, the nicks in them, the scuffs. I've missed my bedroom with all my albums, organized in genres, and then in alphabetical order within the genres, so I can find anything I want at the moment that I want it.

Dad is sturdy and *the same* when I hug him. I've gone off and changed and I'm so grateful that he and Mum haven't. The kitchen smells of sweet plum cake. I introduce Ady and Clem to Berry our dog, Poco the horse, Amadeus the goat. I see them taking it all in and I love them for loving it the way I do.

Clem is actually smiling, which is a huge relief. Ady looks wary, and I wonder if she and Clem are okay now. "She didn't take it well," was all Ady said afterward. "I wouldn't have, either."

"Bathroom through here," I say, opening up the door of the en suite.

"I'm never leaving," Clem says. "I am never leaving."

We walk around the whole house, and I explain that it's big because Mum and Dad sometimes take in boarders when they need money, or use it as accommodation for the seasonal workers. There's heaps to show them and I show it all. The track that leads to the old shed, the gas pump we have on our land, the road that leads to the river, the lavender, the veggie patch, the treehouse Dad and I built with Ben's occasional assistance.

"Who's Ben?" Clem asks, and I tell her that she'll meet him soon.

Get over here, I text him. *Actually, scratch that. Get to the river.*

Be there after lunch, he texts back.

We eat, and then walk there. Down tracks I know by heart. There's a rhythm to the bush that's different from the city. *Slow, dry, and blue*, I think. *Wattle and quiet. Night skies that go all the way to your edges.* I want to bring Oliver here to write, I think, and think at the exact same time that I can't bring him here, because he won't want to talk to me when he knows that I'm not auditioning.

Ben's waiting for us at the river, standing on the side near the eucalyptus. Exactly where he was when we said goodbye. I run over, and he punches my shoulder shyly, and I punch his back. Then I grab him and hug him until he laughs and reminds me that we're not alone.

He, Clem, and Ady hit it off immediately.

In fact, from the way Ben looks at Clem, I know he won't argue when I say that we should go out on the river in two boats. "Me and Ady in one, Clem and Ben in the other."

"Nice move," Ady says, as she and I drift away from them.

I smile, and start to row while she leans back and stares at the sky.

"Are you okay?" I ask.

"I am for now. I'll tell you later."

I understand. She needs this moment. Under this sky.

I need it, too. I row and imagine that things can turn out how I want them. Maybe they can. There's a peacefulness here that makes me think I can talk to Mum and Dad calmly, and they'll understand and help me find a way.

I make myself believe it, so I can carve off some time to think about Oliver, and the kisses we've had. I think about the messages he's been sending.

Him: *Hello.*

Me: *Hello.*

Him: *I find myself missing you. I find myself thinking about Iceland. I find myself thinking about you and me in Iceland.*

Me: ☺

Him: *What is your home like?*

Me: *Trees, birds, sky, cake, open fires, a river.*

Him: *I love rivers. Bring me back a river.*

"Kate," Ady says, her eyes still on the clouds, "I can see now how you got to be you."

"Quiet and studious," I say.

"You're solid. Loyal. Different. Addictive," she says.

I want to find out what's making her sad, and fix it.

If I said that, I'll bet she'd say, "Not all things can be fixed," in her oracle-speak.

I want to fix it just the same.

Clem

Friday, August 26

Ben is the cute guy from the photo on Kate's pinboard. He is standing by the river—like he comes with it. Ady and I watch him and Kate hug. I can tell we're thinking the same thing: that it's strange to have someone else in our sphere. What if it puts us out of balance? What if it's awkward? What if Ben doesn't like us or we don't like him? But we needn't have worried because he's great, funny, lovely—like Kate. And inside of 10 minutes we're all gabbing like mad and laughing our asses off at nothing and everything.

We go out on the river. Ady and Kate, me and Ben. I don't even have to row. I just sit back and listen as he tells me about river sprites and the names of all the plants. When he gets excited about something (land, plants, river, rocks), his cheeks flush a little. It's not unbecoming. As he gets used to me, he stops talking about the natural world and starts asking questions.

"Do you like boarding school?"

I shrug. "It's okay. It was lonely at first. It's getting better."

"I couldn't do it. I know it sounds uncool, but I'd miss my parents. I already miss Kate. I'm a bit lost without her."

I'm quiet for a bit. "It must be good to have someone to rely on."

"Wait—don't you have a twin?"

"We don't really get along." I stir the water with my fingertip and make up a credo. "How about, if you don't get attached, then you can't get lost?"

Ben looks at me. "Nah. I don't believe you think that for a second."

I'm trying to give him a brave stare, but I don't think it's convincing.

"Kate says you're a swimmer."

"I was. But I stopped. I don't want to do it competitively." This is the answer I've been practicing for when I have to explain to Mum and Dad.

"If it was summer, I could show you all the secret swimming spots."

"I've never swum in a river."

"What? Never?"

I shake my head. "Just a lot of pools."

"You'll have to come back. River swimming is the best." He ducks his head and there's an awkward silence—all sorts of thoughts and feelings are swimming in that space—like, is Ben asking me out? Is it crazy to think that maybe I would come back here?

Ben breaks the silence. "What's a Clem dream?"

Stu arrives in my mind. I wish he wouldn't. I think about how, with Stu, I felt like I had to work to hold his attention. Ben's gaze is unswerving.

"Uh," I say. "Pass."

Ben rows us to a point where the river widens. In the middle there's an island. He stills the canoe. Ady and Kate have gone in the other direction. It's so quiet.

"Why are we stopping?" I mock-whisper.

"There was a painted snipe's nest here." He guides the canoe around the edge of the island with the oar. It looks less like an island than a swampland, and is covered in grasses. Ben reaches in his bag stealthily and brings out binoculars.

"Whoa," I whisper. "You brought the big guns."

"Impressed?"

I kind of am. He looks through and then hands them over.

"Do you see him? Look along the ground—more to your right. White on his eye, white on his wing."

"I see him!"

"Can you see the eggs?"

I nod and pass the binoculars back. "The male looks after the eggs?"

"Uh-huh. And they may not even be his. The female is polyandrous."

"What's that?"

"She gets around." Ben uses the oar to push us back into the river. "But it's a good thing, because they're endangered."

My fingers skim the water. The sun is sinking and the sky is changing from blue to mauve; the winter sun is like a low fireball. "It's so beautiful here."

Ben nods. "It's pretty special. There's nowhere else I'd want to live."

"You don't feel like you're missing out, not being in the city?"

"The city makes me nervous. I don't like crowds, and I don't care about having to have the latest whatever. I like space."

I look around. I entertain the idea of living in the country. I could move here and get a job picking fruit or something. I could work and live life moment to moment. I wouldn't have to be anything but present.

"What are you thinking about?" Ben asks. "Sorry. Dumb question."

"It's okay. I was just . . ."

Ben's listening. His waiting face. I don't know why but I feel like I can talk to him.

"Did you ever feel like you *really* got it wrong?"

He smiles. "Which *it*?"

"Love." I shrug, half-smiling because I think maybe I sound stupid, but Ben's considering, his face serious.

"My dad says that matters of the heart are always complicated." He looks at me. "I don't have a whole lot of experience."

"Me, neither. I mean, I've done stuff . . . but . . . I don't think it was love. Not really."

The red rises in Ben's cheeks. "Are you . . . involved . . . with anyone now?"

I hold his gaze and shake my head.

Ben clears his throat, then changes the subject. "Is Kate okay? Do you know Oliver?"

"He's a good guy. You don't have to worry."

I get a lump in my throat because it hits me, the difference: Oliver and Kate, Stu and me. I feel like an idiot all over again. Why did I have to fall for him?

"Did Kate tell you about Iceland?" I ask.

"Uh-huh. I think," Ben says slowly, "there's some stuff about this place that's not so beautiful. Maybe everyone wants to put you in a box and stick a label on it."

"Imagine if we could just live how we wanted to live, without having to explain it or fit it to other people's expectations."

"What would you do differently?"

"I don't know. Maybe I wouldn't feel so bad about myself all the time."

"You shouldn't feel bad about yourself," Ben says. "You're great."

"How do you know?"

"I can just tell."

How do you know if a boy likes you?

Maybe because he acts interested in you. Or he asks you questions and when you answer he actually listens. Because he smiles at you shyly and ducks his head and there's no edge in his voice. Ben's looking at me like he's just given something of himself away. He pulls the oars back and we move with a sudden surge. I close my eyes for a few seconds and feel the trees, the sky, the clouds—all of it gently waving us back to the bank.

Ady

Friday, August 26

We've stayed up after everyone else is in bed to have more of Liz's plum cake, made with the preserved plums that they grow here. (Kate said, *There's always plum cake*, as though it's no big deal.) The music room is at the opposite end of the house from the bedrooms, so we don't even have to be quiet.

"It wasn't even *perfect day* week, it was *retreat, reflect* week, but we had a perfect day anyway." Clem is lying flat-out on the squashy, faded sofa, with an arm extended to scratch Berry, Kate's black lab, who is making a happy, yowling noise.

Clem was having fun with Ben today. Exactly the antidote she needed to fuck-me-but-don't-tie-me-down Stu. Kate is sitting with her back to the piano. She turns around, puts her fingers on the keyboard, reminding herself, plays the first few chords of Lou Reed's song and starts to sing it in her perfect, totally in-tune voice. We listen in awe, and then join her in our not-so-perfect voices.

Clem sings that she thought she was *someone else, someone who wouldn't throw a doughnut at her friend.* She chucks a bit of cake in my direction, and it's snap-caught mid-air by Berry.

Clem and Kate feel more like friends than my friends do because there's honesty here, and I'm not being micro-moment-judged. My friends and I have got into such a habit of doing that and it feels like being smothered. It makes you self-censor all the time, without even registering it.

The song yanks me backwards to being little. I remember thinking the orchestral swell of the music sounded "important." We're laughing now, and Kate makes us laugh more with some hammy pauses and significant looks as she plays. But when the bit about reaping and sowing starts, I start to cry without any part of me warning my eyes that it's about to happen. Clem looks mortified, her eyes shine with sympathy tears, and Kate stops playing, pats my shoulder, and says, "It's okay, Adyadelaidey. No one here but us."

"Sorry."

"Don't say that—you've had a really shit week," says Clem.

"More than you know." I stand up, and sit back down. Where am I going to go? "My dad's gone to rehab. For six months."

"What's his . . . ?" asks Clem.

"Alcohol. And cocaine."

"So, that's . . . good?" Kate offers. "He's getting some help."

"Yeah, I guess."

"Has it been bad living with him?" Clem gives me a tissue she's fished out of her pocket and I blow my nose.

"I'm used to it. It's been there all my life. Mostly in the background. More fighting than usual lately. No money, apparently—we are in deep shit—I have to leave school at the end of term."

Berry comes over, puts her head in my lap and heaves out a big dog-breath sigh that makes me cry some more. Now I have the sobbing breathing that makes its own rhythm.

"Was I too gross—what I said about the up-the-ass post?"

"No way," says Kate, indignant.

"Is that what your friends think?" asks Clem.

"They think what I said was unfair to Rupert."

Clem snorts. "Fuck that."

"Here's what I think about them." Kate lifts emphatic double middle fingers right up at face level.

"And tough, Rupert. That rumor hurt you, not him. And you were right—it's always girls—we're always the target." Clem rolls off the sofa and sits on the floor, resting her chin on her knees. "I really want to know who PSST is."

"It's got to be someone from Basildon, working with people from a few other schools," I say. "There were plenty of Basildons at the Winter Fair who could have taken those photos of you, Clem."

"Ack—it was so crowded, we'll never know who it was." Clem stands up and stretches.

"It's true about the photos, but some of the posts have information that could only have come from inside St. Hilda's and the other girls' schools." Kate is gathering up our plates. "Who would do that?"

"If only we could turn all the hate bombs into love bombs," I say.

Kate opens the door and shoos Berry outside. "Yes, if only the world was not the world."

Kate

Saturday, August 27

Ben calls early on Saturday morning.

He tells me to call him back from the treehouse, which means he has something private to discuss and he doesn't want there to be even a chance that someone will overhear my end of the conversation.

I wrap a blanket around my pajamas, and walk quietly past Clem, careful not to wake her up. She looks like she's smiling in her sleep, but I could be imagining it. Out the back door, down the front path, I veer left onto the grass, my bare feet dodging sticks and pebbles, I climb the old wooden ladder into the gum tree.

Magpies scatter as I settle in on the wooden platform. Dad built it big enough for Ben and me and a third person, which was Mum or Dad in the old days. Ben and I still come up here to look down at the world, hidden by leaves. There's a view across the paddocks. I let myself enjoy the quiet, enjoy my breath, smoky white as it hits the air, and when I've soaked it all in, I call.

"Okay, I'm in position," I tell him, leaning my back against the trunk.

"Tell me about Clem," Ben says immediately.

This isn't unexpected, but now that Ben says it out loud, it occurs to me how complicated this is and how it could end for him. "Tricky, ethically," I say, buying myself some time to figure out the right thing to say. I'm not sure about what I owe Ben and what I owe Clem in this situation.

"No, not tricky, ethically," he says. "I was your friend prior to your friendship with Clem. The ethics are clear. Your allegiance is to me. In any case, I don't want to know anything personal about her. I just want to know if you think it's ridiculous that I'm thinking about thinking about her like that."

"Aren't you already thinking about her like that?"

"*Kate*," he says.

"She was with someone," I say. "She's not with him anymore, but it's still a recent thing. A very recent thing. So you need to be careful."

"Okay."

"You're not going to be careful, are you?"

"She's worth the chance."

"You don't take chances."

"That's how much she's worth it."

"Clem is great," I tell him. "Just know you might get hurt."

"Excellent," he says. "And what of the world of Kate?"

I lean back against the trunk of the tree, feeling the reassuring weight and the oldness of it. I fill him in on the last developments that he's missed. "I'm a disappointment to my parents, to Oliver, to all rebellious teenagers everywhere."

"You're not a disappointment to me," he says.

"Am I doing the right thing?"

"Courage is how bad you want it," he says.

"Muhammad Ali?"

"Joe Frazier. Boxer. Known for his relentless attack. How bad do you want it?" he asks.

That's the question. The problem is the answer keeps changing.

Clem

Saturday, August 27

"So this is Three Rock Hill. I don't know why they call it that—as you can see there are considerably more than three rocks in the vicinity." The four of us are walking with big sticks and Kate uses hers to highlight the abundance of consolidated mineral matter.

"It's when they gave up counting," Ben says.

We've been walking for ages, through pale grass into twilight. The rocks closest to us are huge and look like ancient faces.

"Wasn't it a volcano?" Kate asks Ben.

"Yup. Feel it. It's porous."

We walk around like we're on psychedelics, ahhing and pressing our palms against the strangely Styrofoam-y surface of the rocks. Ben lights a campfire in the gully. We share a bottle of damson gin that Kate swiped from her parents' storehouse. I can feel Ben looking at me. He likes me. I'm flattered, but . . . I don't get it. I'm wearing my slobbiest clothes and zero makeup. I'm so not scintillating—I'm feeling vulnerable, and too sad to try and hide it. Maybe Kate's talked me up. Maybe country boys are more desperate.

The night grows dark around us and the stars are just—there are so many of them—they make me feel tiny and insignificant, but they also fill me with wonder and an aching sort of joy. Beauty exists, and it has nothing to do with people. We're just silly, bumbling humans who come and go, all full of ourselves, and, really, who cares?

Kate says the gin is truth serum, so we drink and tell truths. Then Ben whispers in my ear: Do I want to take a walk? He shines his flashlight on the ground and we walk to the top of a hill, and then climb onto the biggest rock and sit cross-legged. Ben turns the flashlight off.

"So this is an important site," he tells me.

"How so?"

"A local guy, Jim Mulready used to come here on December 21st, 10:00 p.m., every year for 50 years. He'd set up camp and then he'd climb up this rock and wait."

"What was he waiting for?"

"Aliens." Ben stretches his legs out, so I stretch mine out next to his. His body feels warm next to mine. His jacket smells of woodsmoke. "Jim's dead now. He left behind a whole thesis on his theories. My dad's been lobbying to get it put in the library."

"I wonder what he thought was going to happen with the aliens."

"He thought they'd tell him how to have a more evolved existence."

"I'd come back for that," I say. "My sister says I'm primitive."

"What?"

"She's really smart."

"Book smart or life smart?"

"The first."

Ben fumbles for my hand. He finds it and holds it. I let him. "Well," he says. "Sometimes smart people can be really fucking stupid."

We sit like that, waiting. And the stars keep revealing themselves to us, and the soft wind stirs the trees. I can hear the others, not so far away. Happiness is someone to love, something to do, something to look forward to.

"I think we're too early for the aliens," Ben says finally.

"We'll have to come back. Continue Jim's work."

For a second I think that I've said the wrong thing, hitched on to his story too soon, but Ben squeezes my hand and it's like he's given me something to look forward to. Even if it never happens, right at this moment, I'm a third of the way to happy.

Ady's Wellness Journal

Saturday, August 27

That was some beautiful part of the world today, Three Rock Hill. I saw lizards and bright beetles and a wheel of waterbirds writing loops in the sky. I could see that Kate's containment and strength must come partly from knowing this part of the world, living on this land. The sky is so big. Does that make you feel little, or does it feel as though you and your world are boundless? You know this place, and nothing else can compete. Clem definitely came back from her walk with Ben looking happy. She will survive Stu. It's like the same thing that gave her the confidence to chase him will also let her outrun him until he's a tiny speck in her past. I love that about Clem—it's not that she is so sure who she is, it's that she feels free to explore who she might be. Kate knows who she is to her core, but there are things getting in the way of her claiming it. Ben seems lovely. Of course he's lovely—he's Kate's bestie. Thinking about Clem and Ben floats me over to Max Max Max . . . The thought of her has been making butterflies in my heart all week. She had a drama solo rehearsal on Thursday so we haven't seen each other since the party. It doesn't feel as though being with a girl should be a cause for announcements. Is that right? I can imagine that I might love other boys, and other girls, other times. I asked Clare what she thought about bisexuality once, unrelated. She had an opinion: surprise, surprise. She sort of said, Bye bye, binary. For gender, for sexuality, for everything.

She said lots of people can like lots of people. And could everyone please get over it and update their idea of normal. And could I leave her alone so she could get some work done.

Ady

Sunday, August 28

I wake up early to a message from Max: ✌️🌹👯🍰💐☺️👗👠🍲🍟🙏🎈🔥🐧😮👌.

I take it as a date invitation and message back: yes.

Max: *It was supposed to be hot chick, not burning penguin btw. Saturday?*

Me: *Can't, it's our formal.* 💡 *Would you come to the formal with me?*

Max: 👏👏👏😘

The other two are deep-sleep breathing, Clem cocooned in her duvet, Kate with arms thrown out. I slip into Ugg boots and puffy coat over PJs and tiptoe out to pee. I flick on the bathroom light, and I'm looking surprisingly okay for someone who is feeling mildly wrecked. Morning-messy hair is sometimes the best hair of the day; similarly hard to replicate, but also often a good look, is end-of-a-beach-day hair.

I head for the kitchen, Uggs whispering *cup of tea cup of tea cup of tea* as they walk me along paisley hall runners over dark polished floorboards. Pretty.

Kate's mother Liz has just about finished her own breakfast.

"What would you like, Ady—scrambled eggs, omelette, or pancakes?"

"Eggs, please."

The stove is a huge Aga, with double doors. This could be a movie set farm kitchen. It's perfect. There's even a blue-and-white willow pattern *and* flowery china. Exciting for me coming from the land of white china, as I do. We chat about Kate's amazing brainpower as Liz prepares the eggs, setting the bowl next to the stovetop where she slides a hunk of butter, sizzling, into the black frying pan.

"Are you taking the scholarship exam next week?"

"No, I'm not very academic." Come on, get used to it. "And, actually, I'm leaving school at the end of term."

"You haven't been expelled, have you?" She's kidding. Not imagining there's any very bad reason for me going.

"My parents owe the school too many back fees to let me stay."

"Oh, I'm sorry to hear that." Liz looks so sympathetic that my eyes well up and I almost start blubbering. But this is good practice. Find the steel. I'll have to say this lots of times.

She pours and the eggs hit the pan with a gulping hiss. "Your parents aren't alone. It'll make a huge difference to us if Kate gets a scholarship for the last two years of school. Tough times for farmers, these days . . ." She serves a soft pile of scrambled eggs on buttered toast and puts the plate in front of me.

"Okay—enjoy that. There's juice in the fridge. If anyone needs me, I'll be in the vegetable garden." She takes a bucket of scraps from the bench, pulls on Wellingtons at the door, and heads outside.

Later, when I'm reading the paper and having my hundredth cup of tea, Kate and Clem come into the kitchen. When I look up, I have a leap of intuition that the three of us are going to be friends for keeps.

Clem sits at the big table with me, while Kate rustles up teacups and bowls for them.

"Do you know yet where you'll go to school?" Clem asks.

"MCA—if I get in."

They say it at the same time: "You'll get in."

It makes all of us feel better if we can assume that.

"You'll overlap with Max for a term," says Kate. "Max is in senior year."

I've told them every single other personal thing in my life, so I take a big breath.

"Max and I—kissed—at the party. I think I really like her."

"I'm so glad. Max is lovely. And so are you." Kate fills the kettle.

"You should ask her to the formal," says Clem.

I smile. "Tick."

Kate

Sunday, August 28

I get up early again on Sunday to talk to Mum, to test if I have the courage to tell her. Since my conversation with Ben, I can't stop asking myself, How badly do I want it? The answer still hasn't arrived.

Ady is talking with Mum and Ady needs a little comfort, so I let her have that. I stand in the hallway, giving them time, listening to Mum explain how she and Dad are depending on me getting the scholarship because money is scarcer than it's ever been. She says how proud they are, and how she doesn't mean that I have to get the scholarship, that's not what she means, they'll find the money somehow, but it'll be a huge load off their minds when I do.

Ady gives nothing away. She tells Mum about the intimidating nature of my braininess, and Mum laughs and admits she's been intimidated by me since I was about two. "There's a genius a few generations back on her father's side, and I'm pretty sure that's where it comes from."

I want to go into the kitchen, sit next to Mum, and be that girl who had such firm and achievable ambitions, but I can't. I want to go back to my bedroom and reply to Oliver and tell him that I've told my parents everything, but I can't do that, either. So I just stand here on the warm floor, in my bare feet, in a small island of sun, until it moves into shadow.

I hear my phone ringing from my room, and I run back to answer it before it wakes up Clem.

"So are you having fun?" Iris asks, sounding so sick and lonely that I feel like I need to give her something. I tell her I wish she could have been here. "We've basically spent the time cheering up Ady. There's bad stuff going on with her family. She might not even be able to come back to school."

"That sucks," Iris says after I've explained, and I'm reminded again why I like Iris. She's harsh on the surface, but not underneath. In some ways, she's not unlike Ady.

"So we'll be back soon," I say.

Later, lying with Clem and Ady near the river, after we've exhausted the subjects of Ben and Oliver and Max, I ask Clem about Iris and why they don't get along.

"We did a long time ago," Clem says. "We do still, actually, in some ways. It's hard being a twin." She takes a piece of grass and splits it down the center with her nail, then shows it to us, as if she can't put into words what it's like.

Clem

Sunday, August 28

On the train on the way back to Melbourne, a woman comes and sits in our empty fourth seat. She has rings on every finger and a hacking cough and home hair dye.

"You know, girls," she rasps, "Mercury is in retrograde."

We look at her blankly. She explains that when Mercury is in retrograde the world falls into ominous chaos and we can't expect any gifts or resolutions until after October. At the next stop the woman stands up to leave.

"Hang on," she says. "Stay strong."

As the train moves from country green to urban grit, we count the ways of Mercury in retrograde: Ady's dad and Rupertgate; Stu's sleaze, my swim-fail, my cold war with Iris; for Kate, it's all about pressure.

We decide we're going to counteract it and state what we want to happen.

Me: "I want to get over Stu, and get along with Iris."

Kate: "I want Iceland and I want my parents to be okay with it."

Ady: "I just want to know that, whatever happens, I can handle it."

Ady puts her thumb out and Kate presses hers against it. I bring mine into the mix, like we did at the first wellness class—we laugh at our hokey secret handshake.

When we get to Southern Cross, we're exhausted, like we've traveled through time—and maybe we have, emotionally. We catch the tram back to St. Hilda's; Ady leaves at the gate. Everything is normal, but everything is different. Walking up to the dorms, Kate says, "It's quiet . . . too quiet."

Old Joy lets us in, treating me to her jowliest scowl. "Call your parents, Clem. Pronto."

I hightail it to my room. Jinx is still at her aunt's. My phone is plugged in and waiting for me. There are two missed calls from Stu, and a bunch of texts from Mum and Dad. I check the time, then dial their number. I have my line all ready, about how I don't want to be a competitive swimmer, how I don't want it enough, and I just want to explore other activities, but I soon realize they're freaking out about something else altogether.

They pass the phone and it's hard to keep up.

Mum: "You've got some explaining to do."

Dad: "Who is this Stu person. What have you been doing?"

Iris told. I can't believe it.

Me: "He's no one. He's just a joke."

Mum: "Tell me why we shouldn't get on a plane right now and sort this out."

Dad: "What school allows vulnerable girls to roam the streets, to be picked up by ne'er-do-wells?"

Ne'er-do-wells!

"Calm down, Dad. Whatever Iris said, she's lying. Don't call the school."

"If you think you can take this *person* to your formal, think again. No formal, Clem. You're not going to Canberra, either."

"I know I'm not going to Canberra!"

There is silence. Then I'm crying.

Dad gets all uncomfortable. "I'll pass you back to your mother."

"Clem?" Mum says. "What's happening?"

And I start to feel clear, and then I start to talk. I tell her I had a crush, but it wasn't as big as Iris tells it, and I tell her about my bathing suit being too tight, and how I hadn't been enjoying swimming the way I used to. I tell her I've lost my competitive edge, but I don't miss it. I tell her I also felt lost at St. Hilda's, but I don't anymore, and if everyone would just give me a chance, things could be good again. I tell her I'll be honest from now on.

After I hang up, I get a sense of something. Iris! I tiptoe to my door and yank it open—and sure enough she's there, caught in the act. She lets out a little *meep* and starts running back to her room. I call after her with a bounty hunter's relish, "You'd *better* run!"

But I'm too tired to deal with her now. She can wait until tomorrow.

Ady's Wellness Journal

Sunday, August 28, late

My MCA interview is on Thursday. Preparing for a portfolio presentation is a terrifying pleasure. I'll have to remember to breathe slowly. I could easily hyperventilate with excitement talking about my work. I can bring up to six pieces in any stage of planning or completion. It's a specially convened interview because I have to change schools after the third quarter.

I'm going to include the finished birdie cardigan with a piece of writing about the idea of share-wear-ware, something I am planning to do at least once every year. A special piece released into the wild. My influences for the garment itself include a dream of being a bird, an intense day with some inspiring Jean-Paul Gaultier images, falling in love with some wavering black and white lines, and thinking about the differences between black and white, and color. A fragile line, a line that wobbles to find itself, must be one of the most beautiful things in the world. And the birdie stripes have that fragility, created by varying the wool ply and the number of rows in the stripes.

I think I'll include my nine-piece, zip-apart vest/jacket/coat. I made it from some heavy indigo cotton that I washed 20 times before I cut and sewed it. Nearly drove my mother nuts. It bled for at least 10 washes. It's gorgeously strong and soft. And it all zips apart so you can wear it any way you like. It was a one-sleever for a while, which I was totally into, but then I found the lost sleeve. Charlie had been using it, propped up with Legos, as a train tunnel.

I can't leave out now you see me: escape-wear for parties; I have the garment and the concept. Primavera has to go in—the outfit I imagined for Kate. Now that we're friends I'm going to make it for her one day, but for the interview I'll just have the concept drawings and some tearsheets of influences.

So much to choose from for the last two pieces—and perhaps time to design something completely new? Would it be cheating to wear something I'm not formally presenting? No, I don't think so. I have to calm down. I cannot blow this interview. Two a.m. Sleep time. More planning and drawing tomorrow.

WEEK 8

MAPS, TAKING STOCK

Wellness

Monday, August 29
Dr. Peter Malik

Week 8: Personal Geography

Provocation

A map is not the territory it represents.

—Alfred Korzybski

Getting lost was not a matter of geography so much as identity, a passionate desire, even an urgent need, to become no one and anyone, to shake off the shackles that remind you who you are, who others think you are.

—Rebecca Solnit, *A Field Guide to Getting Lost*

Points for Discussion/Reflection

Most people are familiar with the idea of maps as representations of geographical information, but map making can tell our personal stories and help us understand the world around us and our place within it.

- Are you a planner?
- What do you gain from looking ahead?
- What do you gain from looking back?
- Can you think of a time where being lost turned out to be a positive thing?

Task

“Map Yourself”

Make a map that is not for directions but is a work of art and inspired imagination. Use writing, photography, and/or collage, and use memory and emotional landmarks to reveal a journey, past or present.

Clem

Monday, August 29

How are we traveling? Malik asks. But he's not really asking. That is, he's not expecting us to answer. The way of wellness is to let things percolate. Think now, talk later. He walks around the room, weaving through the beanbag islands. Half the class is absent because of the uber-flu—Iris is back, though. She looks pale and depressed. A few times I've caught her looking at me beseechingly. She even left me a note, apologizing, but it'll take more than that to win me over. I still can't believe she told Mum and Dad about Stu. Last night I couldn't sleep. I was picturing interrogation, a doctor's exam, my relocation to a school for wayward girls. I feel Iris's eyes on me. I give her the finger.

Malik is talking about "personal geography"—journeys big and small. He puts a memory map up on the board. It's like a map of his childhood. He talks us through each marker on the map, and each one stands for a story.

"What I want you to do is make your own map. It can be a map of last year or last week, or your life to date—go back as far as you want. Put down all your defining moments—the 'moments of truth'—*el momento de la verdad*—where things changed and put you on a new or different path. As we explore our life continuum, notice that we move through good and bad. We can't map the future, and that can make us worry about all the little possibilities, particularly negative ones. But today's map—*this*—can be both a record of your past, and a tool for the future, proof that you can get over things, through things."

"So . . ." Malik moves up to the front of the room, his shadow blocking the map. "What are *your* markers? What kind of things could you encounter on a map of your history?"

No one says anything. Then Tash puts her hand up. "Success and failure?"

"Right," Malik says. "But be specific. Traditionally, on a geographical map, we have rivers . . ." He draws squiggly lines on the board. "Train tracks, roads, churches, hospitals . . . So think about what kind of markers you might encounter in *psychological* terrain."

"Heartbreak." I say this out loud, without thinking.

Malik ignores the murmurs and draws a heart with a crack in it. And the heat of Iris's stare is too much. I turn to look at her. *Die*, I mouth.

Malik sets us up with butcher paper and colored markers. He tells us to get comfortable. We're going to start our maps in class, but he hopes we'll keep going outside class.

"Once, people used to imagine sea monsters in the unmapped

areas—we still do this now; we have a fear of the unknown. The future is the great unknown, the 'unmapped perhaps.'"

We get started. My life is just a line marked with situations that have arisen from external factors. But maybe that's Malik's point; we can't control anything but our responses. When Mum and Dad made their big announcement at the end of last year, what could I have done? The option of staying at our old school didn't exist. If it had, this whole year would have been different. I chose *not* to share a room with Iris, but what if I'd gone the other way? Would I have even made any friends? Then there was swimming and Stu. He gave me his number, but I was the one who called it. I said yes and yes and yes. My choices did not lead to roses and happily ever after, but major sads—yet even this is changing. I can see from my map how one thing leads to another, how if I hadn't found out about Stu, then I wouldn't have gone to Kate's, and I wouldn't have met Ben . . . and he's already called me. He told me I was pretty, said he was having trouble thinking about anything else. I asked him for a photo and in the one he sent he's fully clothed, facing the camera and smiling.

My symbols are a broken heart (for Stu); a wild wind (for the moments where life went south or north or east or west); I have a lightning bolt marking the swim disaster, but then I add a smiley face, because, really, it was that day that led to friendship with Ady and Kate. For our weekend trip I put three smiley faces on a train. For Ben I draw a little spaceship that has a flight path into the future.

I draw my symbols in a tiny hand because this stuff is private. It's how I really feel. After a while, I look up to see that Iris isn't drawing at all. In spite of everything, I feel sorry for her. She's crushing on a guy who doesn't even notice her. She doesn't have any mementoes of her own; she just has a green eye on everyone else's.

After wellness, I blow off history and go to my room. Jinx is training so I have some uninterrupted me-time. I delete all my photos of Stu. I look at each one for a long time before I delete it. I am building up to there being nothing more of him. He hasn't called or texted since the weekend. He doesn't know what I know. I wonder if he'd care. I can't believe that a week ago I was picturing us in our finery at the formal, imagining it like a fuck-you to anyone who ever laughed at me or called me fat. In my fantasy I looked amazing and Stu's hair was the perfect storm. We stayed at the formal just long enough for everyone to see and then we left for—

But where would we have gone?

There was never anywhere to go.

And now the formal approaches and I don't even have a pity date. I think I'll go with Jinx.

The door opens. I look up, expecting Jinx, but it's Iris.

"Go away," I say.

But she just comes closer. She goes to Jinx's bed, straightens the already straight cover and sits down.

"Heartbreak?"

"How could you tell Mum and Dad about Stu? They want to tell Gaffa. I'll probably get expelled."

"I called them back. I told them I made it up. I told them I was just . . ."

I look at her.

"Jealous," she finishes. She gets up and comes to sit next to me on my bed.

"There's nothing to be jealous of," I say. "It's over."

"What happened?"

"What's the point of me even telling you? You don't get it. You don't know what it's like. You've never even had a boyfriend."

I see the hurt crash on her face and I feel bad for a second, but then I go on, poking my finger in the wound, hooking it around the lip, chucking in salt and capsicum spray.

"I'll bet you've never even kissed a guy."

"I have."

"Who?"

"Theo."

"Theo!" I laugh. "Well, I don't know how you managed to do it for any amount of time, seeing as you're both such mouth-breathers."

"I only came here because I was worried about you."

"No, you didn't. You just wanted to feel good about yourself. And the only way you get to feel good about yourself is when you're watching someone else feel like shit. Well, you're too late. I was heartbroken, but I've decided to get over it. I liked a boy. I thought we were exclusive. We weren't. Map that—it's a short fucking line."

"Oh," Iris says quietly. She's sitting with her hands in her lap, and looking at something—the jar of plum jam Kate's mum gave us. She picks it up and turns it over in her hand.

"I'm glad you were sick this weekend," I say suddenly. "We

would have had to explain everything to you because you're such a freak. You act like you're smarter than everyone, but you're just a lonely loser." I stop, my mouth tastes bitter. Iris's face—I think I've gone too far.

"Friend-stealer!" she hisses.

She picks up the jam jar, and throws it hard against the wall. The glass smashes and jam goes everywhere. Iris looks stricken, then she turns and stomps out, slamming the door behind her. My tears come without warning. I full-on sob. I don't even know why I'm crying. *Again*. Is this me now? I sob into the scarf I accidentally stole from Stu and, even though it's gross, I blow my nose on it, too.

PSST

ADY ROSENTHAL, THE MOST UP HERSELF OF THE WHOLE 10TH GRADE ST. HILDARIAN BITCH BRIGADE, IS FINALLY BEING PUT IN HER PLACE. ABOUT TIME.

1. Her best friend Tash and ex Rupert are now an item. Suck on that, bitch
2. Her father is a cokehead drunk now in rehab—apparently he said, yes, yes, yes, but not before he lost the family money
3. So her family is headed for bankruptcy and she's leaving St. Hilda's. No great loss. Enjoy slumming it in public school land, precious
4. She's a dyke
5. Isn't that about enough to make her the biggest loser?

B@rnieboy: laughing fit to bust. couldn't happen to a bigger bitch
sufferingsuffragette: Ady is nice and not responsible for the behavior of her parents
hungryjackoff: Don't mind watching her eat some pussy tho—3way?
Feminightmare: A friendly reminder that sex between women does not exist as entertainment for boys. Enjoy your next "3way" though, which I expect will be you, a fizzy drink and a packet of chips.

load 220 more comments

Ady's Wellness Journal

Tuesday, August 30

Just when I felt so hopeful and happy about my portfolio preparation . . . Why does PSST hate me so much? I can't even put my head in the space where I'd want to do something so nasty to another human.

My heart has been hammering since I read the post last night. I'm doing Malik breathing—in one, two, three; out one, two, three—imagining the soft hiss of a wave on the shore. It works, eventually.

Wellness class has never been more uncannily relevant. Malik suggests, "Map yourself." Where am I? Where do I want to be? How will I get there? Malik loves a metaphor. The signposts I've missed. The detours. The crossroads. The traps. I'm ready to shake off some shackles, to let myself get lost. I want to be an explorer. I think I am one. But how do I own my map? How do I situate myself when something like PSST can come along and yank me out of my space and put me somewhere I don't want to be?

In one, two, three; out one, two, three.

How will I get by without hearing Malik's calm and hopeful introductions to the week's themes. Lightbulb! He has written a freaking book. If it's on audio, I can get it and have pocket pal Malik with me whenever I need help finding my calm space.

Meanwhile, I reject PSST invading my territory. I'll make my map a coded wonderland, using only my bare hands, optimism, and large sheets of premium-grade watercolor paper (there's loads of it in the school art room). My map is in the form of an old-fashioned spinning clothesline, pegged all over with significant outfits from my past. The point of view is from directly overhead, clothes flying out flat from every direction, so it forms a geometric pattern. As usual, I don't know which way is north, but I know the direction of beauty.

Ady

Tuesday, August 30

Walking into homeroom, there's a gentle crackling, the slightest change in atmospheric pressure, but I feel it. Honestly? They love to see someone fall. Can it really be my turn to get kicked again?

Tash rushes up, excited, though trying not to be too rabid. You never want to look eager for blood. "Babe, I didn't know it was *that* bad. You should have told me."

"You're really leaving school?" Lola wants to know. "Isn't that a bit extreme?"

Tell me about it.

"Can't your gram bail you out?" Bec asks.

They're speaking in important overlapping whispers to acknowledge the disgrace and ensure that everyone will look our way.

I answer each in turn. "It is. I am. Extreme is the new black in our family: All the grown-ups have to act like grown-ups. That means no more bailing out by Gram."

I stand up. "This time it really is true. The bottomfeeders got their facts right. I am in the middle of a family crisis. I am leaving the school. My father is in rehab. I am seeing a girl: early days. That is all. No flowers by request. Any queries can be directed to my press secretary."

I'm acting super nonchalant. What other way is there to be at a time like this? Inside, I'm shuddering and crumbling. Was I wrong about my friends being above all the PSST bullshit? Could Tash have been dripping poison on me all this time?

Only they—and Clem and Kate—knew about most of this stuff. Surely those guys wouldn't have blabbed, would they? I try to think who else, but only they knew about me and Max . . .

But here they are, their faces looking the way I'm not letting myself look. Sad and worried. Kate holding her hand out, touching my shoulder. The large silence. Clem growling, "What are you all staring at? Announcement over."

Tash walks in front of them. "Come on, Ady, we really need to debrief. A girl? What girl?"

I stand with Kate and Clem. "No time for debriefs—we'll catch up later."

I turn away—how right that feels—and walk to English with my thumb-compatibles. Maybe it was one of Clare's friends doing the blabbing about my dad. It could be any kid in the school whose mother is a friend of my mother. There's no real possibility of containing information anymore. That's not the way things work now that we are living in the hate days. Now, because someone anonymous posted this stuff on PSST, the whole world knows all the new and private things about me before I'm even used to them myself, and there's not a single thing I can do about it.

I'm in a pretty significant low here. Malik comes to mind. Wellness wisdom. *An anonymous foe is beneath contempt. Not worthy of your attention.* True, but an anonymous foe can still mess things up, and you have to deal with that.

"It's just—everything at once," I say, tears threatening. I breathe them away.

"I know," says Kate.

"How would they know about me and Max?"

Clem gives me a shoulder squeeze. "It's probably just a random insult—in their fucked-up view of the world."

"We're going to deal with the haters," says Kate. "This is shitting me to death."

Clem

Tuesday, August 30

Laundromat, 4 pm?

The easiest thing would be not to go, but I can't help it. I have to see him. I need to say something—if he's sorry, well, I'm not going to go back with him, but maybe I can believe he's a good guy. If he's not, at least I'll *know*. I'll know that all the things I thought were good were actually bad. All the things I thought were romantic were actually sleazy.

Ady says life's not black and white like that. "And I should know."

I slouch from class to class feeling drained. It's not just about Stu; it's Iris. I haven't seen her since our fight. I keep going over what I said to her. I've been trying to map back to the start of our troubles, and I think it might be me. I might be the evil twin. I was the one who wanted to move away, to separate, cut the cord, whatever.

When the last bell rings, I check in with Kate.

"Seen Iris?"

"Not since this morning."

"How was she? We had a fight."

"Come to think of it, she was kind of quiet—I thought it was just because she missed out on the weekend. Don't worry. She's pretty thick-skinned."

"I don't know. I used to think she was, but I don't know if she is."

Kate tilts her head at me. "How are *you*?"

"Stu texted me. He wants to meet."

"I hope you told him to fuck off."

I don't say anything.

"Clem," Kate says warningly.

"It's okay. It's just for closure."

She's quiet and I know she's thinking about Ben. I have a flash of him rowing. Feel again the silent warmth of his leg against mine on the rock.

"Ben called me."

"I know. He told me he was going to." Kate frowns.

"What?"

"He's my best friend, so don't play him."

"I'm not going to play him. I like him."

"Good," Kate says.

"Great," I shout. Then we laugh.

The laundromat windows are so fogged up that at first I don't see Stu. I feel a bit relieved—maybe I don't have to do this—but then I see him over by the detergent dispenser. When I push the door open, I am assailed by laundry smells: lint, damp socks, eucalyptus wool wash. I'll associate these smells with Stu forever now.

He tips the detergent into the washer and shoves the coins in. He hasn't seen me yet. His face is moody/bored/beautiful. He's set up at the table, the local paper is open, and the brown paper bag with the egg-and-bacon sandwich is waiting for us.

I clear my throat.

When Stu sees me, he looks so happy I could forget everything. Except I can't.

"Where have you been?" He steps forward to kiss me and I step back.

He tries again and I dodge him.

He pauses, reaches past me for the brown paper bag and takes half of the sandwich out. He bites into it and watches me.

"Are you mad at me?"

I nod, once.

"Want to tell me why?"

I feel so anxious. My stomach in knots. I also feel angry. Hurt. Embarrassed.

He searches my face. Then has another bite of his sandwich.

I start, "The other night, at the Blue House, I looked at your phone."

There is a pause and then his shoulders drop a little.

"Zaftig," he says, like he's telling me off.

"I saw your messages, and your pictures."

"Okay." He looks uncomfortable, but not terribly. Not as much as I wanted him to. And he only looks that way for a second before shoring up.

He points his sandwich at me. "We never said we were exclusive."

"I didn't think we had to say it."

"See, that's 'cause you're young." He finishes eating and wipes his hands on his jeans. Then he tries to hug me, but I push his shoulder, hard.

"Easy!" He's half-laughing.

"I thought you *liked* me," I say.

"I do like you. I like a lot of girls." He smiles. "I'm nineteen. I live in the moment. What—did you think we were going to get married?"

"No." I can feel my face burning, because what *did* I think?

I thought I was special.

Stu dips his head, and I imagine that he thinks he's being gentlemanly. "I apologize," he says, straight-faced. "We should have had a conversation about that."

I stare at him and feel myself go hard-boiled.

"Zaftig—"

"Don't call me that."

Stu sniffs and clucks his tongue. "Fine. You're upset."

I get his scarf out of my bag and hand it over.

"Why thank you," he says, acting charmed.

"It's got snot on it."

He nods, smiling, sarcastic. "Great."

I stare at him and he doesn't look so beautiful. He looks

petulant and douchey. I stare until his mask cracks and then I take a mental picture—CLICK—I get the shimmer of regret, the bead of recognition of shady behavior. Then I take my half of the sandwich, bite into it, and leave.

Kate

Thursday, September 1

I want the map of my life to be drawn by me, but the truth is, everyone writes on it. It's not just my map. My personal geography is connected to your personal geography. We're all intersecting.

Later, after I've finished my junior and senior years, I can go to Iceland. After I've finished my science degree, I can study music the way I want to study it. I know I'm lying. I won't go to Iceland, but it makes me feel better to tell myself I'll go back and live that other life.

This is what I need to tell Oliver.

I'll explain that my parents need me.

I'll explain that at some point in the future I will go to Iceland, but it can't be now. At this moment on my map I have to be here, at St. Hilda's, using the scholarship that I hope I haven't lost the chance to get.

It makes sense in my head, but when I phone to tell him, the words won't come.

He starts talking, telling me again that he's sure we're going to win. "No pressure because if we don't win it doesn't matter. But, Kate, I think we might. I mean, I think it's possible."

All things are possible. And all things aren't.

My thoughts aren't entirely making sense.

It's been a long week. I've spent it worrying about Ady and staying up late trying to work out who runs PSST. Because when I saw how hurt Ady was after the last post, I decided enough is enough. The people running it are going down if it's the last thing I do.

"There's something wrong," Oliver says.

"I want to crack PSST. I hate it when there's a problem I can't solve."

"You've been strange all week. Tell me," he says.

It all comes out—not in any logical order. Just out: that I can't do the audition because my parents need me and I messed up the date of the scholarship exam and I know I'm a disappointment. "I'm a total fuck-up."

He doesn't agree, but he doesn't disagree.

"I've ruined it for you," I say.

He still doesn't speak. I can hear him swiveling on his chair. I wish I'd told him in person and not on the phone, so I could explain this better.

Finally he speaks. "Can I use the looping tracks?"

"Yes," I say.

I offer him half the entry fee, and he says, "Thank you."

And then, in a formal way that breaks my heart, he says, "Goodbye."

"He didn't yell," I say to Iris, who wants to know why I'm so upset. She puts her arms around my shoulders and I start crying.

"What did he say?" she asks.

"Nothing," I tell her. "He asked if he could use the looping tracks."

"Did you want him to yell?"

I wonder if I did. I wonder if what I really wanted was for Oliver to make me feel so bad that I chose the audition.

"It's for the best," Iris says, and she takes out her books and thumps them with her fist. "Let's cram."

Her advice is to focus on the scholarship, if that's my choice, and it is my choice, so I cram. I cram until my eyes feel like they're bleeding. I drink so much caffeine I jump every time someone closes a door in the dorms.

Iris is coffee jumpy, too. Every time there's a knock at the door she looks worried. Eventually, she cracks and tells me she had a fight with Clem on Monday. "She didn't say anything?"

"She didn't tell me what it was about."

"I did something awful," she admits, but that's all she'll say. She goes back to the books, and I do, too.

Around midnight, we call time-out and get ready for bed.

"Will you have a coffee with me before the exam?" she asks. "For luck?"

"It's on me," I tell her. "It's the least I can do."

"You're the smartest person I know," Iris says. "You'll make it."

We turn off the light eventually. I can't sleep, though, and Iris can't, either.

"Usually you sleep no matter what."

"I feel bad about Clem," she says. "And I'm nervous."

"You'll get a scholarship. You've worked so hard."

"Did you read that quote, from the wellness sheet?" Iris never mentions wellness. She thinks it's a waste of time. "The one about getting lost and shaking off the shackles that remind you who you are?"

"Do you want to talk?"

"I'm fine," Iris says. "I'm just tired."

We lie here awake, in the dark.

Ady

Thursday, September 1

MCA is in West Melbourne; it's a government school, no fees, but entry is by audition for the performance students and portfolio presentation for the visual arts students. You do the standard curriculum, too, but it fits around the arts stuff, which gets more priority than in a regular school.

This, miraculously, could make moving schools a good thing. And it's Max's school. She's about to graduate at the end of next term, which is basically 90 percent exams, so it's not like we'd cross paths much—and that's better when you're going out with someone, we agree.

Oh my god, please let me get in.

The school itself is a six-story Brutalist building from the early 1970s. So. Cool. It looks more like an office block than a school, to be honest, but over the road there's a shaded park where students go to lie on the grass and stare at the sky, eat lunch, commune with nature, and get inspired to new heights of artsiness, presumably, before returning to the brute.

Art studio time is designed with integration between disciplines, so there'd be a chance for me to work on set and costume design with theater arts students, and do some filmmaking as well as printmaking and photography. I tumble out of the portfolio presentation interview happy-drunk like an overpollinated bee into a world of bigger possibility, brimming with all the next things I might do.

"They liked my *power pocket dress*, too," I tell Max. It's a perfectly simple dress, completely covered in different-sized pockets. You don't even need a bag at all when you wear it. It's actually hyperconvenient. You do need to remember which pocket you've put your transit card in, though. But that's another story, from another day—Tuesday, actually—involving two very rude tram inspectors. I did find it, eventually.

Max slips her hand into mine. "Of course they liked it. It's genius."

"I didn't even need to explain the context of women and not enough pockets; they were all *aha, very witty, empowering* about it." Their response merged "flattering" and "just as well," seeing as I only last week found out about the feminist implications of the tragic absence of pockets in women's clothes—from Clare, natch.

"They said they'd let me know within a few days. What if I don't get in?"

"You were in there for quite a while." Max is smiling. "I take that as a good sign."

Clem's Wellness Journal

Friday, September 2

I've just come back from a Feminist Collective meeting. We watched TED talks about cyber-mobs and online jerkery. And then we watched one about body shaming. The woman presenting said, "So what if someone calls you fat? There's nothing wrong with being fat." And when I think about it, she's absolutely right.

After the TED talks, we discussed the F-word. How some women don't want to call themselves feminists because they think it makes them unattractive. "Fuck that!" Jinx said, and everyone started talking at once.

"Maybe we need a new word?"

"We need a new something. Something has to change."

"All hail the suffering suffragettes!"

I wish Kate and Ady had been there. They would have agreed. Looking around the room, I couldn't help thinking, If we're all on the same page, isn't that enough to change things?

When we'd finished the nachos and our tongues were tired from talking, Lin, one of the Feminist Collective organizers, suggested we get creative about the formal. "Let's gender-flip it! Or, go in costume." The meeting ended with a plan to raid the drama department's costume bins tomorrow.

And now, I can't sleep for giggling. I realize that I've been unconsciously stressed about the formal, about looking "right," about not wanting to be Fat Clam, but wanting to be Zaftig—because even if Stu is a dick, I can still use his word. I don't want to have to regret everything.

Kate

Friday, September 2

I wake up exhausted because I studied late and then I couldn't sleep. I kept thinking about Frances Carter, how she walked into the auditorium that day, all poise and certainty. I lie in bed listening to her music—the beauty and strangeness of it. At least we don't have orchestra this morning, so I don't have to see Oliver.

I cram in as much study as I can between classes. Iris and I look over notes at lunch, and we study at night. She spends time helping me catch up when she should be going over her own work, and I want Clem to see this side of her. The side that doesn't say *I told you so,* but sits with you late at night and explains the calculus problem you don't understand and calmly reassures you that you're doing the right thing, when every part of you screams that you're not.

Our study plan is to work until midnight, then go to bed so we have at least seven hours' sleep. It's about 15 minutes to midnight and we're finishing up a practice exam on our computers, when there's a hesitant knock on the door.

I stop the clock and Iris answers it. We both stare at Oliver in disbelief. My eyes cannot comprehend that he is here, in the dorms.

"Hello," he says. "Please invite me in. I'm scared senseless I'll get caught."

"God, yes, sorry, yes." I pull him inside. "How did you get here?"

"I used the portal. Came across school grounds in the dark. You've been very brave doing that all this time."

"He needs to go or we're both expelled," Iris says.

"Can we have two minutes alone? Go to the bathroom and when you come back, he'll be gone."

"I don't need to go to the bathroom. I need to do my practice exam."

Oliver is holding my hand now. I'm not sure when he picked it up, but I know that neither of us is letting go until he says what he came to say.

"Please, Iris," Oliver says, and she makes a big deal of putting on her robe and leaving.

"Ten minutes," she says, which is so incredibly nice of her. I didn't think she'd give us two.

As soon as she's gone, Oliver kisses me. A full-on, fantastic kiss. A kiss that makes me wish Iris weren't such a stickler for time and we were in his bedroom and the kiss could lead to other things.

"Sorry," he says after. "I needed to do that first. I should have done that before. Earlier. The other day. When you told me. Because, the truth is, I might win because of our work, our song.

I wouldn't have had a real chance without you, hard as that is for me to admit. And you're not a total fuck-up. Not even close. I've met some fuck-ups and you're nothing like them. In fact, when it comes to fucking up, you're a complete amateur."

"Thank you."

"You're welcome. And I get the whole parent thing. I completely understand. I got all worked up because I like you. I really like you."

"It's mutual."

"Excellent. That's really very excellent. Look. I've got a speech here ready, and I feel I need to read it to you, but I wanted to say all that before so you know that, whatever you decide, I'm still with you."

He takes out the paper and starts reading. *"But you have to decide, Kate.* You *have to decide. I wasn't angry because you chose the scholarship exam. I was angry because you seemed to be waiting for me to convince you to choose music. I spoke to Frances Carter that day she came. And she said it wasn't easy to choose music. She had other choices.* The arts are a bitch—they don't pay, *she said.* People think you should do something sensible. *I told her about my mum in the orchestra and she was impressed because that hardly ever happens. But I want to take a risk. I think you want to take a risk, too. But you can't wait for someone to tell you to take a risk. That's the nature of risks: You have to decide to take them.*

"So, to conclude: I really hope you choose the Iceland audition, but that's entirely up to you. And if you change your mind—I mean, at the last minute—I've taken the liberty of mapping out a clear flight path from here to the audition. I'll show you."

He goes to Iris's computer and I sit next to him, a part of me knowing I might need that flight path. I'm thinking about the kiss and risks and Frances Carter, when the screen comes alive and we're looking at Iris's emails. Oliver's about to open Safari, but I catch sight of the subject line of the latest one. The sender is PSST. The subject GFED IS NOW FOLLOWING YOU.

Oliver lets out a long low whistle.

I motion for him to move and lean against the door in case Iris comes back. Why is Iris getting emails from PSST? I type quickly and do a search for other emails, hoping to find proof that it's not her. A heap of PSST emails come up.

"She's got something to do with it," Oliver says.

"She wouldn't do that," I say, thinking about all the terrible things that have been posted. About Ady. About me. About her sister.

I can't read any further because there's a loud rap on the door.

"Under the bed," I whisper to Oliver.

When he's hidden, I open the door, yawning.

"Library," Old Joy says. "No phones. Leave it all here."

She keeps walking and knocking. Angela from next door tells me there's a boy on the floor. "When we're in the library, they'll check the rooms."

"Fuck," Oliver says from under the bed.

Angela looks at me and seems impressed. "We need to get him to the stairs," she says, and grabs a blanket off my bed. "Get between us," she tells Oliver, and together we walk, huddled around Oliver, all of us covered in the blanket.

I can barely breathe because I'm expecting Old Joy to jump out of a doorway at any second. Some girls notice the extra boy feet between us, but there's a code, so they all look out for us, and somehow we get him to the stairs.

"Think about Saturday," he says. "Find your flight path."

He gives me the blanket. And he's gone.

Iris stands next to me in the library, so I can't let Clem know what I've discovered. I don't have my phone, so there's nothing I can do except give Clem looks that she clearly can't decipher.

In hindsight, I guess it's not unbelievable that it's Iris. She hates the popular crowd. She knew about Ady because I told her. She's good technically, and she's a great listener. I still can't believe it, though. Those posts were so awful.

I look over at her, moving her feet around in the cold, and try to see that meanness in her. She looks over at me and smiles.

Who are you? I wonder.

Clem

Friday, September 2

It's just past midnight and I'm lying in bed listening to Jinx—she's snoring in spite of her nose clip (we thought it might help). I'm contemplating throwing things at her, or just smothering her with a pillow, when someone bangs on the door and hisses, "Old Joy's on the beat."

I sit up and switch on my lamp.

Jinx bolts upright and whips off her nose clip. "What's going on?"

"I don't know."

She listens for a moment and her eyes go wide. "It's a round-up!"

She jumps out of bed and pulls her sweater and tracksuit on. She shoves her feet into slipper-socks. I put my robe on and open the door. Girls are whizzing past, faces rippling with excitement. Jinx and I slip into the stream.

I grab Lainie's arm. "Where are we supposed to be going?"

"Library."

Jinx spills as we trot. "Last year there was a bomb threat—they took it seriously because, you know, the world. Turned out to be a lame Basildon douche trying to get back at his ex."

"It could be a fire. It could just be a drill."

"I heard it's a BIB," a seventh grader says in a stage whisper.

"Boy in bed." Jinx's eyes glaze over for a second. "Lucky dog."

I'm trying to imagine which of the boarders would be mad enough to try to smuggle in some salami. It never crossed my mind to try to get Stu in, even though it was possible—the thought of him laying eyes on all the trappings of the dorms was way too creepy. At least I don't have to worry about that anymore.

When we reach the library, we're sorted into years and houses. Iris and Kate are the last to come in. Indra Prahna, Acacia House captain, steps in as Old Joy's proxy.

"It's been reported that there is a male on the grounds. Ms. Reichl's checking the rooms. Anyone got anything they want to confess?"

"I wish!" Someone groans and we laugh.

Iris and Kate look strange. Their body language is out of whack. They're standing next to each other, but Kate's body is aimed at the door, while Iris has the same look on her face that our dog Bananafish used to get when we'd caught him with the empty butter container. Kate catches my eye. She holds her palm out and pokes her finger in it, in Iris's direction. Whatever that means. I shrug, but then Iris turns to say something and Kate turns her hands to fists.

Old Joy takes a while. We're all wondering if she's caught the "male."

"What happens next?" I ask Jinx. "Does she bring him in here so we can all have a turn?"

Jinx looks at me in shock. "Clem!"

"I'm *joking*."

She grins.

We sit, we wait. Indra patrols, in her element. Kate and Iris continue their weird non-standoff. I wonder if they've had a fight. I feel something tugging at my pants leg and look down to see a hand slide me a slip of paper. The passer of the note—an eighth grader who looks like she'd rather be anything but—gives me a covert smile to go with it.

I open the note surreptitiously.

Something BIG. Come to my room tomorrow, early as poss. Kate.

What's big? Does this mean the BIB was Oliver? That would explain Iris's grim face. But if it had been Oliver, surely Kate would have been smiling, or at least looking flushed and tousled. I stare at Kate and she gives me meaningful undecipherable looks.

We stay rounded up for about 10 minutes. When Old Joy comes back, there's this communal effort not to laugh—I can feel it practically holding the room together. She has her sleep mask holding her hair up, and two bits of tape at her temples—I think it might be some kind of old-fashioned wrinkle corrective. Her boobs, usually formidable, are unrestrained, pointing due south.

She says, "You can go back to your rooms."

Someone squeaks, "Any joy, Joy?" And we spill into laughter.

Old Joy closes her eyes, mustering strength, and then flat-out hollers. "GO!"

Something BIG! What is it? One a.m. comes and goes. I push the curtain aside and stare into the black night. There's a moon out, but it's nowhere near full—it looks like something someone started drawing and forgot to fill in. I imagine boys bumped from boarders' beds, roaming around the grounds, horny and unsupervised. I wonder if any of us will sleep tonight.

Kate

Saturday, September 3

Iris is dressed by 7:00 a.m., ready for our "special" breakfast before the exam. I still can't believe it's her. I'm still hoping for an explanation and wanting to give her the benefit of the doubt.

"I'm a bit too nervous to eat," I tell her. "Would you mind if I skipped?"

She grabs my shoulder, squeezes it, and I'm struck again by her kindness. She wishes me luck, smiles, and then leaves to get a coffee. The touch of my shoulder, the wishes of luck, her last-minute smile—they all seem genuine.

Clem arrives not long after Iris has gone. Ideally, I'd break the news gently, but there's no time. "I think Iris has something to do with PSST," I tell her. "I saw her emails last night."

I explain, but she doesn't believe it. "She wouldn't do that. There's no way."

"I'm hoping not, either, but I need her password to find out for sure. I really hate to rush you, but time is running out. Do you know what she might choose as a password? I want to prove she didn't do it, Clem."

She thinks for a moment. Looks around the room. "I don't know what it is, but I'm pretty sure I know where she'd keep it."

She walks over to Iris's closet and looks around in the bottom, sifting through shoes, until she pulls out a black bound notebook. She turns to the back page where the passwords are listed and shows it to me. "It's not her," she says.

I want to believe it. I want to believe that if Clem knows Iris well enough to guess where she hides things, she knows what Iris would and wouldn't do.

I type in the password and get into her emails. And that's when we see the whole sordid exchange between Iris and Theo Ledwidge. Iris has been feeding him information all year.

"She hates me that much," Clem says quietly.

While we're skimming, an email comes in from Theo. I open it and we read. Then there's a terrible silence in which I try to reconcile the kind Iris who stays up late to help me study, with the Iris who would plan this.

"Can you do something?" Clem asks.

I nod and read through the email again, so I know as much as possible about what they're intending. They're putting PSST on the big screen at the formal tonight: TOP 10 PSST POSTS on display for everyone to see.

"Can you shut it down before then?" Clem asks, already texting Ady to let her know what's going on. The two of them are what-the-fucking? to each other via text, while I'm starting to smile.

"I can't shut it down, but if I can get access to the computer I can mess with it." I start grabbing my things. "I'll do it after the exam and before the formal. I've got it figured out," I say. "But first—the future."

I sit at the front of the exam room, listening to the teacher give instructions before she hands out the papers. Iris is three rows in front of me. I stare at the back of her head, at those sloping shoulders. I imagine her sending secrets to Theo late at night.

She turns around and waves. Small face, small life.

Good luck, she mouths.

Good luck, I mouth back, but I mean good luck surviving the shit storm.

The teacher puts my paper on my desk. I stare at the cover, at the place where my name will be, at the dots I will color in, each one corresponding to an answer. I do not want to be here. I want to be somewhere else.

Two roads diverged in a yellow wood.

I stare at the dots.

Dot, dot, dot.

Fuck it.

I took the one I wanted to take.

Choices are all we have. It doesn't matter if things don't work out. It's that we make them for the right reasons—to follow what we think is the best road. I know that when I tell Mum and Dad what I decided, they will tell me that the path of life changes. That the world forks off in inexplicable and unimaginable directions, and you take what seems the right path at the time. It might end, but then there's another one, and another one, and if you're lucky, at the end, you'll look down at the roads you took and they will make the most beautiful, intricate, random pattern.

More beautiful, I think, *than a straight line.*

Whatever happens later, I will never regret this moment. Running hard through the grounds, fumbling with my phone to call Oliver, shouting into the phone that he shouldn't go on without me. Grabbing my cello, hailing a taxi and getting in the back, breathless, leaving the biggest tip I've ever left because I can't wait for the change, cutting a path through the cars, horns sounding, Oliver on the other side, waving at me, the two of us standing in the wings, tuning, breathing—breathe, breathe, breathe.

Play.

Clem

Saturday, September 3

I'm sitting on Iris's bed holding her journal in my hand thinking, *Ahem, I've been here before.* History always repeats itself. You would think that Iris would learn not to write down her deepest secrets for other people to find them. You would think, but you would be wrong. I knew her passwords would be on the back page—Iris has always kept her passwords on the back page—but as to what else the journal contains, as much as I'm dying to know, a bigger part of me is resistant. Rhapsodies about Theo. Rants about me. I open it again, just for a flash and a piece of paper falls out. It's a letter and it's addressed to me. So I guess I have to read it.

Dear Clem,

I know what you think of me. I've known it for ages. I knew even before we came here, when you were so eager to share a room with anyone but me. You've been screaming for freedom for a long time. It hurts that you don't like me, that you don't want to be around me. I lean toward you and you lean away. It's always been like this. I'm not me without you, but you don't give a flying fuck.

First of all, know this: I only told Mum and Dad about Stu because I was worried about you. You changed when you met him and I don't trust that. I don't get why you would willingly give up the one thing you're good at. I don't even get how you could sleep with a guy you'd only known for a minute, who's so obviously not boyfriend material (even I can see that) . . . I'll admit there was a bit of jealousy there. Why are things so easy for you? You going away to Kate's was like the last straw. Did you have to take her away from me? My only friend here, if she ever truly was. Did you laugh about me together? I bet you told her all my embarrassing stuff. Well, sister, you don't know the half of them.

You know what I do to make myself feel good? I got the idea in wellness. Dr. Malik was talking about depression, ways to lift yourself out of the swamp. He said we should think about people who are having a worse time than we are. Or maybe he said we should think about being grateful for what we have? But it made me think of that word schadenfreude—taking pleasure in other's misfortunes. You were right when you said that I was only happy when I was looking at someone else's sadness, and it made me even happier to know that I could share it. Who doesn't want to feel better about themselves? Who doesn't want to feel that those perfect people suffer, too?

It's the rule that fuels a hundred gossip rags—and, okay, we don't have any celebrities at St. Hilda's, so we just have to make do with our own social pecking order. But I think you should know that the first time I shared something on PSST it was an accident. I was with Theo, studying. I was telling him about how some eighth graders had ordered sex toys online and had them sent to Old Joy. Do you remember the week after there was that thing on PSST about Astrid Martin and her peppermint lube? That was the start. I'd see Theo every week and tell him things—sometimes they were true and sometimes I made them up—and I guess it hit the same part of my brain where chocolate does. Theo loved my "work." He flattered me and I was ripe for it. I'll bet even the most terrible evil tyrants start small. I'll bet things just snowball and, before they know it, the thing they've made is alive and hungry and they have to keep feeding it. Malik said that, too—energy flows where focus goes.

So there you have it. A confession. I'm not proud of myself. I know that Theo isn't actually into me. (Why would he be? Why would anyone be?) He's using me—maybe in a way I do know some of what you're feeling with regards to Stu. But beyond all that, I know that I've hurt people—friends, strangers, family (sorrysorrysorry). This thing Theo wants for Saturday—the big reveal, PSST's Top 10—I can't believe I've contributed to it. I don't know who I am anymore. What I wish, what I wishwishwish, is that I could get a time machine and take us back to age 11, to sporty Clem and brainy Iris, and our old bedroom with the two alcoves Dad made us—mine mint green, yours sky blue—and that we could be in our bunks laughing like we used to, sharing like we used to.

And now it's 5:00, and time for study hall, and any second Kate'll be back. So I'm signing off with love and shame, and I'll never show you this.

Iris

Ady

Saturday, September 3

We're at our tech run-through for the formal, and everything's looking good. I've never had to fake being pleasant to this extent before. I could happily kill Iris Banks and Theo Ledwidge with my bare hands right now, but my job is to keep my eyes open and my mouth shut. So I fake it with the smiles and make like it's any other day. Not the day that PSST is about to come undone.

My backdrop images have a luscious, trancelike quality—clouds scudding across skies, flowers popping into bloom, abstract swirls doing their psychedelic things. Theo has actually been *pleasant* and *helpful*, talking to our drama teacher Ms. McKeen about the lighting program. Iris is hanging around like his little shadow. I suggest that we put the admin passwords for both computers on the table where they're set up in case we need to do any adjusting to the film or the lighting tonight. Theo says no need, but he'll be around to help. Ha! I made sure I saw him entering the password. So long as he doesn't pull a late change, I can give Kate what she needs. We're running the film and the "Moments" PowerPoint on the Basildon computer—it's their art department graphics laptop, the fastest hard drive for the job.

We double-check, plug in, and tape down the leads into outlets and into the data projector and lighting board, and we're set.

Tables are having their cloths laid and chairs, glasses, and dishes are all being unpacked and unstacked.

I say goodbye to Iris and Theo, nice as pie, feeling a surge of excitement that they have no idea they've been found out.

And I'm meeting Max here in just four hours.

Ady

Saturday, September 3, later

Last year, the formal was the big thing. Our first proper formal. All we talked about. Who was wearing what. Who was partnering up. Who was going solo. Both okay options because we were a group, a happy unit at the center of the universe. Me and my gals. The best pre-parties, the best afterparty. Hair. Makeup. The most enviable selfies. The most ridiculous rumors on PSST about the group sex that, of course, didn't happen. We did play Twister while drunk, and Bec sprained her little finger.

This year I'm waiting on the wide marble doorstep of Tash's house, alone. Max needs to get some studying done, so no pre-party for her.

Last year I was in purpose-bought Scanlan Theodore. This year I'm in altered vintage.

If it hadn't been for the kind-but-fake rallying that followed the latest big PSST outing, I could have huffily ignored this part of the night.

Tash's mum, Sherry, answers the door, head immediately on the side and sympathetic smile applied. "Your poor, *poor* mother. How is she?"

"She seems okay, thanks Sherry."

"Let's hope things pick up."

Stepping inside, I see that a lot of my friends' parents have been invited for drinks, too.

"I didn't ask your mother, Ady. I thought she had enough on her plate." That's true, and she does not need a giant helping of insincere sympathy dumped next to it. But, still, it seems rude not to have asked her.

I look at Sherry, remembering my mother's report to my father after she first picked me up from this very house, soon after Tash's family moved here when we were in seventh grade. *Your daughter's friend Tash lives in the most comically vulgar faux-Georgian house in Toorak, and that's saying something.*

And my father, always vague, asked: *Which ones are they again?*

The social climber and the nose droner with hair implants. And they both laughed.

They have a way of being mean together that seems bonding. When I told them not to be so judgmental, my mother said, *Sorry, darling, very naughty, you're right.* And they both laughed again.

"Yes," I say. "She does have rather a lot on her plate."

Inside, most people have already arrived. Everything looks the way it always does, but this doesn't feel like my world anymore. My head and my heart are with Kate, who is right this minute trying to work out the best way to smack down PSST.

The boys are drinking beer and the girls prosecco and Aperol with a mint leaf in each glass, which will be the only thing that some of them eat tonight. The boys are in suits, and the girls are zippered and dieted and taped into some pricey and very bare evening wear, and I'm a bit *one of these things definitely doesn't belong*, but happily so.

I'm wearing an evening jumpsuit from Gram—a wild geometric pattern—that she bought at Biba in London in the late 1960s. It's sleeveless with a diamond shape cut out at the back and the front, and has a high, bead-encrusted collar. I've got a big, messy-teased down do, Jean Shrimpton smoky eyes, and nude lips.

"What are you wearing, babe?" Tash's routine *Am I safe to ridicule it?* question.

"Vintage Pucci." Hard burn.

Tash is forced to admire it. "Amazing."

"I love it," says Bec.

I sip my (color-coordinated—there's orange in the jumpsuit pattern) drink and wander into a group talking about the PSST post. Everyone becomes awkwardly quiet.

"Don't stop because I'm here. It's not just me they hate—they disparage girls every single week. I mean, who are these misogynists? Is this the actual Stone Age?" It's quite a relief to be coming on super feminist, thanks to listening to Clare and my mother, but still, I 100 percent believe it.

Nick Fergusson says, "Oh, come on, Ady, where's your sense of humor? My father says we're letting political correctness rule us."

"Political correctness is not a pejorative," I counter. (Clare again.) "It's just people being switched on enough not to further vilify groups that are already under attack."

"What? Like girls? You all look okay to me." It's delivered like a joke-sleazy compliment. And there's a general sense that the boys are agreeing with him.

"Don't be a douche, Nick," Rupert says. "You only have to look at domestic violence stats to know there's a massive gender problem, and things like PSST contribute to it."

Rupert's mother is a social worker. He gets the lowdown from her, the same way I get it from Clare. He gives me a half-wink and I smile back, feeling that he and I can maybe be friends again one of these days.

The guys claim they don't know who PSST is, and I believe them, hugging to myself that I do know, at least a couple of them. The trouble is, these guys are on the fence. They'll laugh at some of the misogynistic crap, but get defensive if you confront them about it because they didn't actually say it or write it.

Malik says the standard you walk past is the one you accept.

My phone vibrates with the text from Kate that I've been waiting for, and I step away to text back what she needs.

Kate

Saturday, September 3

I type fast, writing the browser extension. Clem isn't here, but she left her room open for me. It's the one place Iris won't think to look. I know what I'm doing, but I have to concentrate. I haven't written one of these before and I need it to work.

There are a few variables, even if I get it right.

I don't want these people to win. I want that feeling I had at the audition—the hum of doing something, being something; the hum of having friends, a boyfriend; the hum of feeling fantastic about yourself—I want that hum to go through everyone at the formal.

What I don't want is some manipulative fuck to win tonight. My hands are aching. I can't type fast enough.

When it's finished I copy it to the USB stick and kiss it for luck.

Done, I text Ady. *Can you send password? And what's the browser?*

I stare at the three dots and imagine Ady typing.

Please, please, please, I think as her reply pops up.

Password is Art Department. Browser is Chrome. See you there.

Ady and the rest of the committee have done a brilliant job. Fairy lights lead the way to the door. I walk past the photographer's corner, a cloud of silk and hairspray, where people are lining up to have their official memory of the night taken. One after the other they stand close to their tuxedo-clad date and smile like this is the best night of their lives.

Please work, browser extension. Please, please work.

I'm helping Iris with tech, so I have access to all areas and all equipment. I walk backstage, grabbing an appetizer and drink on the way, and announce that I need to do some sound and computer checks. Ady has taken care of Theo, luring him outside.

There are others standing around me, though. Guys from Basildon who are probably in on the whole thing, so I hope they're not technically savvy. It turns out that, even if they are, they're too busy talking to the band members from Hoxton to worry about me.

I'm just mute Kate, I guess.

But it's the quiet ones, don't you know?

Hoxton start up their first set while I'm working, and it gives me the cover I need. They're playing one of their louder songs—the perfect soundtrack—all guitars and fuck yous.

"Fuck you, Theo and Iris," I say calmly, as I type in the password and plug in the USB. It feels like forever until it pops up in the menu, and then forever between opening it, clicking on the file, and installing the plug-in on the browser.

Done, I text to Ady and Clem.

I do some pretending—act like I'm checking lights, mics, sound.

Oliver appears after a while, stepping over cords and past speakers. He's still grinning from the audition. "I don't want to jinx us, but we were brilliant," he says. "I mean, we were absolutely brilliant."

"We were indeed."

I look him up and down. He's wearing an old blue suit that belongs to his grandfather. His shoes, as I would expect, are shined. "You look very beautiful," I tell him, straightening his tie.

"You look very beautiful, too," he says.

I feel good—the silk dress that Ady gave me is cool against my skin. My hair is done the way she did it that night at the club—piled up with flowers through it. I've left off the crimson lipstick for practical reasons: I have plans for kissing later.

Hoxton take a break as Theo walks backstage with Iris. "I've got it from here, Screamer," he says.

Loser, I think, and squeeze Oliver's hand so he doesn't say anything. The payback will come, but it will be later.

Iris is with Theo as his date—at least she's clinging to his arm, desperate to be that. "We want to check the computer," she says.

"I've got it covered," I tell her.

She nods, and looks worried, and I wonder if she's having second thoughts. I want her to have them. I want to know that she's the person I thought she was. If she doesn't say something now, I can't talk to her again. I won't. This is her chance. Anyone who would do this isn't someone I want to know.

Please say something.

But she walks away, telling us she has to go to the bathroom; she'll see us later.

I call out goodbye.

"So, you'll start up the slide show?" Theo asks.

I tell him he's welcome to start it himself. "I'll be out watching. When you're ready, just hit PLAY."

The formal is in full swing by the time Oliver and I leave backstage. Hoxton are taking a break while the main course is served. Ady's taken my advice on the music and Mazzy Star is coating the room in low velvet voices. Oliver and I take a seat at a white-clothed table marked by the Ady touch—flowered centerpieces wild with color.

"Which fork?" Oliver says. "I always forget."

"You start from the outside," I tell him.

I wave at Clem, who's laughing hysterically as she tries to get her paella past her beard. "Who's she supposed to be?" Oliver asks.

"Herself," I say, as my food arrives.

"You don't seem nervous at all," Oliver says, nodding to the screen that's onstage, ready for the presentation. "I eat when I'm nervous," I tell him, forking up salad that's left on his plate.

I wasn't looking forward to the formal. It wasn't even on my radar. For the last few months, the other sophomores have been planning dresses and dates and makeup and nails. I've been in music-land, Kate-land. But now that I'm here in the middle of it all—the school transformed into elegance and glamour, thanks to Ady—it feels important. It doesn't matter whether you're subverting like Clem or embracing like Tash and her friends—it's a moment. And it's not the waiters or the tablecloths or the silverware or the amazing food or the fact that Hoxton are here. It's that we are here.

And if my plan fails, then Theo ruins it all.

"I'm actually beyond nervous," I tell Oliver.

After the main course is done and cleared, Tash heads to the bathroom, a sign that the presentation is about to start. I imagine her in front of the mirror, checking her lipstick, checking her teeth, checking her hair, practicing her smile, before she's in front of everyone, onstage.

I watch her sauntering through the crowd, stopping to hug and kiss people on the way. Backstage, Theo is waiting—laughing—the shithead. I can't tell if the other guys here know what he has planned. Oliver thinks most of them don't and I want to believe that.

Tash walks onstage. There's electricity in the air. She swings her whole body and flirts with the room until we're quiet. "We love you, Tash!" a couple of people call out, and she waves at them, then taps the microphone and everyone goes quiet.

"The St. Hilda's formal committee would now like to present for you a slide show. 'Moments,'" she says, with a hand flourish that convinces me she has no idea what's about to appear behind her on the screen. She's just as likely as anyone else to be in the Top 10. "This year's highlights—St. Hilda's and Basildon."

She nods offstage, to Theo, just before the lights go out.

I shift nervously.

The familiar PSST page comes up on screen, and then PSST BEST OF.

There's a collective inhalation of breath, no cheering, just hushed silence broken by some fucks and oh my gods. I can see the shadow of Tash, hovering on the side of the stage, freaking out. I can see the calm shadow of Ady, her hand on her arm. I imagine Ady looking at the screen and telling her to watch.

The posts roll.

Guess what ❀ put on ✸ at Jonno's party?

Helena Parks—total ❁ body

Who is the biggest ✸?

Angela Bannon— ❀ hot and number one

Clem Banks is so ❁ I can't stand it.

Who gave who a ✸ at Tash's party?

Kate Turner— ❁ but if you're ✸ it's the ❀ that really ✸

Patrons at St. Hilda's Fair were ✸ by a mass. It came of out of the water and remains a ❁.

Ady Rosenthal likes ❀ courtesy of ✸ Rupert.

I would like to give Kate Turner a huge ❁

Every slut is replaced by a flower. Every fucked-up thought replaced by a star. Whores, blow jobs, fat, rape, bitch: They're all gone, wiped out by us. And a little technical know-how.

I raise my hands in the air and cheer with everyone else.

Everyone in the room is going crazy with happiness, with the feeling of telling the things and people in the world that try to trap you to go ❁ themselves.

Everyone except Theo and Iris, that is.

But as Oliver tells me I'm spectacular, I really couldn't give a ❀ about them.

Clem

Saturday, September 3

Formal notes:

- The table bearing your nametag may not be the table where you end up sitting.
- That curious smell is two parts hormones, two parts hairspray, and a dash of anticipation.
- Vegetarians always get a bum deal.
- Boob tape is hazardous.
- Beware of over-manscaped Basildons bearing gifts.
- And this one's important: Who you arrive with does not dictate who you leave with.

My table is the best table. It's the funnest, the most raucous, the best-dressed, and the worst-behaved. The Feminist Collective went nuts in the drama department and, as a result, I am dressed as the lovable Russian Jewish village milkman, Tevye, from *Fiddler on the Roof*. That is to say, I am wearing baggy pants, a jerkin, and a full beard. Lin Barlow is dressed as *Kenickie* from Grease and she can't stop leering and grabbing her crotch.

The presentation is supposed to happen after the band, between the main course and dessert. Ady and Kate have been hovering around the computer. Theo Ledwidge is there looking officious. He posed for his photo with Iris with the cheesiest smile in the world, and then, as soon as the flash disappeared, so did his teeth.

Iris looks really pretty, but she also looks really sick, and I know she's thinking about what's going to happen. I'm trying to work out what I'm going to say to her. What and where and how.

After I read Iris's letter, I put it back in her journal, so she has no idea that anyone knows anything. I gave Kate and Ady the *Cliffs Notes* version. And we were all quiet for a bit, thinking about it. Thinking that even after what she's done we can't completely hate her. I feel sorry for her. I feel a bit responsible, but when I said that to the others they were adamant.

"This is not a twin thing," Ady said. "This is on Iris."

But maybe if I'd been nicer to her. If I'd made more of an effort to include her . . . She's at Theo's table, but he's not there. At the opposite end, there are a couple of Basildon boys ignoring her. Iris looks small, and angry, and watchful. Theo has clearly deserted her. Even when the main course is served, he stays AWOL.

I feel as if I've got eyes everywhere; I'm watching Iris, Theo, Ady, Kate. Cool, cryptic texts circulate between me and my thumb-compatible comrades. In between *OMGs* and *Soons*, and

Yassssses! there's *Check Theo's boys looking so self-congratulatory* (Ady), *superbia et ante ruinam exaltatur* (Kate).

I'm going to say something to Iris, I text.

Make sure she's watching, Kate replies. *Don't let her leave.*

And then I get the text that makes me rise to my feet. *"IT'S GO-TIME."*

"Iris. Wait—" I catch her arm as she's trying to run away, as the first slide comes on, and in the hush that goes with it I feel like my heart might have stopped, just for a sec. Iris tries to pull away, but I grip her arm and together we watch PSST's TOP 10, the flower-bomb version.

I see the PSST page swamped with daisies and tulips and bluebells and roses.

And people are going, *What*?

And people are going, *Awwwwww*!

My tablemates are high-fiving and giving up bro-tastic, chest-bump action. Theo Ledwidge is trying to get to the computer, but Ady and Max block him with their folded arms. The teachers are way behind us—trying to figure out what all the commotion is about. And as each post scrolls, we know what they're supposed to say—but with the flowers replacing the offensive words, the display becomes like a surreal, incoherent rebus. It builds and builds, the laughter, the cheering—and it feels like such a win after all the stabs and hits and taps and sluts, and it's kind of galling, to see just how many flowers appear.

Iris is mesmerized. Then she turns to me. "That's genius."

"That's Kate," I say. "You were right. She's the smartest girl in school, and if you think she's going to want to spend another night sharing a room with you, you're crazy. We *know*, Iris. You're the snitch."

Her chin starts to wobble. "I'm sorry," she whispers. She looks up and her eyes are glistening. "Are you going to tell the other boarders? Does everyone have to know?"

"I don't see how there's any way out of it."

"They're going to hate me."

"Probably."

Then she looks scared. "Are you going to tell Gaffney? The scholarship—"

"That's the thing with fallout—you don't know how far it will reach."

She's getting paler by the second.

I give a philosophical sigh and pat her shoulder. "This is probably the worst of it."

You can pick them off—the Basildons who are involved. You can see them huddling and conferring and looking dark and thwarted. Theo comes up to Iris and grabs her arm and hisses something in her ear. "What have you done?"

"Nothing," she whimpers.

"Not Iris," I say. "Kate Turner." And Kate's right near us now, with Oliver. He taps Theo on the shoulder, and when Theo turns, Oliver—mild, straight, music nerd Oliver—punches Theo in the nose. Theo falls across the dance floor and while he's down, sprawled, glaring up, blood gushing onto his white shirt, Jinx does a neat sidestep over and takes a picture.

Then the screen goes black, the show is over. Iris is looking at Kate but Kate's shaking her head. Iris runs for the bathroom.

Malik is walking over to Theo. Someone puts on "I Gotta Feeling" and everyone rushes onto the dance floor.

And it's not just a good night, it's a GREAT night. It's almost perfect—there's only one thing missing. I am literally thinking this as Ben walks through the door. He's not a bit put off by my beard.

Ady

Saturday, September 3

If I look back at the formal when I'm old, old Adelaide, I will remember these things particularly:

Max arriving in a killer tux—jacket, trousers chopped to knee-length, long black lace-up Doc Martens.

Luring Theo Ledwidge away from the computers with false smiles, giving him lots of detailed instructions about the location of a nonexistent afterparty so Kate could download her magical browser extension.

Dancing to Hoxton, out of control with relief, delirious in anticipation of the PSST annihilation. Max and I laughing our heads off and, later, dancing slowly, close and whispery.

Making sure we were at the computers when the time came, so Theo couldn't wreck Kate's plan.

The cheer that built up and exploded when Kate's amazing flower-bombed version of PSST appeared on the screen, post after post covered in flowers, not a vicious word to be seen. She is the hero of the entire school. It warmed my heart to see that the guys were cheering just as hard as the girls. It really has been a few shithead trolls: Theo Ledwidge and associates.

Malik's look of puzzlement quickly graduating to happiness, as he realized what we'd done.

Going to Malik with Kate and Clem to give him Theo Ledwidge's name and asking him to make sure Basildon would be told, and PSST shut down.

I'm generally no fan of violence, but it was a triumph for good over evil when Oliver clocked Theo.

Clem being very gentle with a crying Iris.

Tash, a few too many drinks on an empty stomach, slurring to me that we'd always be friends, and me privately doubting that very much.

Ben walking in right at the end, and the smile on Clem's bearded face.

Me, Max, Kate, Oliver, Clem, and Ben piling into an Uber, going to the breakfast truck on St. Kilda beach, and watching the sun rise eating French toast and waffles and drinking outlandish milk shakes. Mine was Jaffa, sprinkled with popping candy.

WEEK 9

LOOKING FORWARD

Wellness

Monday, September 5
Dr. Peter Malik

Week 9: Looking Forward

Provocation

For now she need not think of anybody. She could be herself, by herself. And that was what now she often felt the need of—to think; well not even to think. To be silent; to be alone. All the being and the doing, expansive, glittering, vocal, evaporated; and one shrunk, with a sense of solemnity, to being oneself, a wedge-shaped core of darkness, something invisible to others . . . and this self having shed its attachments was free for the strangest adventures.

—Virginia Woolf, *To the Lighthouse*

Nothing is absolute. Everything changes, everything moves, everything revolves, everything flies and goes away.

—Frida Kahlo

Points for Discussion/Reflection

We've come to the end of our wellness journey: What did you think about it in the beginning? What are your thoughts now, after "all the being and the doing"?

- What "strange adventures" do you hope for in the future?
- If you had a time machine, would you go forward or back?
- Frida Kahlo says, "everything flies and goes away." What, if anything, comes back?

Task

Write a letter to your future self. It can be as long or as short as you want. You can keep it in a special place, or post it on https://www.futureme.org/ (they'll send it to you at your appointed future date), or burn it after writing it. Think of it as a portable time capsule, linking who you are right now to who you hope to be. You can use this letter as a place to express your goals—by making yourself more conscious of your goals, you can start imagining the steps toward them. You can summarize your current self: What are you happy about? What do you wish to change? Who are your friends? What are your dreams?

Ady

Monday, September 5

Letter to my future self . . .

I think that's what Malik said: Imagine what you might like to remember, looking back.

So, sitting in the Oak Parlor for the last wellness session on a comfy moss-green beanbag, next to Kate and Clem, thumb-sisters, I listened as Malik recapped.

He spoke about being kind to ourselves and to other people, about finding our authentic selves.

He made a big deal about what Kate did at the formal, taking down PSST, and she said Clem and I helped, and we all clapped and cheered Kate. It got pretty rowdy.

Iris wasn't there.

He emphasized again the thing about the standard you walk past. I'm going to really try hard on that one. And he talked about going easy on our families; everyone is probably just doing their best.

I think about my father, doing his best, facing up to rehab. I hope it works this time.

I've taken my time, and taken this assignment home; Malik said privacy might be beneficial.

So, wow, dear future self, what do you want to know, exactly?

You're me, so I'm guessing—everything. That would take more than a letter. That would take a whole book.

Malik said to set the scene. So, here goes. As I write this letter, I'm:

Listening to: The Cure, my father's favorite band when he was my age.

Feeling: Elated that I got into MCA. Also a teeny bit scared shitless. Just heard this morning. Kate and Clem and Max are coming over for a celebration dinner tonight. I'm making spaghetti carbonara. An early night so we don't bug Clare.

Also feeling: Thrilled and shy about spending more time with Max.

Eating: I have made myself a big plate of nachos with loads of jalapeño peppers and guacamole, and, boy, is it good. Malik would approve of this mindfulness because I am truly living in the mouthful.

Sitting: In the living room, overlooking the garden, and it's coming to life again after winter. The smallest, clearest, brightest leaves are out, and I love that.

Smelling: I've picked a fat posy of violets that smells so sweetly of itself, as sweet as a bagful of lollipops, as sweet as icing on a cake, as sweet as the end of winter, as sweet as purple.

Feeling: Relieved. I had a proper talk with my mother last night. She's proud that I investigated and prepared the whole MCA thing, and she said it was the best surprise. I told her stuff I'd seen, and stuff I'd heard, here, and she was honest with me and said to ask anything about Dad. She assured me that nothing I did contributed to his problems. Adults were completely responsible for themselves. And she said that he thought having kids was the best thing in his life. We didn't thwart him. We've made our "clear up the closet" date for Saturday, but it doesn't have to involve any throwing out, unless I want that. And there will be Figgy's apple cake.

Topic for this letter: "Why Can't I Be You?" (Spoiler: I can be.)

Older me, I hope you're a clothes artist for real, or another sort of artist, and that you love your days and you spend them dreaming and making things. Please be a maker. Be a creator. I hope you have a studio where the sun pours in, and you have a little dog with you while you work. I hope you live with someone you love, or love living by yourself with your doggie.

These are some things you learned when you were 16:

Family: Strangely, it's a relief to have it all out in the open. The months of half-knowing everything was wrong and getting worse, and my mother pretending that it was all systems go, and me having to guess, or find stuff out from Clare, and pretending to my friends that everything was okay—they were the worst.

Even Charlie is at home a fair bit now, proof of habitat improvement. We just found out that we can stay in our house, for the time being. My mother has arranged for a mortgage moratorium with the bank for 12 months, and she thinks she can probably get a job before then, so we might not have to sell.

Sex: I—you (we) haven't had it yet. Unless we count autosexuality.

Friends: It seems so simple it's dumb, but it took you a while to get onboard—a friend is someone you can be real with. No games, no faking it, no showing off, no putting down, no power plays. Not cool or hot or mean or popular or fashionable or competing with each other. Just being true. And how that makes you feel is . . . relaxed.

Older me, please remember how great it felt to have real friends for the first time. Remember that it felt like something cracking open to give you the wider view, and more oxygen. Remember that it also, contrarily, felt like a nest where you were comfortable and safe and restored. Remember that it felt so loose and free when you could let your guard down and stop performing that popular girl version of yourself. I hope we've never had to perform that again. Bad for the heart.

Love to you from me X

Kate

Tuesday, September 6

Dear Future Kate,

At this point in time, you are sitting on a beanbag in wellness. The sun is streaming in and you are basking. Who are you currently? You are the hero of the moment. Even Tash is talking to you. It's nice, but not important. What's important is that you stopped PSST dead in its tracks.

Other things that have stopped dead in their tracks—there's no more sneaking out of the portal. I felt the need to tell Mum and Dad everything—from beginning to end—and that included Orion, Oliver, and swapping scholarship study for audition practice.

You know this already, but they didn't take it well.

I think we'll remember all our lives the way Mum sighed, and said, "Katie," and handed the phone over to Dad. "It's not the money, it's the lying," he said. "You lied, for six months, over and over."

They're angry about the sneaking out, too.

They called the school.

(I'm practically locked in at night by Old Joy, now.)

They still love us, though. They call us every day to tell us—and to check that we're behaving.

I don't know who we will be. I know that we don't have a scholarship for next year, but I know that Mum and Dad are in serious talks about how to help us stay at St. Hilda's. There's talk of applying for assistance because we're from a country area. There's talk of a state school with a good music program and boarding with a friend of Mum's.

But at the moment the future is unknown. I love that. I'm not making long-term plans. I'm playing cello with Oliver, kissing him quite a bit (cello, kiss, cello, kiss), seeing him during the times sanctioned by Mum and Dad.

There's been no sex yet. But I am greatly looking forward to it. What's it like? Actually, don't tell me. I'd rather find out for myself.

I don't know if we won the scholarships to Iceland (you know that, future self, but I don't). Maybe we change again along the way. Maybe in the future we're playing cello onstage at Parliament House with Oliver, or maybe we're accepting the Nobel Peace Prize for something scientific. Maybe we're still in love with Oliver, maybe we're in love with someone else. That's an unsettling idea. That past me is falling for Oliver while future me is falling for someone else.

Good exercise, Dr. Malik. It's making me think.

We can be anything, Future Kate. We're allowed to change our minds.

So, if you're looking back and thinking, I didn't get Iceland, I didn't get the scholarship, don't regret it. We got more out of this year than money or pieces of paper.

We got the future. Whatever that is.

Love,

Kate

Clem

Tuesday, December 20

Dear Future Clem,

Sorry I took so long to write to you. Malik set the assignment back in September and now it's December. I'm writing from seat 14A of the train to Shallow Bay. Iris is in Singapore with Mum and Dad, and I'm going to Kate's for Christmas. I'll be staying at Kate's, but Ben is just across the fence and we've got a date with the aliens on December 21st.

Ady says I am living proof of the indomitability of youth: One week I'm a wreck over Stuart Laird McAlistair and the next I'm kissing Ben Tran on the dance floor at the formal. But while it was happening, I felt it all. What can I say? Time is trippy.

Two weeks ago I was walking past the laundromat and I saw Stu with a girl in a Sacred Heart uniform. I went in—she looked about 14. Stu goes, "Uh, hi?" I ignored him and patted her hand and said,

"I'm telling you this as a sister—sure, he's cute, but he sleeps around. Use protection. I'm not just talking about your lady parts—I'm talking about your heart."

I don't know if she believed me. Probably thought I was an unhinged ex. But I hope she did.

Ben and I are having an epistolary romance. On the night of the formal, he said he knew that I was brokenhearted and he wasn't going to be pushy. He said if he had to settle for being just friends, well, he wouldn't love it, but he could stand it. But then I kissed him, and since then we've written letters and sent photos. I send him silly selfies and he sends me photos of rocks and clouds, and baby birds. I can't wait to see what happens.

Future Clem, where are you? What do you do? Are you happy? I wonder if you're married with children, or single with a great collection of shoes. When I think of all the possibilities for you, my brain can't cope. You're in Paris or you're in Melbourne, you're on the Trans-Siberian Express, you're making pancakes for your children in an apartment in Frankston, or you're getting a back rub from a masseuse before your next important meeting. The truth is, I can't really imagine you at all.

This is me, now, Clem-at-16: I love my family, my friends. I maybe have a boyfriend. I know good things are coming.

I promise to look after me so you can become you.

With love and selfies,

Clem

Acknowledgments

Our thanks to Claire Craig, Katelyn Detweiler, Georgia Douglas, Catherine Drayton, Amarlie Foster, Minna Gilligan, Melita Granger, Jill Grinberg, Philippa Hawker, Alana Kelly, Michael Kitson, Julie Landvogt, Louise Lavarack, Ali Lavau, Mark and Willeford Luffman, Chris Miles, Reba Nelson, Cheryl Pientka, Denise St. Pierre, Libby Turner, the Crowley family, the Howell family, and the Wood family; and Writers Victoria, Iola Mathews, and the National Trust for the Glenfern Writers' Studios.

DISCUSSION QUESTIONS

1) During the first wellness class of the year, Dr. Malik discusses the topic of identity with his students (see page 5). How did the identities of Ady, Kate, and Clem change over the course of the novel?

2) When Clem is trying to decide if she should stay on the swim team, she wonders if being good at something means you have to keep doing it. Do you think that having a talent for something means that you have to keep pursuing it? Do you think Clem would have eventually left the team even without her interest in Stu or her negative experience with her bathing suit?

3) How does Kate's love of science influence her love of music (and vice versa)? Does her love of the country influence her feelings toward the city?

4) Clem, Ady, and Kate each had some of their perceptions of other people challenged over the course of the story—most notably, they realized that they'd misjudged each other. How did their perception of others change over the course of the book? Have you ever misjudged anyone or been misjudged yourself? If so, did your relationship with that person change once perceptions shifted?

5) For their second wellness class, the sophomores are expected to bring in an item that is meaningful to them so that they can share it with their class. What item would you bring?

6) During one of their wellness classes, the girls discuss the idea of perfection and what a perfect day would look like to them. What is your idea of a perfect day? Do you think perfection exists?

7) One of the girls' assignments for wellness class is to make a map of their lives (see page 348). Clem makes a timeline with meaningful symbols to represent important decisions in her life, and Ady uses a spinning clothesline. If you were to map out your own life, what form would you give it? What "landmarks" would you include?

8) This book is told in alternating points of view between Ady, Clem, and Kate. Each narrator gives a different perspective and adds new details with their retelling of events. If you were to add another point of view to this book, which character would you choose?

9) At the end of the novel, Ady, Kate, and Clem work together to take PSST down and keep the website from hurting more of their classmates. Do you think they should have told someone about the website sooner? Why do you think the students kept the posts a secret from the adults in their lives? What would you have done in their place?

10) One of the central relationships of the novel is the complicated relationship between Iris and Clem. Why do you think Clem keeps pushing Iris away? Why does Iris keep seeking Clem out anyway?

11) How does the setting effect the story? Would the story be different if it weren't set in a boarding school? How would the story change if it were set in the country instead of the city?

12) After the "Rate the Boarders" list is posted on PSST, Clem wonders if she should be worried that her name wasn't on the list: "Not that I want to be on it but, at the same time, am I so forgettable" (see page 160)? Do instances of cyberbullying and harassment effect the bystanders along with the people experiencing the harassment? Do you think this is affected by the internet and social media?

13) The central conflict for Kate's section of the novel is her desire for two different futures and the necessity for her to choose between them. Have you ever had to make a similar decision? What choice would you make in her place?

14) At the end of their wellness program, Dr. Malik has his class write letters to their future selves. What would you say in a letter to your future self?

15) Ady, Kate, and Clem were each facing a major decision or adjusting to a major change in their lives as they began to spend more time together. Do you think this contributed to the development of their friendship? How do you think their interactions would change if they'd been assigned these groups earlier in the year?

16) In her letter to her future self, Ady says that she felt she had to perform the "popular-girl version" of herself when interacting with her old friends. What do you think she meant by that? Do you think there were times where Kate and Clem performed different versions of themselves as well?

17) When Clem and Kate discuss the possible PSST perpetrators, Clem tells Kate that they can't rule girls out from their list of suspects, because, "It's not acceptable for girls to act on their aggressions, so we have to get creative." Do you think that this is the case for Iris? If so, in what other ways could Iris have vented her frustrations?